GRAN

Flynn

ff

faber and faber

LONDON BOSTON

First published in 1991
by Faber and Faber Limited
3 Queen Square London WC1N 3AU
This paperback edition first published in 1992

Photoset by Wilmaset Birkenhead Wirral
Printed in England by
Cox & Wyman Ltd, Reading, Berkshire

A CIP record for this book is available from the British Library

ISBN 0–571–14463–2

For Marsha Hanlon

There were three of them, three young men with bitter hearts and greedy hands. They were coming down the aisle of the tube train, fast, intimidating by their very presence, terrifying by the ease with which they plundered.

I spared a single glance before dropping my eyes to the floor, the slatted wood and the ranks of shoes of the other passengers who were also looking at the floor, schooled in avoiding eye contact with villains, scared into awaiting fate. That brief look made up my mind. The first one, the brute with the bull neck and the heaving muscles straining the sleeves of his leather jacket. The ringleader. Oh God, oh St Lucy, will you let him keep his thieving hands off my chain?

God and St Lucy weren't listening. A handbag, emptied of its purse, was kicked away over the slats. Beside me, the knees of an old man were trembling beneath threadbare serge, and then the youth was wrenching a watch from the mottled wrist, and then . . . He was in front of me, his fingers clawing at my throat.

I sprang. As he leaned over I bulleted from the seat, my head cracking under his jaw and my knee rising to his groin. He roared, falling backwards off balance. I was after him, pumelling him to the floor, to the wooden slats and the immobile rows of shoes. 'Help me!' I gasped. 'Hold him!' And when no help came. *'Please.'*

Politeness paid off. The spell of fear and inactivity dissolved. Shoes moved, the marauder disappeared from my sight as people grappled with his battling arms and legs and pinned him into submission, face down, nose grinding the slats. Near the doors passengers had grabbed the other two, less dramatically but grabbed them all the same.

The train was coming into Highbury station. A woman pulled the alarm, to warn the driver of trouble aboard, to stop him opening the doors and allowing escape. The message was late and the doors opened. One of the youths tore free and was gone.

I went too, running, pounding along the platform, threading between home-going commuters desperate for fresh air. Up above would-be carol singers, charity collectors rattling tins, a flower stall, and pedestrians waiting for a green symbolic man to signal safety across a busy road. A time for peace and goodwill to all men, and a fine time to go thieving on the London Underground when you were needy and greedy and everyone else was loaded with what you wanted for Christmas.

I jinked down a passage that wasn't the exit route, cutting time, aiming for the escalator that might or might not be working. It was. It was crowded. I ran up the stone stairs beside it. People on the way down were glistening, dark clothing made pretty by fine rain. The tiled floor of the entrance hall was wet and I skidded.

In my head I heard the tone of my Irish grandmother. 'Laura Flynn, where in the world is your dignity?'

Then a hand fell on my shoulder and I jerked round, to see a breathless Detective Sergeant Ray Donnelly. He's wiry and fleet, and at that moment he looked triumphant too.

I went on the attack. 'Now don't you dream of arresting me for assault, Ray. Where were you when the travelling public needed you? The police should . . .'

He held up a hand. 'Laura, I want to talk to you . . .'

'It's like travelling in Fagin's kitchen. They come steaming right through, one carriage after another, and never a sign of the police . . .'

He's not actually much older than I am but he has a way of talking that pretends he is. He wagged a finger. 'Laura, will you let the adrenalin subside just a little? I want to talk to you about Kate Mullery.'

'That's a fine way of changing the subject, Ray. The subject was thieving gangs on the Tube, remember?'

We were blocking the exit, passengers leaning past us to drop tickets into a cardboard box where the West Indian ticket collector ought to have been if London Transport weren't so understaffed. Ray Donnelly took my elbow and steered me aside.

He was saying, with laboured patience: 'All right, Laura, thieving gangs. We were on the train, the transport police and I were. These steamers are organized. It's no use catching one here and a couple there. We want to trail them all the way to Fagin's kitchen. You get the picture?'

'In full colour: I stopped them, you didn't. May I go now? I have an appointment and I'm late.'

'Then you're going to be later. Mullery, Laura, I want her.'

Impatient, I shook my head. 'A client, Ray. I can't talk about my clients. Golden Rule.'

He smirked. 'Ah yes. Your hypocritical oath. You talk to me about them when you want information I might get for you, but when I want something you fall back on that secret-of-the-confessional line.'

My watch had stopped. I was twisting round to look for a station clock. 'OK, have a good laugh, Ray. It would suit you to laugh more. But I won't talk to you about Kate Mullery and I do have to go now.'

'I could detain you, you know.'

'Assault, like I said.'

'Preferably for a witness statement.'

I shouldn't have let myself look horrified but I did. He'd known I would. The last thing I wanted was to appear in court as a witness. Bad for business, that would be. I run the kind of business that profits from a low profile.

Ray Donnelly was enjoying himself. 'Look at it my way, Laura. There's a fellow downstairs, an old boy who had his wrist watch plucked and would you believe the fool is claiming he flung himself on the prisoner and is therefore the hero of the hour?'

He didn't wait for my reply. He said: 'No, and neither would I and neither would a magistrate. Our chief witness would lack a certain credibility, wouldn't you say?'

'Ray, there were around fifty people in that carriage. Any of them would tell you differently.'

He laughed, not mirth but irony. 'Oh yeah? Fifty different stories, and all from people who were so frightened they had their eyes down and suddenly it was bingo and in truth they don't know the how or the who of it.'

The station clock had stopped. I shrugged, about the clock and about Donnelly's exaggerated difficulties. 'Ray, the prisoner, as you politely call him, won't go along with being felled by a geriatric. He knows what happened.'

'Trouble is, Laura, he can't tell us. He has a broken jaw.'

'Oh.'

'So, er, when do we talk about Kate Mullery?'

Resignation set in. 'Blackmail.'

'No, no, hardly that. Just getting you to see things my way for once. What time will you be free this evening?'

I thought fast, looked vague. No way out. We both had decisions to make and I had to make mine first. I capitulated, never a nice feeling and I especially disliked giving in to Ray Donnelly. Or to blackmail. 'Say nine-thirty,' I offered. 'But not at the police station.'

'Of course not. The house? The office?'

'I'll be at the office.'

'Good.' He moved away from me. In the background was a commotion as the prisoners were escorted from the escalator to the street. I shifted, to avoid them noticing me. Besides, I felt bad about the broken jaw and I couldn't bear to see it.

Donnelly turned back briefly. 'Nine-thirty at your office, Laura. Otherwise it'll be a squad car at your front door and a ride to *my* office tomorrow morning.'

I swung round and went out into the evening air. A bitter

black night, people and vehicles reflected in the sheen of the road and the puddles on the uneven pavements. No carol singers, no rattling tins, perhaps they were trying their luck elsewhere. A police van was easing into traffic on the round-about. By the time I'd walked past the man clearing his flower stall for the night and started along Upper Street, the rain had turned my hair into an untameable frizz.

There's nothing that Chris Ionides doesn't know about cars and what he knows about my car is that it's finished. He also knows I can't afford to believe it, so he patches and doctors and we both pray.

This time it needed an unpronounceable spare part and would have to stay in his garage at Highbury Fields until he found one. He said all that in a heavily accented message on the telephone-answering machine in my office.

I pulled a face at the machine and replied wearily: 'Thanks, Chris,' and I continued to rub a towel over my hair. It's long hair, it corkscrews at the front and it tangles at the back. I hate rain. Another thing I hate is being without that car and Chris had hinted at a long wait. Maybe he wouldn't be able to devote himself wholeheartedly to the search for the unpronounceable. His brother had gone home to Cyprus for Christmas and Chris was singlehanded.

Then Mrs Lotti came on the tape, grumbling in a good-natured confusion of English and Italian that I hadn't been in contact to say whether I'd found her cat. What I *had* told her was that I didn't look for missing pets but she'd refused to accept it, and anyway I felt sorry for her. All those children and a dreary husband and now the cat runs off. But I hadn't looked. Not really. Guilt tweaked at me.

There were other messages but the one I wanted wasn't there. No word from Kate Mullery. Detective Sergeant Ray Donnelly of the Met., wasn't the only one wondering. I'd mislaid her too, and she owed me money.

I threw the towel back on the rail in my tiny washroom and

checked the time on the church clock across the street. Until the Big Storm the Big Trees had obscured it, but now I had my own personal version of Big Ben. Late, of course I was late. That delay at the solicitor's office in Holborn, and then Donnelly accosting me – events had conspired to make me late and now there was no car to help me catch up. I locked the office door behind me, listening to the thrum, thrum, thrum of music from the ladies' gym down below.

The shops were shut, except for the supermarket that traded late. Lighted windows flared yellow across wet pavement. I ran, dodging puddles and pedestrians with savage umbrellas.

'Forget it,' I told myself. 'It doesn't mean anything. Pretend you never heard it.' But I couldn't; it might; and I had. His voice on the tape, after Mrs Lotti and before the one from the bank. His familiar, threatening voice. Promising to kill me.

Anna Lee let me into the house in Liverpool Road, the reassurance of her welcoming smile exactly what I needed. She's a big woman, it makes her appear protective. She said: 'Laura, you're drenched! No car again?'

I noted the 'again'. She was right. I needed a new car. I dripped all over the hall rug and mumbled about repairs and liking the old car, when it was going, and said it would be a shame to sell it and rob Chris of the challenge of keeping it on the road.

Anna tutted and took my mac to carry it to the basement kitchen where there was a peg in a warm place. The heat of her Aga stove funnelled up the tall narrow house and drew us down. She stopped on the stairs, her sweater striped with the shadows of banisters, and she said: 'Sue's out. It's OK.'

I opened my mouth to say it would have been OK anyway, but it wasn't wholly true and I said nothing. In the kitchen were Jennie and Ruth and a woman whose name I instantly forgot once we'd been introduced. We all chattered about the weather and who'd got wettest, and I drew up a chair to join them around the scarred pine table. There was a half bottle of Bulgarian red wine on the table. Anna hung my mac near the

stove and came back with a
it.

Time was, and not so long ago,
moved out and the woman whose
remember was the latest occupant of my
go, Anna's friends, but she bestows the wor
I do. In her mind she's the benificient member
finding room beneath her roof for those who need a with
the caring support of other women. In reality, she ge used.

Jennie fetched another bottle of wine from her room, Anna scattered cutlery around the table and plonked a steaming casserole in front of us, and Ruth and the newcomer accepted without appearing to notice, their minds on the iniquities of husbands. Anna and Jennie and I talked together. By my definition, we three *were* friends, had known each other a long time. We trusted and were worth of trust.

Even so, it was only Anna I'd tell about Kate Mullery, for instance, because her discretion is reliable and because everyone, after all, needs to tell someone what happens in her life. Anna dispenses comfort and common sense in equal quantities. We talked over coffee. Jennie had drifted out to meet a friend and Anna and I went up to her room on the pretext that I wanted to read the story she was working on. She writes for children. That part of her world is a mystery to me but it provided our excuse.

Anna's room is the spacious one right across the front of the house on the first floor. We flopped into armchairs and she flicked on her coffee-maker. Guiltily I kept an eye on my watch. Her cat came and curled on my lap. I was comfortable and relaxed. I didn't want to go home and I didn't want to go back to my office. I didn't want any more frustrating or ridiculous or threatening telephone messages, and I didn't want to think about anything stressful.

She said: 'I let Sue know you were expected this evening. She thought it best to be out.'

who never faced anything if she

at I'm telling you.'

...ere's no need.'

'I told her that.'

'I'm not married to him any more. He can see who he likes.
Sue. Anybody.'

'I know.' Anna gave the slightest sigh. 'Trouble is, you know
how Sue likes to dramatize.'

The machine began to hiss and splutter and we talked above
the noise, Anna saying she doubted Sue's affair would last any
longer than her earlier ones, and me saying Sue had a fine
imagination if she thought I'd be upset at her taking up with a
man I'd ditched years before she met him. We knew we were
both lying.

With the coffee poured, it was a convenient point to drop the
subject and turn to Kate Mullery.

'I did what she asked,' I said. 'I found out what she wanted
to know and I gave her the information, a proper written report
and a nice clear bill attached to it.'

'These big names are all the same,' said Anna, although it's
doubtful this view was backed with authority. 'They're the
worst at paying up.'

'I've phoned, but it's demeaning to chase.'

We both thought about the mortgage on my flat, the lease on
my office, the cost of running a car that wanted to quit running.
Anna asked whether it was, in fact, a big bill and when I told
her the exact amount she pursed her lips in a tight little Oooh
that showed she thought it a great deal and not a sum I could
allow to escape. Justifying it, I suppose, I told her of the weeks
of work; the intricacies of unravelling the ownership of a
company when someone has been to great pains to conceal it,
and the way I'd been obliged to march into places where I
wasn't wanted and ask questions people plainly hoped no one
would ever raise. For Kate Mullery, and for a lot of money, I'd
done all this.

I didn't tell Anna everything but I told her more than I told Detective Sergeant Ray Donnelly later that evening. He was waiting across the road in his car, when I splashed back through the drizzle to Upper Street. He let me get the street door open before he came over.

'Donnelly rubbed a finger over the diminutive brass plate. Flynn Detective Agency, that's what it says. A few months ago it said somebody's employment bureau. Funnily, I still get visitors who climb to the first floor convinced I'm prepared to find them a job. I send them right back down with a smile and a quip about my usefulness in solving everything except the problem of mass unemployment. It's higher than 20 per cent around here and rising – or falling, depending on how you choose to play with the numbers. Sometimes those visitors ask whether I need staff myself, but those who look first at the tatty desk and chairs that came with the lease don't bother to ask.

Ray Donnelly took my chair and sat at my desk. He absorbed the drab detail of the place with a practised eye and a face that avoided comment.

'OK, Laura,' he said. 'To the point. I'd like to speak to Miss Kate Mullery and she's not to be found. But you've been working for her. I'd like to know where she is and why she hired you.'

'Who told you I'd worked for her?'

He said he wouldn't go into that and please would I answer his questions so we could both go home. That's when I told him I'd last seen her three weeks ago and that I wouldn't discuss why she'd sent for me, except to assure him it was a business inquiry and I had no reason to connect it with her disappearance.

Donnelly was making a chain of my paperclips. He cocked an eyebrow. 'Disappeared, has she?'

We wrangled about who'd introduced the word and whether it was apt. I said: 'My only interest in her now is that I haven't been paid. She's had three months and I've been handed a series of excuses but no money.'

9

'Show me your file on the job you did for her.'

I shook my head. 'Confidential,' I insisted. But it was unavoidable that my eyes flickered towards the scratched filing cabinet where her folder lay.

He held up a necklace of paperclips. From the gym downstairs came the beat of reggae. 'How did she seem when you last saw her?'

'Embarrassed,' I said. 'Why not? She owes me.'

The necklace was twirling gently. 'Not worried? Or scared? Edgy, maybe?'

'Just embarrassed. She apologized about the cheque, said there'd been a mix-up and she would put it in the post right away. The usual noises people make in those circumstances.'

Donnelly waited and I said: 'Sorry, Ray, I can't tell you any more.'

Briefly, his eyes lingered on the filing cabinet. Without a word he got up, looped the paperclip necklace over my head and opened the door. Then he said: 'If you think of anything, you know where to reach me.'

We should both have said more and we could both have said less. He left me guessing I wasn't the only one chasing Kate Mullery for money. That's how it started: money. She was canny but I wouldn't have said short. And she'd have been a dolt not to have checked out the financial security of a company to which she was about to entrust the future of her business.

With Donnelly's lace-ups beating a retreat on the stairs, I stood at my window and watched the rain slanting between me and my personal Big Ben. Ten o'clock on a dreary Tuesday a few days before Christmas. A taxi hissed towards Highbury Corner and then Donnelly skipped across to his car. I waited to see his lights switched on and his car snaking away. When none of that happened I went to my filing cabinet and I spread the contents of the Kate Mullery file over my desk.

Kate Mullery was a dress designer. Maybe I should have told you that before, but maybe there were reasons I didn't. Dress designer – it has the wrong ring. It conjures up glamour and catwalks and the breath of expensive perfume and insincerity. It doesn't drum up Kate Mullery, at any rate not the impression she gave me.

Her call had taken me by surprise but I'd gone right round to her house. One of her staff had escorted me through rooms with fabrics draped over chairs, with cutting tables and drawing boards. I'd been led to a room of thick carpets, cut flowers and Kate Mullery Petite, Irish, blonde, she was exquisitely dressed and yes, if I concentrate hard enough, sure I can remember expensive perfume.

Success had come in Ireland and success had brought her to London. Odd to think of so small a person as such a big name, hard to make the connection between the talent that excited fashion editors and the reticent young woman holding out her hand to me in a house in Canonbury one humid Friday afternoon.

'I'm Kate,' she'd said. 'We have friends in common, Laura.'

So that was it. That's how she'd picked me. The old tribal thing of going to somebody you know and if you can't do that, then you go to somebody known to somebody you know. I didn't ask who the friends were, it made no difference. I just wanted to hear what the job was.

'You'll find it trivial and dull, I'm afraid,' she said, apologizing in advance, 'but it's important to me.'

Then she'd explained about Bethesda, a company that hoped to produce a range of her designs for the chainstore market. Part way through she'd coughed, a delicate hand fluttering to her mouth, and she'd excused herself and taken a long drink from a glass of iced water before going on: 'My financial advisers say the deal's sound, and I intend to move into that sector of the market – without losing my grip on the customers I've already won over, you understand.'

In her way, Kate Mullery was as innovative as Katherine Hamnett with her sloganed T-shirts, or Vivienne Westwood who put the seams outside. Why should only rich bitches get to wear Kate Mullery? She was good enough for the street too.

'What do you want me to do?' I'd asked.

'Find out everything you can about Bethesda.'

'But surely your financial advisers have already . . .?'

'Oh yes, that's true, but I want to be sure. *Extremely* sure.'

Of course I'd said yes, although doubting I'd unearth anything to show that her accountants and her bank had goofed. I offered to report in a week's time.

'No, come back when you've done everything you know how to,' she said.

I didn't expect to prove Bethesda were shaky or crooked, and I didn't expect the inquiry to run into months. The other thing I didn't expect was that I wouldn't be paid.

Crossing to my office window I checked on Donnelly's car. It was still there, by the gardens across the road. The driver's window was wound down an inch. I guessed he was having a cigarette before he moved off, and I imagined him mulling over Mullery the way I was. But if he was loitering in case I had second thoughts about opening my heart to him, he was destined to be disappointed. After putting the file back in the cabinet, I played through the answering-machine messages for a second time. Chris Ionides and the saga of my car, Mrs Lotti and her missing cat. And then the long pause, until you'd think there was no one there, before a whispering voice threatened to kill me.

'Flynn,' it said, 'you ask too many questions. It's not a good thing to be asking questions. But you Flynns, you never learn. You've had your warning. Now I'm going to kill you.'

Then there was another pause before he hung up, and next came the call from the bank. I played the Whisperer through a few more times, but the whisper so distorted the voice that identification was impossible. Over the months he'd left me four messages, the first suggesting death was imminent, the others of the 'or else' variety. Now we were back to imminent.

A crank, of course. Probably an old man with a bee in his bonnet and nothing more constructive to do with his time than

12

leave silly messages on strangers' answering machines. Even so, I wished he hadn't.

It crossed my mind that if he were a regular, then Ray Donnelly might recognize his voice. But when I looked out, Donnelly had driven away. Soon after, I headed up towards Barnsbury Square. Donnelly didn't know I'd moved. Earlier, he'd referred to meeting me at the office or 'the house', meaning Anna Lee's place, and I'd chosen to let him assume I was still there. The fewer people who knew about my flat the better.

It's the top half of a four-storey brick house in a typical London terrace. Nothing fancy, but I'll be staying there. The good carpet I paid for proves that. I have the basics and I'll take my time buying the rest. I didn't come well out of the divorce.

Home. A word with resonance. Sanctuary, for instance. A place where you shut the world out and do what you like, providing it doesn't bother the neighbours. A place where, if you're lucky, you make unfettered choices.

'Japanese,' said Anna Lee, inspecting the flat after I'd moved in. 'A very Japanese lack of clutter.'

But there were no prized possessions behind the doors of my cupboards, no treasures I displayed briefly and otherwise kept safely out of sight. I'd walked away from a lot of things when I'd walked away from my marriage.

The home I'd shared in those days had just been a gadget-filled place I'd lived in, in a way no better than the room I'd had at Anna's house. Worse, maybe, because at least that room was my own personal space. Everyone needs that. Or do they? Home – I mean the one I grew up in – was a clamour of people: parents, brothers and sisters, and then grandparents and aunts and uncles always dropping in, plus friends and neighbours. Not much personal space, not a glimmer of selfish choice.

Somehow we'd all spun away in different directions, like sparks from a Catherine wheel. Two sisters went to Australia, a brother to California, another to New York, yet another to Geneva. My mother took herself off to Ireland to hook up with a cousin starting a business. Grandfather died. I only see my grandmother these days. She stayed, living it out in her great house, squabbling with her lodger, knowing nowhere better to go. Besides, she'd settled down to wait. Wait, that is, for my father to come back.

Climbing the stairs to my flat I heard Gran's voice in my head again: 'Laura Flynn, will you leave it alone now? There's not a soul on God's earth can have the answers to everything. Was there ever a child like yourself for pestering?'

Her remembered words gained a curious significance. 'Flynn,' the Whisperer accused, 'you ask too many questions.'

They were both right. I always had.

Propped against my door was a white envelope. The shy couple who live downstairs often take the mail up for me and leave it like that. But this envelope had been delivered by hand, and it contained a note from Kate Mullery.

'It's very important I see you tonight, Laura,' she'd written, and she'd given me an address at Arkley on the outskirts of north London. She promised to explain when we met.

Some detectives I know, especially in fiction, would have dashed off right away in a state of high excitement. Me, I poured myself a drink, ran a bath, read a novel and went to bed. Mullery could keep. She hadn't said anything in the note about handing over the money she owed and I'd been messed around by her too much to want to call on her for any other reason. And if she seriously thought I was going to undertake any more chores for her, she was wrong.

It was a good novel, about one of those super sleuths who triumph where the police fail. You know the type: a courageous figure, a lone ranger operating outside society, untrammelled by friends and family and any consideration but Getting His Man and Seeing Justice Done. I like a little fantasy before I fall asleep.

Wednesday morning. Still raining. I asked the woman downstairs whether she or her husband had seen who delivered the white envelope but they hadn't. I rang Chris Ionides and begged to borrow a car. He stuck his tongue in his cheek and said there was only his motor bike to be had.

'Some other time,' I said, and he 'remembered' his old Ford and told me to call in and pick it up. Some other time I might surprise him. What's so special about riding a bike?

A memory. I'm out in a summer place, an old wartime airfield in Hertfordshire, I think, and the boys are teaching Tim, the youngest bar me, to ride a bike. I'm twelve, something like that.

Tim's straddling the great thing and kicking and jumping on it until we can none of us stand the roar, so Danny grabs it from him and forces life into it. Then Tim's on and away. It's like he's transformed into a smear of fair hair, dark jersey, silvery bike. 'There was a whirr and a blurr and then he was gone.' That's not me, that's P. G. Wodehouse describing sudden speed. And that's Tim exactly, a whirr and a blurr.

Danny and Desmond are hurraying that he's got away and they're making a great hullaballoo about it the way boys do. Me, I'm tired of it all. You see, I know well enough it's never going to be my turn. When was it ever Laura's turn? I'm fine to go up on the pillion with either of them and to look out the spanner they need for tinkering, but will they let a girl ride? Indeed not. I understand it, and the knowledge wearies me.

There are two bikes. Tim came on the pillion with Danny and I was up behind Desmond. Danny's bike's better because he's the oldest. Of course, they aren't trusting Tim with Danny's machine. That one's leaning against the wall a few yards from me.

All of a sudden the lethargy seeps from me and I take a step towards Danny's bike. Before the boys realize what's going on behind their backs, I'm away after Tim.

The memory shuts down abruptly at the point where I'm trundling back to face my brothers' wrath, wheeling the thing because it's no longer running and there's a nasty twist in a piece of chrome that was nice and smooth when I set out, and

Danny's livid and screaming: 'Mam would have killed you if you'd injured yourself!'

It was round about that time that Gran started to complain about my harum scarum ways.

After the call to Chris Ionides I threw my kit into a bag and headed for the office, by way of the gym downstairs. Going early, I could have the weight machines to myself. I like that, sometimes preferring solitude to the obligation to chatter for fear of being labelled unfriendly.

When I showered and dressed after an hour I felt wonderful. Maybe it was the sheer physical involvement plus the achievement of pulling more than I'd once believed possible for a woman of average height and build. Maybe too it was the thinking time it allowed me. Nothing narcissistic about this, I solved more than one of my cases while sifting evidence to the regular rhythm of my pulse and the resisting machines.

That morning it helped me decide what to do about Mrs Lotti. She'd have to be persuaded that it wasn't practical for me to scour London for her missing moggy, and I could drop in on her *en route* from Chris's garage to Kate Mullery at Arkley.

Mrs Lotti lived in a walk-up block, in Holloway, named Nonesuch. Someone with a cruel irony had named all the piles on the estate after royal palaces. Windsor, Buckingham, Hampton, Hatfield, that sort of thing. I wondered whether Mrs Lotti and the other tenants knew how they were mocked.

Parking Chris's car by some graffiti-daubed garages alongside a greyish grass playing area, I started up the concrete stairs. Youths looking down from a landing watched with more interest than made me comfortable. When I reached that level they'd gone. I glanced down at the Ford. No one was interfering with it, no one was on the playing area near it unless you counted two lascivious dogs. I began on the next flight of stairs.

Nonesuch had always given me a sinking feeling. It was no uglier than its neighbours but it was the block you saw most prominently from the road and it didn't have a single pleasant feature. From way back it had bad associations. Hazy about detail, I recalled a fuss over the building of it, something to do with corruption, I thought, but that hadn't been rare in the rush to throw up cheap homes in the sixties. Lately Nonesuch had been recognized as substandard and there was a campaign to get it demolished. Meanwhile it housed council tenants with the least choice about housing. No one would ever have chosen to live there.

I paused on the next landing and looked at the view. Pooter country. Young Lupin, archetypal yuppie that he was, said Holloway was a bit 'off', which his father took to mean 'far off', especially as Lupin's pronouncement accompanied a move to the racier milieu of Bayswater. Somewhere down below me, to the south I'd say, was the Pooters' house: The Laurels, 12 Brickfield Terrace. I know the house well, although it isn't there. I see it in all the streets around. *'A nice six-roomed residence, not counting basement, with a front breakfast-parlour. We have a little front garden, and there is a flight of ten steps up to the front door which, by the by, we keep locked with the chain up . . .'*

They weren't all bombed in the war or bulldozed later to make space for horrors like Nonesuch. Mr Pooter paid £80 a year rent for The Laurels, today he'd have to find at least £250,000 to buy. That's one joke the Grossmiths missed.

Mrs Lotti was a caricature of an Italian *mamma* with a cluster of children. 'My cat, he'sa gonna,' she sighed, and I'll swear she managed a tear. 'You finda my cat, *sì*?'

'No,' I said. 'Impossible.' And I caught myself exaggerating regret and waving my hands about like she did. So I pulled myself together and gave her the postcards I'd typed for her to put in local shop windows pleading for the return of the cat should somebody in the neighbourhood be feeding him.

'This cat,' she said, 'isa not English.'

I floundered.

She said: 'I show you, Laura. Isa beautiful cat. *Sì*, isa pedigree.'

Now all this seemed highly improbable. Folks like Mrs Lotti, who live in places like Nonesuch, don't by and large own

17

pedigree pets. But Mrs Lotti fetched me a photograph of her cat and lo and behold he was a most singular creature. When I say he was big I just know you won't understand that he was *extremely* big. And when I say he was tabby with long, long bristling fur, and that his ears were huge and pricked, and his eyes were close together and he . . . Well, as you see, he was no average puss.

Mrs Lotti couldn't tell me what breed he was, but believed he was American and she had a rambling and unhelpful story to explain how she'd come by him. Reluctantly I handed back the photograph. Reluctantly, because I wanted to run to Liverpool Road and thrust it in front of Anna Lee who's the most cat-loving woman I know, and say: 'Now that's what I call a cat!' Only it wasn't. It was more what I'd call a monster. Especially if I met it in the half-dark.

The photograph did the trick. I left Mrs Lotti's having promised after all that I'd go to some trouble to locate her cat. Jaguar, she called him.

That crazy cat was still on my mind as I turned into Arkley Lane, an unmade road trickling out of suburbia into the city's green belt. Bungalows, the haphazard acretion of past decades, hedged it. Then they ran out and I thought that was that, no house of the name Kate Mullery's note had given me. But slowing by the deer farm, looking for a safe place to turn, I spotted the gabled roof of a Victorian farmhouse hidden behind ragged hawthorns. Knights End. This is what I'd come for.

Kate opened the front door while I was getting out of the car. I didn't apologize for not rushing to her the previous evening and she didn't grumble. We got down to business. Her business, not mine. There was no mention of the unpaid bill.

She said: 'I expect you'll find this absurd, Laura, but I've been forced to go into hiding.'

I answered her with all the surprise she hoped for.

'Phone calls,' she said. She was pacing the kitchen, striding back and forth between a solid pine table and an attractively

18

decrepit dresser. A hand went to her neck in search of stray hair but the upswept style was perfect. She coughed once. Twice. I waited. She explained: 'Threats, that's what they were.'

I remembered that cough, that fidgeting. Apparently I'd lied to Donnelly, unwittingly misled him with my assurance that Kate Mullery hadn't been nervous when I'd last met her. She was doing the same things now, and I've seldom seen a woman so agitated. I said: 'Who?'

She denied knowledge with a shake of her head. The hand checked the hair again. Still perfect.

'All right,' I said. 'Tell me this. If you're being threatened, why am I here and not the police?'

The look she gave me suggested she was properly aware of me for the first time, I might have been wallpaper until then. She pointed at a chair. I'd hoped to go through to the sitting room and talk more comfortably in there. That would have reassured me that there was no one listening the other side of the partly opened door. I suspected I'd heard movement in there. Accepting her terms I drew the chair out from the table and sat down.

'A man,' she said. 'A man with a muffled voice rings me. He does it late at night and he speaks softly.'

I decided not to tell her I had a Whisperer of my own, for all I knew perhaps the same one. 'What does he say?'

'He tells me to leave well alone, to stick to designing frocks and keep my nose out of other people's business.'

If only she'd stop that pacing, it was like trying to eyeball a metronome. My eyes refused to follow her any more and my index finger drew a matchstick man on the table. 'Go on,' I said. It didn't seem much of a threat so far.

Kate came to rest against the dresser, arms folded protectively around her. 'It escalated, Laura. In the last two messages he threatened to kill me, said I was putting my life at risk because I hadn't taken the warning to stop meddling. He said I should seriously think about going home to Dublin if I wanted to go on living.'

'Did you record any of this stuff?'

'No. I said he rings late, and the machine isn't in the bedroom.' The farmhouse kitchen was warm but she was shivering.

'A crank, I should think.' I said. 'Why leave home because of a crank?'

Kate flared at my dismissal of her fears. 'That's easy for you to say. You haven't heard him. There's menace in that voice, and . . .'

'And?' I forced her to the end of her sentence.

'And I found my cat dead in my garden.'

I'm afraid I laughed. I mean, here she was, a grown woman allowing herself to be scared out of her home by a few not very specific threatening phone calls and panicking because a dead cat turns up in her garden. Half London would be on the move if we all reacted in that way.

The laugh was a mistake. She crumpled. She cried. She slumped on to a chair across the table from me and wailed. I didn't know what to do. She was a client, not a friend, and a comforting arm around the shoulders might be out of keeping. Also I wanted her to snap out of it and not assume my pity. And besides that I was wondering whether it mightn't be an act.

Eventually I did what lots of people do when they don't know what to do. I made tea. She dried her eyes. Her sobs diminished as she warmed her hands around the mug I set on the table in front of her. I heard a sniff mixed up with a thank you and then she accepted I wasn't letting her off any hooks. I wanted the full story, from the very beginning to the very end.

It got interesting only when the cat turned up dead. This wasn't an exceptional cat, except that it had been shot. The man on the phone had promised her that soon she'd get a different kind of message from him, and that was it: her cat shot through the back of the head and left on her front path.

'That's when I fled here. It belongs to a friend and it was the best I could do for a hiding place at short notice.'

I thought she'd done pretty well. 'When did you come here?'

'A few days ago. I skulked at home before that, not answering the door or the phone and hoping people would think I was away. But it was unnerving, listening to people trying to contact me and then giving me up.'

We drank the scalding liquid, Kate keeping her eyes down and me watching her. I dusted off my first question and tried it again. 'Why me? Why not the police?'

'You've already done some work for me.'

I hoped that reminded her I hadn't been paid. 'Not as a body guard,' I said. There had to be a better reason than that.

If there was, she hadn't decided to tell me. I asked whether she'd been interesting herself in anything apart from her new collection and fretting over Bethesda, the company who wanted the franchise to take her into the high street.

Kate set her empty mug between us, her fingers busy stroking the pattern on it. Pink elephants, holding each others' tails with their trunks and circling the mug. Round and round and round. Pink elephants.

She said: 'I can't afford a mistake with that franchise, it'll make or break me.'

Yet what did this have to do with husky callers and dead cats, and an objection to calling in the police? She fastened on to Bethesda again. 'Laura, that business with Bethesda has taken all my energy. They *sound* good. They *look* good.' She hesitated and there was a 'but' in the room. I grunted and pushed her on. She said: 'You were clever to find out their true ownership.'

'Diligent, that's all.'

'It didn't produce any reason for me to avoid getting involved with them, and yet I know something's wrong. I feel it. Maybe it's idiotic to let feelings influence judgements in business, but I can't help that.'

I didn't mind we'd stuck on Bethesda, it could revive her

intention to pay me. I said: 'You didn't go ahead with them then?'

'Oh yes, I did. At least, I've agreed I will and matters are in hand. It's only that . . . Oh, Laura, I wish I could like them more. The people there, the superbly charming Mr Elvy and his colleagues doing all that smiling and reassuring . . .' Distaste expressed itself in a shudder.

Rejecting the notion of telling her that what she required of them was a professional relationship and not a love affair came easily. I was still hoping to be paid sometime. But my opinion of Kate Mullery had shifted. Today she didn't strike me as stable and sensible, and apart from that it was irritating that she was withholding something from me. I tried my question again. Third time lucky.

'Why me and not the police?'

'Every time he's called he's told me not to inform them. To begin with, when I didn't take him seriously, I saw no point in bothering them.'

'And later?'

'Later, the evening after I'd found the cat, he rang and said I was to stop you working for me. Or you'd be killed too.'

I strained to hear sounds in the next room. Kate, I guessed, assumed I was reeling from the news of a second-hand death threat, and one delivered, by her account, a week ago. I let her assume it. I had plenty to think about and her reactions to *my* reactions were irrelevant. The one decision I took while I was with her was that I wouldn't own up that I'd had death threats of my own.

Telling me we were on the same hit list cheered her up a shade. There was the ghost of a smile. 'Now you see why I wanted you and not the police.'

I didn't, not entirely. But she was making assumptions and didn't register the ambiguity of my murmured reply.

Kate said: 'You're supposed to be good, Laura. Find him. And stop him.'

Just like that. I studied the fingers fondling the pink elephants and I warned her: 'The police are already interested in why you're not at home.'

This was intended to persuade her that the wisest course was to call them. Unfortunately, it convinced her she'd be better off with me, because they'd failed to trace her and because I was apparently privy to their every move. Recovered from the weepy stage, she was single-minded.

Pride lured me on whereas common sense urged me to keep a grip on common sense. Pride won. 'OK,' I heard myself say. 'I'll handle it.'

Even now there are nights when I wake in a cold dread and regret that decision.

She said: 'That's great, Laura, I knew you'd . . .'

'There's a condition, though.'

'Which is?'

'That you tell the police where you are and that you're safe.'

'Oh but . . .'

'Listen, Kate. Someone's already told them you've strayed. When you stay hidden the pressure will build up and there'll be a fully fledged missing person inquiry. And you're too famous for the story not to be played up by the press. That's not the sort of publicity you want, though, is it?'

This time she took the point. 'Tell them I'm safe, but not where I am. I want to feel secure here until the man's caught. If no one but you and the friend who owns this house know I'm holed up here, that's better than it being gossip in every police station in London.'

So that's the way it was. I was to call off the police and go sleuthing after the man who'd threatened her. Oh yes, we agreed a rate for the job and she had the grace to apologize yet again for her tardy payment for the Bethesda inquiry. There wasn't a lot I could say about that because she claimed she'd gone into hiding without her cheque book. No, I didn't believe it either.

I carried the pink elephants and my mug over to the kitchen sink and I said goodbye and went outside. The morning was achingly cold. Frost lingered palely in the ditches and bluetits quivered along the hedges. Rural pretence was sustained for a good few hundred yards before I hit the Barnet road and traffic spilling into London from the M25.

Driving was slow and troubled right into Barnet. Near the church I parked in a side street and walked the rest of the way to the library. I looked up farms in the *Yellow Pages* telephone directory and found a number for Knights End Farm, a number Kate Mullery had refused to give me saying I could drive out there whenever I needed to see her.

A number wasn't enough for me. I wanted the name of the owner too. The Arkley Lane entry in *Kelly's Directory* of businesses provided that. Robin Digby.

The name I'd remember, the number probably not. That's why it was only the number I wrote on the slip of paper I zipped away in a compartment of my shoulder bag. It would be safe there and only I would know what it meant.

Afterwards I rewarded endeavour with an *espresso* and a creamy pastry before trailing back to the car and rejoining the flow downhill towards central London.

Chris Ionides was glad to see us, the Ford and me. Relieved, I might say, because he'd promised it to a friend for the afternoon. He had news. He'd discovered where the unpronounceable part was to be had for my own car and I let it look as though this encouraged me hugely, while knowing we'd both be anxious until it was actually in his workshop or, better still, in my car.

Then I wrapped my scarf tighter round my neck and set off from Highbury Fields for Upper Street and my office. The route took me close to Highbury Corner Magistrates Court and on impulse I made the detour.

I owed Ray Donnelly a favour for not making much of my heroics on the Underground, and I was uneasy at having fobbed him off with scant help the previous evening. I never knew when I might need him. He wasn't one of the police officers who, against all the rules, are prepared to moonlight for detective agencies but he had his uses. As the court was sitting, there was a chance he'd be there and if not then one of his colleagues might tell me where I could reach him. Better that than ring the police station. Like Kate Mullery, I favoured discretion.

Breezing in, I met a man with answers. 'Donnelly's case is in there.' He jerked a thumb. 'He should be finished any time now.'

'Thanks.' I entered the courtroom, just checking. Ray Donnelly was there all right, holding his peace while a deal of argument went on about two black youths and whether they ought to be remanded in custody. The boys' solicitor was doing a valiant job but not good enough. The magistrate was geared up to speak, he'd made his mind up and didn't want any more on the abstruse point the man was developing. Donnelly knew it too. A glint of satisfaction came to his eye.

The magistrate got his word in. The solicitor subsided. The lads stood up and were remanded in custody. A court officer led them towards the cells. And Donnelly turned and saw me. I anticipated recognition, a wink, but he was startled. And then I looked past him and saw the prisoners clearly, saw their faces for the first time. One was a brute with a bull neck and heaving muscles. He didn't look delighted to be heading for the cells, but on the other hand he wasn't wired and bandaged. No broken jaw.

'You lied!' I accused, pursuing Donnelly out of the room.

'Laura, what are you doing here? I thought you wanted to keep out of this.'

'That's no answer.'

'I don't owe you any answers.'

He was needled at being caught out, he wasn't talking in the superior way he usually did, as though I were young and silly and had to have things explained simply. He was too annoyed to bother with that.

I let his pace outstrip mine and then he was through a door where I couldn't follow. I went out into the street. He'd lied to coerce me and I didn't like that, but his lie freed me from a debt. My guilt dissolved and with it my intention to tell him he could stop wasting his time hunting Kate Mullery.

I've mentioned there's a women's gym below my office. That's true, but it's at the rear of the building. Fronting the street, directly underneath me, is a boutique. I allowed myself to be enticed into it, not an infrequent diversion, and treated, myself to a pair of long, flashy titanium ear-rings.

Trying them on before the mottled mirror above the basin in my washroom, I complimented myself on my trashy good taste. I flicked my long black hair over my shoulders and admired the way its colour set off the winking greens and purples and pinks of the metal. Slipping a hand inside the neck of my black blouse, I drew out the only piece of jewellery I habitually wear, unless you count the Spiro Agnew watch that I'd bargained for on a stall in Camden Passage for the pleasure of hearing people ask 'Spiro *Who*?' It wasn't a watch stall, it was ephemera. 'Interesting Ephemera', the sign said. Ah, the vagaries of the political life.

I stared into the mirror at the reflection of my gold chain and St Lucy on the medallion that swings from it. When I was four years old I'd been given St Lucy. She was a present from my father, although my mother decided she was too old for me and had put her away, in tissue paper, until the years had spun by. My father hadn't been there to argue. Soon after my fourth birthday he'd left us.

He'd walked out of the house one Friday evening to buy a packet of cigarettes, and he'd never come back. The classic desertion.

Too young to remember the shock and the anguish, all I have of him is a scattering of unreliable memories and St Lucy.

I shook myself out of this mood, got busy on behalf of Mrs Lotti and telephoned the Wood Green Animal Shelter to check their countrywide register of missing pets. But they had no monstrous Jaguar for me. They did, though, offer the opinion that it was an American breed called a Maine Coon. This apparently signified a creature crossed with a racoon and originating in the state of Maine. Having seen its photo I was ready to believe anything.

After registering the cat with them, I got out the Mullery file and went through it again considering everything from a fresh angle, the one that might toss up the identity of a man who'd make her nasty phone calls.

Her staff were out for a start, at any rate the ones I'd met. Chief assistant was a camp young man who regarded her with doggy devotion. Scuppering Kate would ruin his career, and rob him of a friend he variously described as wonderful, marvellous, tremendous, fantastic etc. No, Keith Jay was out.

The rest I'd encountered were women, and again they were people who needed a job and would stand to lose if Kate moved from London or, worst of all, died. Rivals, then? Other fashion businesses who were scared of her competition if she moved down to street level? I'd have to find out.

Islington's crammed with tiny businesses you don't notice if you don't choose to. I walked around the corner into Islington Park Street, up past the Oddball Juggling Company and the health food shop, and through the door of a clothing manufacturer, which is to say the wholesale front of a sweatshop. A lugubrious middle-aged Turk, with tight curls and no time on his hands and drivers to chase up, heard me out and promised to talk to me about the clothing industry.

Why did I pick him? Not purely because he was nearest but because I passed that shop window every day and couldn't help but be aware how the expensive clothes that were in *Vogue* one month would be hanging there, in cheapo high street mode, the next. He was a man who'd know about the world Kate Mullery was planning to enter, and it might even be that he knew a thing or two about Bethesda that my first round of inquiries hadn't revealed. All I had to do was get him to tell me. We fixed a time to talk.

In the busy run up to Christmas he was going to spare me half an hour. If he'd known it was for Laura Flynn, detective,

I've no doubt he wouldn't have troubled. It's illegal to pretend to be a police officer, but it's easy to lie about being a journalist. The police do it themselves. I let him think I was a freelance writer working up a story for *Time Out*. I said *Time Out* because I'd written one or two pieces for them.

By now I should have spelled out for you the intricacies of the Bethesda business but they make dull reading unless you've a taste for business and the shenanigans accountants get up to. Let's put it briefly, like this. On the face of it Bethesda was a modest business in north London making up garments for the fashion industry, but it was actually a subsidiary of a development company. That's virtually all you need to know.

The rest, if you've a yen for more, is that Bethesda was financially sound and had approached Kate Mullery for a contract to manufacture for her. There was no secret that she hoped for a chainstore range; she'd said as much in an interview with the trade press when she'd moved from Dublin to London, and Bethesda hadn't been alone in following up the tip.

Bethesda was impressive and Kate had gone along with it in preference to other companies, and it had been at a late stage that she'd recognized the degree of her uncertainty and had turned to me. What I'd found was that the company had been in trouble a few years back and had swapped names with a sister company called Larches. Originally it had been Larches that manufactured and Bethesda that had supplied fabric to Larches and other manufacturers. The switch meant that Larches' debts had been cancelled out and both companies could continue in business and continue to borrow. The people were the same.

Well, there was no shame in a clothing business getting into financial difficulty and accountants doing fancy footwork to get it out again. A common story. Except that when I'd dug around a while I noticed that a firm called Bagel Delight owned both Bethesda and Larches. From there I'd sauntered down the byways of the food industry, discovering that Bagel Delight was associated with a company that catered for barmitzvahs and weddings, and that this was owned in turn by a small hotel group, and so on and so forth. At the end of the line they all belonged, one way or another, to a property company called Shirlands.

It takes a few lines to convey all this, but it took me months to uncover it, although I'm no novice at revealing the truth about companies. With a number of local councils determined to ensure their contracts aren't awarded to businesses tainted by apartheid, there's plenty of this kind of work available to detectives.

My report to Kate Mullery was a model of economy. Bethesda, I said, was as safe as Shirlands wanted it to be. Presumably she discussed this with her financial advisers, confirming what I claimed for Shirlands and what, being new to this country, she might not herself have known. It's medium sized but it's solid and it's been competing in London with the big developers.

No reason to worry Kate with the outstanding puzzle, but it had niggled me that while most growing businesses have rationalized lately, Shirlands was attempting to make the big time while hanging on to an extraordinary diversity of bits and pieces. Bethesda, Larches, Bagel Delight . . . What on earth did it want with that lot? She didn't ask and I couldn't have told her.

Here I was then, one Wednesday morning in December with a keen wind sneaking under the window frame in my office and lifting the papers in the Mullery file. Here I was, back at square one. I pulled a thick cardigan out of my bottom desk drawer and twisted my scarf around my neck too. The electric fire was already doing as much as it was prepared to do.

I was getting no help from the file, either. None of the people I'd met at any of the businesses, from the casually chatted-up minions to the executives with dark suits and formal appointments, seemed a contender for the role of Kate's threatening caller. Imagining them growling down the line at her late at night was impossible, picturing them shooting her cat was laughable.

As I sighed, flipping the file shut, my breath misted in front of my face. That was enough to allow me to lock up and leave. Nothing more would be gained sitting there staring at old information, except perhaps hypothermia. And I knew a place which was warm and welcoming and might, in an admittedly oblique fashion, help me cast light on my darkness. I trotted off to visit my grandmother.

Gran. A dumpy old-fashioned woman living in a big old-fashioned house with an old-fashioned fortune stashed away. Or so they said. Gran didn't say.

When I arrived she didn't say hello, either. She was crouched forward in her chair, reading the palm of the cherubic Father Mahon. Ada, Gran's lodger from the rooms at the top of the house, let me in, her clatter and fussing designed to show disapproval of the art of Cheiro and Kitty Flynn both.

Ada had curled over with the years; her spindly body makes me think of an umbrella. She clumped about the sitting room, setting upright the Christmas cards that had toppled on to their robined, hollied, snowy faces. 'It's Laura to see you, Kitty. Haven't you a word of welcome for your own kin?'

Gran rejected both of us with a wriggle of her hunched shoulders.

Father Mahon was having nothing to do with us either. 'Is it gold you see now, Kitty? I could be doing with a portion of gold.' He laughed but there was a keen edge to his voice. He wanted the gold.

Ada snarled. She's as old as Gran, possibly more, and they've known each other since they were girls in Wicklow. That means they never stop fratching but are allowed to go on being friends all the same, suspicion and insult being no more than common currency and not a matter for taking offence. A truce is called for Father Mahon's visits, but it's an uneasy one.

Gran jerked the shoulders again, irritated by Ada's open disapproval. Her finger moved up the centre of the priest's palm, not exactly touching but close. 'Your Line of Fate, Father, makes it plain you're a man of strong character but there are few of those little influence lines.' She shook her head in regret.

He said: 'Is the lack of little lines a bad thing, Kitty?'

'It means you're to lead an isolated, lonely sort of life.'

Who could deny it, in his sort of work?

Well, Father Mahon did. He cocked his head and he chuckled. 'Ah, the lines haven't run true then!'

Gran moved her hovering finger. 'Success now,' she said, ignoring his challenge. 'Cheiro called this the most mysterious of the signs . . .'

Ada came to life, richly sarcastic. 'The whole thing is most mysterious to me!'

Gran went on: 'We call it the Sun sign. It brings success. You see here, Father? The way it curves from the Line of Fate? That's where it tells me plainly that you're to look forward to gold.'

Ada kicked in another protest. 'Ach, make it pounds and pence will you, Kitty? How's the man to go down to the shops with gold about him?'

Gran withdrew her hand and was turning to Ada, but Father Mahon smoothed things over. 'Shall we say wealth? Will that satisfy you both?'

Gran said: 'Tea please, Ada.'

And Ada Carey was sent servant-like from the room leaving Gran and Father Mahon and me to say our belated hellos, and Gran to murmur modestly at his compliments on her skills as a reader of fates. There's something deep in her that hankers to reach beyond the limits of everyday human understanding, but she'd reached no further than this. Tea came and the four of us sat around the fire with Gran's favourite porcelain, all that remained of a long-ago tea service, for three of us, and a chunky china willow pattern for Ada.

Gran said: 'Would you believe it, Laura, I was saying only twenty minutes ago that I entirely expected you to call in on us this afternoon and take a drop of tea.'

Ada's expression disproved this.

Gran continued. 'I knew you'd not let me down, Laura. Isn't that what I was saying, Father?'

He gulped and nodded and splashed his tea. Ada's chin came up in triumph, the priest's clumsiness apparently making the point that Kitty Flynn's premonition was news to him too. I mumbled that I'd meant to drop in before but had been tied up, the kind of thing one says.

Gran addressed Father Mahon. 'Today is the day, you see, and Laura is always sure to come by on the very day itself.'

'Oh,' I said. 'Er . . .'

'Is there some doubt about that?' Gran asked me, but I dared not argue with her. Sometimes she goes like that, talks cryptically not to say confusingly. It's all of a piece with her being in the mood for premonitions and reading palms.

Father Mahon was shaking his head, assuming formality. 'A sad, sad matter it was, Mrs Flynn. A great trial to you, a burden you have borne down the years.'

Gran said: 'And the same for Laura.'

'Yes,' he added quickly, 'and for Laura.'

Of course I'd caught on by then. She was talking about my father. My mind filled with the picture of a gently smiling man, a happy man. But it was nonsense that Gran and I shared a miserable vigil on the anniversary, waiting for him to walk back into the house or speculating why he didn't. As a matter of fact, I didn't think it *was* the day, but I was going to let that pass.

Not Ada Carey, though. 'It was the eighteenth, Kitty. This is only the seventeenth.'

Gran went tsk tsk to show what a fool Ada Carey could be. 'Father, I will never forget the anguish in this family on the Wednesday before Christmas when Joseph Flynn . . .'

Ada intercepted. 'You always say it was on a Tuesday, Kitty.'

I headed off trouble. 'Well it was such a long time ago . . .'

I hadn't headed off trouble.

Gran bridled. 'Would you say so, Laura? Well you were only a dot of four and to be excused on that account, but that

Christmas is one that nobody else in the family is ever likely to forget.'

Father Mahon and I exchanged cautious looks. I'm always cautious with Father Mahon. For one thing, I never know what nonsense Gran and Ada have been feeding him and for another he's a person I'd prefer to keep at a distance. I'll hazard he's around fifty, which is more than twenty years older than me and more than twenty years younger than Gran. But he has an innocent air that I imagine him to put on in the morning and take off at night, all part of his professional guise.

Gran's hobby, apart from sparring with Ada, is telling people their destinies. More truthfully, she short-changes them by not relaying everything she claims to see and then hinting wildly to the rest of us about the dramas and catastrophes her clients, whom she almost but never precisely names, clutch in the palms of her hands.

Also she has a disconcerting way of drawing her breath in sharply while watching television so that anyone who didn't know her would think a pain was stabbing in her side. She'll say: 'That one now . . .' And you'll know the person on the screen is one whose hand she'd like to hold in hers. She spotted Margaret Thatcher in the early seventies as a woman with a destiny that deserved examination, but quite often she lights on people who've yet to make their mark. They don't have to be on the telly though for her to fancy them.

'Whose hand,' I once asked her, 'would you most like to read?'

'Mozart,' she said without hesitation.

Until this afternoon I hadn't trusted the rumour that Father Mahon went round there to have his palm read, I thought he was round there to prise money out of her. But I didn't expect him to get it. Kitty Flynn's nobody's fool.

She got rid of him after his first cup of tea and Ada faded away. Gran popped out of her chair and fetched a bottle of whiskey from a cupboard and splashed it into her tea. In the evenings she's prone to a cup of hot milk with the whiskey in it.

33

Her Irishness intensifies as she ages. In recent years she's thought nothing of taking in the *Irish Times*, detailing me to bring her black and white puddings from the butchers near my office and setting Ada Carey to bake soda bread. My mother is appalled by this regression.

'Laura,' said Gran, her eyes blue and clear as the hand-painted anemones on her Spode teacup. 'Will you settle to something, please, and make a go of your life?'

'I work, Gran, I'm useful. You can't demand more than that.'

'I can so.' Tutting, she rattled the cup down to its saucer. 'It's a waste to be merely looking for cats and dogs.'

'And stolen children, and missing money, and fraudsters and thieves in the night and . . .' I recited some of my recent cases.

She pretended not to hear me. 'Let folk chase after their own pets, your talents should be better employed.'

My talents? She was referring to what she'd seen in my hand, long ago when I was impressionable and curious and let her look, before my mother interrupted and blamed us both for foolishness.

I fingered St Lucy on her chain around my throat and I smiled. What, I wondered, was in Gran's own hand? She'd never confessed what she read there.

'You're like your father before you,' Gran said suddenly, and smacked her hand against the teapot to check for warmth before pouring a refill I was unable to refuse.

'Gran, you're funny about my father,' I said. 'For years you wouldn't have his name mentioned and now you keep bringing him into conversation.'

She narrowed her eyes and said she thought I was bright enough to understand. 'Age gives fresh perspectives. And the anger dulls, the way people tell you it will but you're never ready to believe. I haven't the anger with him now, but I need to know what's become of him.'

'He was supposed to be in America.'

'So we heard. And before that we heard he was in Ireland.'

A ripple of apprehension ran through me as I feared she was going to ask me to look for him, that the gibe about seeking out cats and dogs had been a prelude to asking me to look for her son. Gran claims powers, she doesn't need to speak the words for you to know her will. As I tried to read the expression on her face I couldn't satisfy myself whether the thought inside my head was mine or hers.

But when she next spoke what she said was: 'I have the need to know where he is and what he made of himself. I can account for all the others but not for Joe. The anger of it has gone but not the pain of it. Now it's the ache of unfinished business. Laura, I'm an old woman and I will not have long to finish it.'

Gran didn't say any more, there was no request that I was forced to acknowledge with a yes or a no. But in the firelight her eyes beseeched me.

I shifted in my chair, eager to change the subject, but as I deftly accomplished it my mind was elsewhere. The movement had sent my medallion sliding an inch along its chain and I was conscious of the fire-warmed gold touching my flesh. St Lucy. My father's last gift to me. St Lucy, the saint you pray to for help in finding that which is lost.

TWO

There are seventy bodies taken out of the River Thames in London each year. Kate Mullery's was one of them.

I was there. That's coincidence if you enjoy coincidences, but it needn't be if you don't. We can argue it either way.

I knew why I was there but I couldn't say why she was. Kate was supposed to be hiding out at Knights End deer farm at Arkley, I was the one meant to be creeping about in the shadows and upsetting people who had secrets.

Actually when they found her I was at Wapping Old Stairs quizzing a man from the Thames River police force about access points to the water, ownership of riverside sites and so on. Mundane but for all I knew crucial stuff. He didn't mind, I'd helped him once, when I was working as an investigator for a big detective agency, and now it was his turn to help me. While we talked, somewhere out on the threatening water his colleagues in the Underwater Search Unit were tracking a body that tourists in a pleasure boat claimed had hit the water earlier in the evening. Kate's body.

They came in close with their sodden cargo and I looked down into her savagely contorted face and I knew her. I didn't say so.

Perhaps I should have done, should have got involved in making witness statements about when I'd last seen her and why she'd employed me, but I didn't. I steeled myself to thrust another question at my helpful contact and when he'd rambled to the end of his answer I strolled away pretending total preoccupation with my inquiry, no feeling for the awful thing in the boat or for the sensibilities of the men whose grisly work was to bring such things ashore. Gulls keened above us the whole time I was there.

I got back up the precipitous steps hanging over the greedy water and I walked up the narrow alley. It's a forbidding place, one where hanged bodies used to dangle in chains from a gibbet until the tide had washed them three times. When I reached the pub I shut myself in the lavatory and I was sick, very sick.

Kate Mullery dead! Sweet Jesus, what was going on?

Underlying my revulsion there was fear. Her caller had threatened us both and now she was dead.

Someone grumbled through the door and I hurried up and rinsed my mouth and blundered out to find a telephone and a taxi. 'Canonbury,' I told the driver. And got him to take me to the end of the street where Kate had lived and worked for that brief sequence of her life that promised a bright future of fame and fortune but had this night ended in murder.

Oh yes, I was sure it was murder.

The cloakroom window opened easily and with a bit of a struggle I eased myself through the gap and stepped down on to the edge of the wash-basin and then the floor. I pulled the window shut after me, then felt my way in the near dark to the beautiful room where Kate had stood one day back in the summer and held out her hand to say hello for the first time.

London helps on occasions like this. It's never entirely dark, too many powerful street lights and security lights for that. And so I moved through the rooms, the ones with the cutting tables and the ones with the drawing boards and I came to the beautiful room. The carpets were just as thick as I remembered, but the cut flowers had gone. What I wanted was Kate's desk and the information she'd elected not to give me.

Now what she'd left behind in Dublin I couldn't guess, but in London Kate Mullery wasn't a woman who surrounded herself with personal snippets. No photographs on the desk or mantelpiece, for instance. Nothing on view looked personal instead of professional. With the thin blade of my torch I checked letters and notes of telephone conversations, all neatly paperclipped and waiting for her. Everything was related to orders and availability of fabrics, or invitations to fashion trade events. That left the desk diary.

I skimmed it, from the beginning of the year when she'd come to London. Entries were terse and gave away nothing beyond names of individuals, names of companies and times of appointments. My own name featured in the identical cryptic manner.

After the diary I went through the desk, hoping for anything that would flesh out this enigmatic woman and illuminate the nature of her fear, the reasons for her death. Here I was luckier. Kate Mullery had written a dozen cheques, attached them to bills and then drawn back from sending them. So this is what had happened to her cheque for me.

I stood with it in my hand, the temptation to slip it into my pocket rising to insurmountable. And that was when I heard the noise.

In the passage outside the room someone was moving, softly. My torch flicked off, I glided to the black corner behind a bulky armchair and I crouched there. I was hidden but unfortunately I couldn't see. The merest draught alerted me to the opening of the door, I sensed a figure moving over the carpet to the desk and I recognized the gentle protest of a drawer being opened and one brief, brushing papery sound. The sequence ended with a sharp click and then there was a repetition of the draught and receding, furtive movements in the passage.

I counted twenty and risked peering around the chair. A street lamp flung a grey haze down the centre of the room. I was alone again.

Back at the desk I tried to open a drawer, discover what had been slid into it. But my suspicion about the click proved correct. The desk was locked.

Whoever had crept in had locked it and left me with Kate Mullery's cheque in my hand. Now this might appear the answer to a prayer. Hadn't Fate intervened and recommended me to keep the cheque and go on my way and cash it? Who, now Kate was dead, would know she hadn't sent it to me herself?

The person who'd been through the desk before me, that's who. Besides, at that moment I was more interested in finding out what had been added to the contents of the desk.

Lock-picking is not one of my skills. I know a man who's brilliant at it but this was no time to ring him up. For one thing it was late, for another I couldn't risk sending for company and anyway I wasn't certain whether he was still in Pentonville. So it was just me and that desk.

I twiddled a bit with a hairpin but it was Kate's own paperknife that did it. In the top drawer I found a folder. This, then, was how Kate Mullery had coralled all the scribbled notes and reminders that had made up her working day.

To go through that pile was going to take more time than I was willing to spend there. That's why I took the file away with me. Reckless, perhaps, but hindsight is great for pinpointing recklessness. I wanted to be away home with what I'd been seeking, not tiptoeing around a house where I knew I was not the only tiptoer.

The cloakroom where I'd climbed in was a dangerous distance away so I opted for the sash window in the beautiful room. This had security bolts, unlike the cloakroom window where security had been overlooked the way it often is in cloakrooms. In seconds I'd unscrewed the bolts and swung up the sash. As I swung, the alarm went.

Tossing the file out into the garden, I tumbled after it, shut the window and went pell-mell down the front path and across the street, getting away fast, hugging whatever shadows were available until I came near the traffic lights. Red. Nothing moving at all and they'd lodged on red. A warning? Too late if that's what it was. Too late for me and my client. My client was dead and I was being careless.

The junction forced a decision. Straight on for home or sharp right to the office? Oddly I turned right, although I could read a file at home as easily as in the office, and in greater comfort too.

I smoothed a finger over the plate that said Flynn Detective Agency, and made a vow to polish it one day. Then I was through the street door and up the stairs and wondering at the broken lock on the door to my office.

Annoyance first, nervousness second. Nobody had needed to do *that*. They hadn't made a mess of the street door, so why wreck this one? Unless, of course, someone wanted me to understand very clearly indeed that an intruder with a violent streak had been there.

The nervousness began as I shoved open the door and stretched out an arm to grope for a lightswitch. Could be somebody was still in there. No one was. Just my chipped desk and chairs and my scruffy filing cabinet. The desk was clear, no message waiting on it for me. The drawers were untidied but nobody had bothered to steal my warm old cardigan from the bottom one.

The filing cabinet then. The top drawer was where I kept my instant coffee, along with the more expensive filter stuff and the sachets of fancy tea in case I ever got a prospective client who looked as though he'd rear away if offered anything worse. The intruder hadn't fancied any of it.

The middle drawer had files on current cases, in this instance Kate Mullery and Mrs Lotti. My visitor had squandered several minutes on this drawer. Both files had been emptied out and the contents jumbled up.

The bottom drawer contained my small tape recorder and a few other bits of equipment (yes, all right; I do own a magnifying glass), an umbrella and, sometimes, my gym kit. At the back were details of completed cases. These files seemed to have been examined but were only mildly disordered.

I sighed and pushed the drawers shut. Well, I wouldn't have to worry how I was going to occupy myself when I got to the office in the morning. It was going to be a day for doing the filing . . .

Meanwhile I had another file to concentrate on. Kate Mullery's own, the folder from her desk. I began reading through, setting aside anything that looked halfway interesting. This amounted to a very small pile indeed and I wished I had her desk diary for cross reference. No, even I didn't consider going back to fetch it.

My name cropped up again, on a piece of paper along with one other, that of a man I used to know. I frittered several minutes wondering what that could signify.

A lurking worry, that if I left my office unattended the burglar might return and mess things up a bit more, kept me there. Finally I realized, around 2 a.m., that I'd do better to go home and get some sleep. But I wasn't going to endanger Kate's folder or the muddled contents of my own file on her. In the washroom was a plastic carrier bag. I went to fetch it so that I could bundle everything in there and take it with me.

The message was on the mirror in the washroom, the one where I'd admired the twinkling titanium ear-rings and my own curling dark hair. It was written in lipstick in livid capitals: TOO MANY QUESTIONS FLYNN.

And that's when my guts turned to water and I had to snatch at the door frame to steady faltering knees. The Whisperer! The growling old man who'd left messages on my telephone accusing me of asking too many questions and had threatened to kill me if I didn't stop. He'd been in here. In the office, in the filing cabinet and the desk, and then here in the washroom to scrawl his challenge.

A crank, I'd told myself. I'd said it to Kate Mullery too when she'd confessed she'd been scared out of her home by threatening calls. I'd played it down when she'd warned me her caller had included me in his threats. And now . . .

I gulped air, forced my eyes to meet their reflection in the mirror, my mind to absorb the significance of everything that had happened this night. Kate's face, ugly in death, would look to anyone else like a simple case of drowning but my instinct had insisted from the first that she'd been murdered. Now I'd discovered that my Whisperer had chosen the night of her death to rifle my file on her and the Bethesda inquiry. The words on the mirror gave away his identity beyond doubt. Therefore my Whisperer and Kate's caller were probably the same man. And if it was the caller who'd killed her . . .

It was no good. There was too much information reeling around in my brain for me to make sense of more than a smattering of it. I was making conjectures and leaps that the pure facts didn't justify. Yet what came through repeatedly and urgently was my need to escape home.

I ripped a couple of sheets of toilet paper off the roll and started to wipe the words from the glass. But after the TOO had gone I stopped, realizing it might be best to leave it there however much I wanted the place clean and the memory fading. The writing was evidence and might the time not have come to think of calling in the police? Bewildered, I shook my head. Two in the morning and too late for difficult decisions: I lobbed the paper into the loo and shut the washroom door.

I was going to go home. I stuffed the documents into the carrier bag, and then checked on what I knew needed no checking. *Red for Danger*, it was called. I kept it in a quilted purse in the desk, with a spare comb and a nail file. I'm careful with my lipsticks but now *Red for Danger* was worn to a blunt end. What I hadn't used myself was smeared over the washroom mirror.

Seven-thirty in the morning by my Spiro Agnew watch and my phone was ringing. I croaked into it, mouth dry, trying out my voice for the first time that day, making sounds and not words.

I heard Debbie, one of the women from the gym. Something about taking my post upstairs, something about my office door being smashed open. Debbie trying to be helpful but ruining the only bit of sleep I'd managed to scrounge.

When she'd rung off I lay there on the hard narrow bed and let the events of the previous day flood back into my mind. Then I headed for the kitchen and some reviving coffee. I needed to think. *Still* needed to think, despite hours of it during the night.

Before dropping off I'd made a plan. I was going to come clean, go to see Detective Sergeant Ray Donnelly and hand over the whole shebang to the police: Kate in the river; her flight to Arkley; her Bethesda doubts; my Whisperer; the Whisperer's break-in at my office and my break-in at Kate's house. Everything.

Daylight revealed this as an appallingly bad idea, an idea born of fatigue, one that would wreck whatever reputation I'd won for persistence and discretion. So I changed the plan.

I decided that whenever it came out that Kate Mullery was dead, then I'd have to co-operate but it could be days before the police discovered the identity of the drowned woman. That was time on my side.

I spent a little while on my appearance, taming my hair, drawing it back sleek and tight from my face and smoothing it into a plait. I wore the new ear-rings, a fair bit of make-up and a severe wool suit with hight heels. Vanity? No, disguise. I was going straight round to Kate Mullery's house and I preferred not to be recognized as the fleeing figure of the night before.

Kate's chief assistant, Keith Jay of the doggy devotion, was on the telephone when I was led past an artistic and symbolic Christmas tree, all white and silver purity, and shown into the room where he worked. Young and camp, he waggled his fingers at me in greeting and went on cooing down the line at someone called Dearie who'd sent him buttons of the wrong hue. He finished the call with eye-rolling resignation.

'Honestly, Laura, some people! They don't know their aqua from their peacock. What's one to *do* with them?'

I smiled and shook my head, which passed as a suitably sympathetic response.

'Coffee, love?' asked Keith and without waiting for me to say no thanks he called through to the next room: 'Glenda? Two coffees soon as you can, love.'

'Well, now,' he said, with the merest glance at the watch on his bare freckled forearm. 'What can I do for you, Laura? Kate's not here, you know.'

I said I did. 'Do you know where she is?'

He was sitting at his desk, hands stroking the arms of his chair. 'No, actually she's being a wee bit naughty. I've told her. I mean, she took off all of a sudden, phoned to say it'd be for a few days and here we are three weeks later and . . .' He ended with a shrug. 'She phones me. Well, she's got to, hasn't she? I mean, she's supposed to be running this business, not me.' Another quick look at his watch.

The doggy devotion, I registered, was slipping a bit. I asked whether she'd told him why she'd gone away and when he was reticent I explained she'd told me.

Then he relaxed. 'Oh that's all right, then, Laura. I thought you were here about the Bethesda thing, not about Kate's panic attack. She's a marvellous person but I feel she's over-reacting to this phone call problem. Running off and all that. It's not like Kate, really. I've been with her for years and she's tremendous to work with, steady as a rock, not like some in the business. Now, out of the blue, this happens. I said to her, Kate, my darling, I simply don't understand it.'

'Does anyone else here know why she's away?'

'Lord no, only me. We don't want them all jumping about and cutting the cloth anyhow because their minds aren't on the job, do we? Mind you, she wouldn't have told me either if I hadn't found her all broken up over her cat getting shot. Then it all came tumbling out.'

Glenda arrived with the coffee, just when I hoped Keith Jay was also going to let it all come tumbling out. After Glenda stole a few minutes of my time with questions about milk and sugar, I tried to get Keith back on track but the moment had passed and if there was any more to the cat business than I'd already heard from Kate, he'd decided against going into it.

Instead, I asked him about business rivals or anybody else he thought could possibly be behind the calls that had intimidated Kate Mullery. No use. He said he hadn't a clue, assumed it was the work of a weirdo, that the fashion trade was as cut-throat as you like but not into the type of nastiness that had unnerved Kate Mullery.

I finished the coffee, made out I was ready to leave, then threw in a half-hearted request for the money owed me. 'I don't suppose she left my cheque lying around, Keith?'

He hesitated. Just a fraction. Just enough. Then he said no, and became embarrassed and finally said yes he thought he had in fact seen it.

Naturally I brightened at this and said well OK then, let's have it, please.

Young Mr Jay was torn between loyalty to the marvellous but tiresomely absent Kate and decency to me. I wasn't asking for anything that wasn't mine by rights. While he wrestled with himself I muttered that three months had been too long to wait and it would make a very nice Christmas present if he could get it for me. Now.

Decency won. 'I'll see whether I can put my hand on it, Laura.'

I think he expected me to wait where I was but instead I trailed after him, all the way to the beautiful room. Curious to think I'd been in there, illicitly, only hours earlier. There was the chair I'd hidden behind, there was the sash window and there, obvious in daylight, was the burglar-alarm system I'd activated.

The bolts had been secured once more. I waited for Keith to make some reference to the drama of the night before, but he said nothing. Who, I wondered conversationally, normally lived in the house apart from Kate Mullery? He did, he said. He had a flat there, and so did a couple of his colleagues although in their case it was supposed to be a short-term arrangement until they found an affordable alternative in the district.

He was by Kate's desk, pulling at a resisting drawer. Then he put a hand in his pocket and found a key. A minute later I was walking away from the house with the cheque in my shoulder bag.

Success in getting hold of it buoyed me up all the way to the bank at Highbury Corner. I checked the date on it – three months ago almost to the day – and then wrote out a paying-in slip, backdating it a couple of days in case it mattered that I was presenting it after Kate's death. Then I detoured to arrange for a new lock to be fitted to my office door, and after that I called on Chris Ionides and begged the use of his car for that afternoon.

I caught Chris having a mug of tea, a mug smeared with engine oil and heaven knows what. He knew why I refused his offer to join in his mid-morning break. Chris rubbed hair back from his face with a blackened hand and the jet eyes shone happily at me. 'Your part, Laura, I think she comes soon.'

Excitement always ruins his English.

'Good,' I said. 'How soon?'

'Two weeks. Three?'

My face showed I didn't think it was all that soon. He said, crestfallen: 'She's a difficult part to find. We're lucky, Laura. One day maybe not, but this day we're lucky.'

Good old Chris. Who else would bother to keep the old crate on the road? I said as much.

'New cars,' he said, and came close to a sneer. 'What good are they? Nobody makes cars like yours any more.'

Most of my friends could think of several reasons for that. Reasons like petrol consumption and reliability and comfort. But Chris and I didn't think that way. No, let's be truthful. Sometimes I did, but then I'd remember that swapping my car would rob Chris of a challenge and a hobby and I'd never had the heart to do it to him.

Propped on a shelf of greasy gadgets was a postcard sent by his brother on holiday in Cyprus. Chris showed me, with pride.

'Kyrenia,' he said, as if that explained everything and it certainly explained much. Kyrenia, which was home but no longer home because the boundary had been redrawn and now home was on the wrong side of the Turkish border.

'It's beautiful,' I said, which was no more and no less than the truth.

Chris set the card back in place, leaving me to invent the village where the brothers had grown up, white-walled houses with a taverna in the shade of a plane tree. He was saying: 'One day, Laura, you will go to Cyprus, yes?'

'What for? You're all over here.'

'But not so much as the Irish, I think!' And he gave his barking laugh.

We fixed a time for me to pick up his car and I took one small peep at my own invalided vehicle in a corner. It's a fine car for two people and a legless dwarf. There's not much room in the back. The shape looks as though it means to go somewhere: light the touch paper and stand clear. And it's stripy, like the toothpaste with the built-in mouthwash. Gran refers to it as 'that old humbug' and has never been brave enough to get into it. Given a free hand it would have been a three wheeler. It's inclined to behave like one, with a temptation to overturn on roundabouts.

I wrote 'Laura' with a fingertip on the dusty bonnet and then went back out into the crisp morning. Exhilarating, that was the word for it. Exhilarating because of the weather and because it was only days before Christmas and because I'd got my money for the Bethesda job and because Chris was going to mend my car, and because I was young and busy and independent. Extremely exhilarating.

Highbury Fields seemed almost pretty as a thin sun brightened the stucco of the buildings around it and people walked their dogs on the bit of grass left over when they built the tennis courts and the children's playground and the swimming pool. Even the blue plaque showing where Sickert had his painting school seemed a decorative addition.

And so the morning passed in this lively mood with things apparently going right for once. The door was mended with commendable haste; Anna Lee invited me to eat an Indian meal with her that evening; and I had a useful meeting with the long-faced Turkish clothing manufacturer in Islington Park Street.

In the guise of a journalist writing a piece for *Time Out* I sat in the showroom with him and learned how the designs that appeared on the catwalks were translated into inexpensive versions for the average woman. I didn't pin him down about the legitimacy of all this. For the sake of the interview I was happy to go along with the notion that it was always thoroughly above board and to forget that the fashion houses live in terror of their designs being stolen.

His story was that skilled sketchers attended the designers' shows and noted salient points that allowed companies like his to work up similar designs, and in no time at all. He reminded me how it could be done, citing royal weddings where sketches were taken from television screens and crude imitations of the bridal gowns went into production before the marriage services ended.

Bethesda's coup in getting a contract to produce a high street line for Kate Mullery was well-known in the trade, and he had a few comments (careful ones, I thought) about that. I let slip that I knew about the Larches-Bethesda background and the antics the accountants had performed to keep both businesses out of financial trouble. And he hinted at the fierce competitiveness Bethesda had shown since the turn-around. But he had nothing specific for me, nothing that told me I wasn't wasting my time querying Bethesda.

Maintaining the pretence of the magazine feature, I shifted ground and got him to talk about Kate Mullery instead and asked how marketable her high street line might be. He laughed at my naïvety, saying she was one of the most interesting new designers and it was a shame she'd been perched at the top end of the business for so long. The 'so long' amused me. Kate hadn't been around very long at all. Apparently things were expected to move fast in the fashion world.

I ended our talk on a light note. 'So if she'd walked through your door and asked you to do what Bethesda are going to do, you'd have been delighted?'

He pursed his lips and suddenly there was merriment in his eyes. Obviously I'd said something exceptionally stupid. 'You haven't been paying attention, Laura. Come.'

He beckoned me through a door at the back of the showroom and we abruptly left behind the world of pastel walls and clean uncluttered surfaces and charming window displays. Rack upon rack of garments were crammed into a long narrow room. Unshaded light bulbs hung from a high damp-stained ceiling, and carpet had given way to bare boards.

We stopped by a rack bursting with flowery dresses and he tugged one free and held it up in front of him, like a woman before a mirror. He didn't say anything. He didn't need to. The dress had all the hallmarks of a Kate Mullery design.

I fingered the fabric. Synthetic not silk, but only the touching told me so. I murmured that it was a lovely dress.

He said: 'Look.' There was a mirror on a wall between two of the racks and he pushed the dress into my arms and there was nothing I could do but look. I liked what I saw. 'Yours,' he said. And when I started to stumble a reply he said: 'A free sample for a journalist. So what?'

Ungracious to argue, I accepted despite a vigorous undertow of guilt.

While he slipped the dress into a bag for me, a velvety grey cat curled in the window. It prompted me to show the photograph of Mrs Lotti's cat and ask whether he'd seen it or heard of one like it in the area. Cat owners pay more attention to cats than the rest of us do.

'Magnificent!' he cried, studying Jaguar. 'No, I've never seen a cat like this, but I'll be sure to remember if I do. This is a very striking creature.'

His own plush grey looked with disdain and then gave its attention to a van pulling up outside. A man came running through the door, with a collection chit for an order. I said my goodbyes and went out, having scribbled down my office telephone number and address in case Mrs Lotti's cat put in an appearance in Islington Park Street.

The cat, the dress . . . One proved a good idea and the other a very bad one. But how was I, then, to know that?

My drive to Arkley and the meeting with Robin Digby came into a different category. Eighty per cent of me knew all along that they were blunders. It wasn't that I was chewed up with guilt at pressing on with inquiries while Kate Mullery was lying in a morgue unidentified, although I don't doubt I ought to have been. No, the 80 per cent was caused by my being thoroughly ill-prepared to confront the man. Who exactly was he, apart from a deer farmer? How did he know Kate, and know her well enough for her to decamp to his place when the going got tough? They were things I could have – I *should* have – found out before setting off. But the other 20 per cent was pure optimism, based on the flimsy excuse that I was having a good day with everything going my way.

We got off to a very bad start, Robin Digby and I. He caught me halfway through his kitchen window.

You'll be thinking by now that I make a habit of this kind of thing, but it isn't true. Getting into the house in Canonbury I'll explain away on the grounds that it was my client's house and I was acting on her behalf, even if I know full well she wouldn't have sanctioned it. My 20 per cent optimism was enough to stretch a point and claim that getting inside Knights End amounted to the same thing: a bit of effort on behalf of Kate Mullery.

There I was, having given up the door bell, with one leg over the sill into the kitchen sink and suddenly a big, florid man was charging round the end of the house and yelling blue murder. It would have been funny if he hadn't had the dog with him.

I'll gloss over the swearing (Digby's and mine) and the persuading (all mine) and the fury (Digby's, mine and the dog's). Let's skip to the scene in the kitchen once we'd all gone in by the door determined to pursue the matter like reasonable creatures.

Robin Digby huffily examined the scratch he claimed I'd made on the window sill. I lamented the run in the skirt of my good wool suit where the dog's teeth had lodged in it. His scratch was disputed, my damaged skirt wasn't. The dog thought about taking another bite and was banished to a utility room where he growled intermittently throughout the rest of my time at Knights End.

'When did you last see Kate?' I tried.

Digby was washing his hands at the kitchen sink. His hair was thinning over the crown. I put his age somewhere in the fifties. He said: 'What's this? A bloody inquisition?'

'Look, Mr Digby, Kate asked me to make inquiries . . .'

'Not about her, I bet.'

'What does that mean?'

'It means you were paid to do a job . . .'

'That's what I'm attempting.'

'. . . and that job wasn't to badger Kate.'

Digby was loud in a peculiarly English way, the type who might have a decent army background or anyway be a bore down at the golf club. He wore a soft checked shirt but from first acquaintance I knew there was nothing cuddly about him. I never actually saw him with a large whiskey in his hand and his back to a log fire in a country house but he had a quality that suggested that was his natural stance.

Perhaps his attitude to me struck *him* as ridiculous too because he snatched at a towel, scrubbed his hands dry and flung the towel down on the draining board without challenging my silence. 'All right,' he said, turning to face me. 'Let's get down to it. You came here assuming you'd find Kate Mullery because she's supposed to be holed up here. Instead you find me and you find Kate's gone.'

Summed up perfectly. I nodded. 'Where? And when?'

'Yesterday evening. I came back from seeing to the stock and she'd left a note.' Then, registering my expression: 'No, I haven't got it. It just said she was going out for the evening.

51

Business, she said. Someone was picking her up, she didn't say who. I threw the note in the boiler this morning.'

I asked whether it was usual for Kate to leave the farmhouse. He said not, that this was the first time.

'Weren't you worried about her?'

He shrugged. 'The thing is, Miss . . . er . . .'

'Laura Flynn.'

'You see, Miss Flynn, I never set much store by Kate's idea that somebody meant to harm her. The phone calls and that. Lots of women get funny calls, quite nasty they can be, but they don't leave home because of them. Nothing happens to them, does it?'

This was rather perplexing. Knights End was a near perfect bolt-hole but Robin Digby was hardly the most sympathetic friend she could have run to. I dug around, trying to discover how close they'd been, how long they'd known each other, how far she'd confided in him.

What I learned was that Digby classed himself as a friend of Kate's family, but more than that: he'd put money into her business and made the move from Dublin to London smoother than it might otherwise have been. Something deep inside me responded to this. I saw Kate and Digby as unofficial niece and uncle, and I was happy with that. I'd experienced it myself. Fatherless girls frequently do. Some, of course, marry their older men and are accused of winning father substitutes. Maybe it was my stubbornly questioning streak, but I could never have fallen into that.

I'd no idea what kind of husband Kate would have settled for. I knew too little about her to form an opinion. Every time I learned something, something else cancelled it out. Digby had a good point when he said she hadn't hired me to ask questions about her. She was a woman who'd given nothing away if she could help it.

I concentrated on keeping her in the present tense while we spoke. It wasn't easy but it was essential. Kate's death was news somebody else must break to him.

He took the mug with the pink elephants off a hook and filled it with tap water. No large whiskey, no log fire. Digby leaned his back against the sink and gulped water. I tried to squeeze some more information out of him but he'd decided he'd said enough. In five minutes he had me out of the back door. The bolt slammed home. The last thing I heard before I turned Chris's car round on the unmade road was the dog barking inside the house.

Bambi's to blame for my sentimental ideas about deer and all that relates to them. Digby had adjusted my soppy notions about the gentle folk who might take up deer farming. He was gruff and brusque, solid and, yes, *hard*. How in the world had he become a close friend of Kate, *the* friend to whom she'd run? Had she truly put up with him just for the money? I hoped not, and it seemed I'd never know.

I coaxed Chris Ionides into letting me keep his old Ford until morning. I was cheating letting him think I was away on a big job. In truth I was in a pub half a mile from his workshop, but the evening was damp and blowy and I'd arranged to go out later on. This wasn't any old pub, it was one of the Irish pubs and I'd dropped in to see whether an old man my grandmother knew was there. Using the phone was just an excuse.

Old Gerry MacGuire was precisely as I'd always known him, a wily and wheedling little man, not the company I'd choose to keep. He slumped forward over a cigarette and a pint of dark beer, his rheumy eyes blinking through smoke.

'Hello, Gerry,' I said in a bright sort of way. He'd always been Gerry to everyone of every age.

'Is it Laura Flynn, you are?'

Good. He'd remembered me. 'Sure, I'm Laura. How are you doing, Gerry?'

'Moderate fine,' he said, and he jiggled his glass just a quiver. I took the cue and ordered him another. Tinsel was twisted around the necks of the optics and clusters of balloons against the yellowed walls were stealthily deflating.

'How's Bridie?' I asked.

'Bridie's herself,' he said. His wife had been dotty for years, in and out of hospital.

We talked while the barman poured and I paid, and then I cut through all the flim-flam and asked Gerry MacGuire to cast his mind back twenty years and more to a Christmas when a young Irishman had walked out of his house one Friday evening to buy a packet of twenty and had never come back.

Gerry drew a raw red hand over a bristly chin. 'Ach, let it be, Laura Flynn. Why be fretting now?'

'It's Kitty, Gerry. She's old. She wants to know where her son got to.'

'He'll not come back to her.'

'Before she dies, she needs to know where he is.'

Gerry MacGuire coughed. Heartbreakingly. Then he gasped at his cigarette like it was a lifeline and not the very thing that set him wheezing. Smoke obliterated his face as he struggled to speak. 'Tell her to leave it, Laura. Her Joe's gone, that's all.'

'But it isn't all. He must be somewhere. There must be a reason he went. Would you see old Kitty go to her grave with the question on her mind?'

He mocked that with a chesty laugh. 'There's plenty I've seen go to the grave more troubled than that.'

I sat across the table from him and I ran a finger round and round and round the rim of my glass, waiting. In a while he stubbed out the cigarette and as his other hand went automatically to his pocket to light its successor, he said: 'Your mam, Laura. Has she no answers at all for ye?'

I shrugged. 'She's in Ireland. Works with her cousin over there. It's Kitty I'm asking for.'

He lit a match, held it in front of the new cigarette in his mouth and said: 'They were bad days, Laura. People coming and going, coming and going. You're too young to know about it, but they weren't easy times.'

I'd been told though. Gangs and street fights and the Irish clubs burning down each others' places given the chance. But nobody had ever accused Joe Flynn of being part of that.

He said: 'He told your mother he was out to the pub to pick up a packet of cigarettes and he went away.'

Exasperated I snapped: 'I know *that*! That's the part I've always known.'

He rubbed the bristles again: 'Ah, but did they ever tell you he didn't go alone, Laura?'

I stared at him, understanding well enough the insinuation but not believing.

He said: 'Perhaps they should have told you that too.' And when I opened my mouth to speak he got in first. 'Kitty must have heard. Did she try to protect you, do you think?'

'Er . . . yes,' I lied. 'That would be it, I imagine. Where was it then, Gerry? Another bit of England? Back to Ireland? Or off to the States? Where did he – *they* – go?'

More sucking on the cigarette. A long drink from the beer. Gerry MacGuire screwed up his eyes, thinking hard. 'It's the divil of a time ago to be remembering details, Laura.'

'Well you think about it, Gerry. I'll look in again soon and see if it's come back to you. Will you have another now before I go?'

Unsurprisingly he said he would. I got to my feet, my purse in my hand and the barman poised to serve me. 'One thing more,' I said looking down through the haze of smoke. 'Who was she? That's the kind of detail nobody ever forgets.'

'Her name now?'

He was blinking rapidly, the smoke seeming to bother him too. I said: 'Ideally her name, but if not anything you can tell me about her.'

He came out with it then. She was half Irish, he said, and married to a man called Cotton. They'd kept a pub in Canonbury.

And so I was on the trail, not one I'd ever have chosen for myself but one Gran had begged me to take. Nobody had heard a word of Joe Flynn since he'd left home but perhaps somebody, somewhere, had heard what had become of Mrs Cotton. It was a start.

Waiting in the car to join the flood of traffic in Holloway

Road, I fingered St Lucy. 'We don't have to believe old Gerry MacGuire if we don't want to,' I assured her. 'He's a rogue and a gossip but that's why he was worth asking. Gossips are gold dust when everyone else's lips are sealed.'

A bus driver did his good deed for the day and let me into the flow. I continued lecturing St Lucy. 'I wonder why I've never heard of Mrs Cotton before? Obviously Joe Flynn went off with another woman, what other reason would anyone suspect? But I've never heard anyone put a name to her before. Hmmm.'

And as I neared Highbury Corner I added: 'Don't worry. I won't breathe a word of this to Gran until I'm absolutely certain.'

St Lucy preserved her usual discreet silence.

If Anna Lee were not my special friend I'd describe her as blowzy. Think of a wartime film, an ample barmaid, and you're thinking of Anna Lee. Except that in her case it isn't artifice. Anna achieves the effect without in the least knowing she's done it. Her shape's to blame, the full-breasted generous shape that sculptured bras are destined to exaggerate rather than quell. Anna, enthralled in her children's fiction, is delightfully unaware that dressed up she inevitably looks like a cartoon strip busty blonde. Most of the time she favours long loose skirts and dresses, and the effect is merely of a large, comfortable woman. The first time I saw her smartened up for an evening out, the contrast was a shock.

She phoned after I got back to the office and she said: 'We're invited to a party tonight. Friends of Jennie. But I insist we have our Indian meal first.'

'Will Jennie's friends want either of us after an Indian meal?'

She said ha ha, very funny and would I pick her up an hour earlier than we'd agreed? I decided to wear the Kate Mullery dress I'd been given, and to depend on the heater in Chris's car for warmth because I hadn't a coat that looked good with the dress.

Jennie has friends who live in smart addresses in the

neighbourhood. The party was a few houses from where my grandmother lives. Quite probably Jennie's friends would tell me about the extraordinary old Irishwoman who refused all enticements to move out and sell the place to folk like themselves who'd bring it up to scratch, in line with the rest of Gibson Square.

This had happened to me more than once, but how would I handle it if the subject cropped up again? Agree the house was crying out for modernization? My grandfather had been a builder and he'd modernized it in the fifties but nothing, apart from redecoration, had been touched since. I could admit kinship and defend Gran's right to live how she liked in a house she owned outright. Or pretend mystification that one old woman (and her lodger; don't let's forget the gamp-like Ada Carey) could want to hang on to such a property?

I was chewing over the alternatives as I drove up to Anna's house and spotted a gap in the parked vehicles outside it. I did one of those textbook manoeuvres, pulling forward and wiggling back into the space. Only I didn't make it. A speedy hatchback dived in nose first and blocked me.

No doubt there are clever ways of dealing with this situation but mine has always been to protest. With a turn of speed that took me by surprise, I was out of the car and looming over the other driver's door ready to tell him (somehow I knew it was going to be a him) what I thought, when . . .

'Oh!' I said.

'Laura?' he said.

And we were gawping idiotically at each other, Mike Brenan and I.

The Mike Brenan I'd been divorced from for three years. *That* Mike Brenan.

My voice was finding cutting banalities about his driving not having improved one iota, but I wasn't listening to it. I was dismally self-conscious about the wind playing havoc with my hair and pressing the silken cloth tighter and tighter round the contours of my body. My vulnerability, my sexuality, were exposed in a way that frustrated and angered me.

With excruciating timing Sue appeared on Anna's doorstep, ready to meet her date. She became rooted by what she saw. I thought perhaps I should say something, to Mike, or to Sue perhaps, but couldn't muster anything intelligent so I backed off and got into my car.

I started the engine and was ready to pull ahead when it got through to me that this was ridiculous because Sue was now in the car with Mike and he was signalling he was moving off. So then I put the car into reverse to take his space – *my* space – and then I knew that was daft too because Anna Lee had walked up to my car and was about to hop in.

'Oh dear,' she said, scrutinizing me.

I dredged up a shred of nonchalance. 'We were bound to meet again one day, I expect most couples do.'

'But a warning would have been nice. Sorry, Laura, it's my doing. If I hadn't switched the time . . .'

'If you hadn't, it would have happened some other day.' I adjusted my seatbelt, smoothed my hair. 'Besides,' I continued, 'you and I can't be expected to organize our social lives to accommodate Sue's arrangements with my ex.'

'True,' said Anna. She flicked a hair off the shoulder of her dress, a green cross-over number with cleavage. 'And it's not as though you feel anything for him any longer.'

'Quite,' I said.

We were both lying again.

'That dress,' said Anna, changing the subject, 'is superb. New?'

I told her the story of the dress, except that I didn't tell her how much it had disturbed me to be wearing that of all things when I'd collided with Mike Brenan. Practically anything else I owned would have made me look a more grown-up, serious, independent, modern woman. Just my luck to be caught in the one garment that gave out all the contrary signals.

The chance of rejecting the dress was lost the moment the

Turkish factory owner had made me hold it against myself and look into the mirror. I certainly hadn't shrunk away from decking myself out in the flowery silkiness, wrapping myself in its emphatic femininity.

Chapel Market is an ideal venue in the evening, the stalls have been wheeled away for the night and you can park right outside the door of the restaurant without restriction. Anna and I go to the Indian Veg frequently.

Anna likes excuses to celebrate and this evening we were there to mark her eventual payment for a short story. I believe it was the one about the lollipop lady and the cat.

'But I'm buying supper,' I insisted, and told her I'd been paid at last for my work for Kate Mullery. Oh yes, I told her all sorts of things that evening, but I didn't tell her my client was dead.

Not saying it made the fact unreal. It excused me from doing anything about it. Or so I was inclined to believe. Anyway, Anna was far more interested in Gran coaxing me to look for my father and my basic reluctance to do that.

'How would you feel if you found him?' she wondered.

'I don't know. I grew up in a house that was learning not to care that he wasn't there.'

'Hmm.' She splintered a wafer-thin *paper dosa*, topped it with coconut *sambal* and chewed it. Then: 'You'd do well to think about it, though. It's a very tricky situation to get into, for both you and your father.'

'And I should be armed with self-knowledge? A fine theory, Anna, but I can't imagine how I'd feel and in any case I can't be sure that if I met him a flurry of entirely unexpected emotions wouldn't surface.'

Anna nodded wisely and broke off another piece of *paper dosa*. We were being unusually solemn, growing philosophical.

We talked about betrayal, whether, as Fay Weldon wrote, the perception is that women betray people and men betray ideals, or whether, as Jennie and Sue would have it, men betray everyone and everything in sight. We came to no conclusions, unable to fathom the betrayal that leads a man to walk away from his family without a word.

Betrayal, though, is a slippery word. Look it up. It has several meanings and you can mean any or all of them when you use it. How to simplify? 'You have betrayed me in the second use of the word as expressed by the *Shorter Oxford English Dictionary*'? Here you must imagine me shrugging and skipping briskly on, because I have no suggestions, except to treat betrayal with caution. Let's say I seldom feel betrayed so much as let down, like a blind or a bucket in a well. It was Anna who introduced betrayal into the discussion of my reluctance to meet the man who'd been no more than a nominal father to me since my fourth Christmas.

We got to the party late, long after Jennie who was slightly drunk and overlooked her responsibility to introduce us to people. I worked out who the hosts were and Anna and I introduced ourselves and then settled in to chit-chat with a series of strangers, most of whom wanted to talk about house prices and traffic plans and Porsches or the perils of foreign servants. It wasn't our kind of party.

But the house was lovely and the drink was good, and when Anna became snared in a long conversation about one of her more controversial books, with a couple who were reading it as a bedtime story for their five-year-old, I floated through into the conservatory. Far too cold to be outside at this time of year, but there were fairy lights in the garden to ensure we appreciated the spectacle of the terrapin pond, the late flowering roses and butter-coloured winter jasmine cascading down a brick wall.

'Laura!' a voice exclaimed from beside a massive yucca near me. I tensed, unwilling for another startling meeting that evening. But it was Keith Jay that I saw, Kate Mullery's assistant. He peeled away from his companions and came to me, the wine having flushed his fair freckled skin, his diamond ear-ring twinkling at me in the lamplight. 'Fancy seeing you here.'

Explaining my tenuous connection with the party-givers, I was conscious that Keith was less interested in what I was saying than in what I was wearing. He leaned over me, conspiratorially: 'Laura, you look divine, my darling. But do tell me, love, wherever did you buy that frock?'

I fell back on feminine giggles and coyness and refused to say. But Keith seriously wanted to know. 'Laura, I'm really interested in this.' He was between me and the doorway to the sitting room and he was fingering one rose and purple sleeve. Difficult for me to walk away.

'A girl has to have her secrets,' I said.

'Tell me, love.'

Only that morning he'd done me a favour and given me the cheque I'd asked for. One good turn deserves another?

I said: 'It was given me by a manufacturer I was interviewing. I don't think I ought to mention his name.'

'Because you know it's a rip-off of one of Kate's designs.'

'Well yes, I suppose I do.'

He let go the sleeve and leaned back, looking me up and down. I didn't mind. He was a professional studying a garment, it didn't disturb me. As far as Keith Jay was concerned I was a mere clothes hanger.

'Well, the thing is, Laura . . .' His voice had dropped to not much more than a whisper.

'Yes?' I had to lean forward to hear the rest.

Anxiety had replaced curiosity. 'The thing is, we haven't shown this dress yet. It's from the collection Kate's working on at present.'

'Oh.'

'You see . . .'

'Yes, I see. You're telling me someone's stolen the design.' My voice was as low as his.

'I can't think of any other explanation.' But he was bewildered because he wasn't satisfied with this one either.

We couldn't go on whispering like this in the conservatory so we arranged to talk again the next morning, at my office rather than his as he didn't want the staff to overhear nor, indeed, wonder why I was there yet again. He rejoined his friends behind the yucca and I retreated to the sitting room and plunged into the party again.

Anna was ensconced with a band of admirers whose children were growing up with her stories, and Jennie was drunker and telling an indiscreet tale about a woman who used to live at Anna's house. Sober, Jennie is hot on solidarity among women but after a glass or two all that goes to the wind and she's carelessly disloyal. That's why it's Anna and not Jennie who's my confidante. With Jennie one never quite knows.

I haven't given away much about Jennie, I know, but only because at this time of my life it's Anna Lee that I'm closest to. Yet I've known Jennie longer, Jennie who'd led me into consciousness-raising groups and feminist battles, Jennie who'd been the chief support when my marriage was collapsing, and Jennie who'd introduced me to Anna and secured me a room at the house when I needed one.

She's a college lecturer with a huge range of friends who appreciate her liveliness and her determination, and forgive her foibles. Like being unable to hold her drink.

'I'll take her home soon,' I thought, and got hooked into conversation with a television producer who wanted me to help with research for a programme she was making. When I next spotted Jennie I knew I ought not to delay.

I cast around for Anna and caught her eye. She began to disentangle herself, understanding the familiar signal. Then I broke in on the story Jennie was telling, with an invented reason for us to go. She came without a struggle, as the police say.

A nice smooth exit and we were all three hurrying in thin party dresses to where I'd parked my borrowed car when the door of Gran's house opened and her doctor came out. I remember gasping and running forward to demand he told me what was happening, then realizing he didn't know me and trying to explain I was Kitty Flynn's granddaughter, and then trying to take in that Gran had suffered a heart attack and an ambulance was on its way.

Next I was in the house, with frail, stooping Ada Carey wringing her hands and Gran lying silent and unfocused in the great bed she'd slept in most of her married life and all her widowhood. *Gran* to be lying there like that, bluish, features sagging, eyes unseeing. Oh God, not Gran!

'Ada, what are you saying?' I was impatient with her moaning.

'Father Mahon. Will I call Father Mahon?'

'No. Yes. No. God, I don't know.' I fixed Ada with an angry eye. Why was the old woman pushing me for a decision, hadn't she lived long enough to know about death for herself and not rely on my inexperience?

Death. The thought banished every other thought. Gran's death. Like this, with a despairing lodger and an incompetent granddaughter at her bedside. No daughters or sons, especially not Joe she'd asked me to trace for her, none of her other grandchildren, not even . . . She'd come to this and it was nothing like good enough. All right, then, send for Father Mahon. If she can't have her family at least she can have the professionals.

Ada, hunched over the bed end, had quietened her hands by gripping it. I said: 'Ring him. Father Mahon. Get him round here.'

'Oh Laura!' Ada winced at my instructions, but she fled and from the hall downstairs I heard the plastic clatter of the telephone receiver lifted.

'Oh God,' I prayed, and didn't know how to go on. 'Give Gran time,' I managed. 'Just a bit more time. That's all. Until they get here. Just enough for them to get from the States, and Ireland, and Australia, and Switzerland and . . . And enough for me to find Joe for her.'

My fingers had gone to my chain, St Lucy was in my hand. 'Just enough for me to find Joe Flynn for her. If you'll do that for her, I'll . . .' But of course there was nothing I could offer in exchange.

The doctor was back and the ambulance arrived before Father Mahon. The result was a farcical scene on the pavement as Gran was being carried into the ambulance and the cherubic priest was calculating whether he should say a word over her there and then or whether he'd have time to pursue her to the hospital. In the end he went to the hospital and I hitched a lift with him.

Chris Ionides's car had gone from where I'd parked it in the square and Anna and Jennie had vanished too. Presumably I'd flung the keys at Anna. I don't recall it but it must have happened.

Now Father Mahon and I are not each other's favourite company. I distrust his air of innocence – no man has the right to look so unmarred, so unworldly, especially not a priest – and he's wary of me. I would love to know the full story of what Gran read in his palm.

We went most of the way to the hospital in silence and as we got out of the car again he touched my arm in a gesture of condolence and said: 'A difficult time, Laura. A difficult time.' Which I thought was crass and unctuous.

'How difficult?' I responded. 'Will she be going home again?'

'Did the doctor not say so?'

'He very carefully said nothing, therefore I know nothing.' My frustration and fear was breaking out in anger, the way it does.

The irritating man touched my arm again and hurried ahead. I loitered in a corridor, blind to the casualty queues of broken arms and bloody faces and the squeal of trolley wheels and the odour of polish and disinfectant and stale food.

They let me see Gran but she was wired up and asleep and they said there was no point in staying but they'd call me if need be. I looked at Father Mahon to interpret this and he nodded and said: 'I'll drive you home, Laura.' Outside the ward was a bedraggled plastic Christmas tree with only half its fairy lights working. I noticed it was the green ones that had broken.

On the return journey I couldn't stop talking. It felt awful to be leaving Gran among strangers and I started by saying that.

He said: 'Your grandmother is quite elderly, Laura.'

Sharp I said: 'Oh yes, it's absolutely normal, but I don't have to like it. I hate it. And we can none of us avoid it, can we? That ultimate betrayal of the body, when your own flesh fails you. Look what she's become. Within minutes she's stopped being a person, she's reduced to some doctor's case. All that personality and individuality gone into hiding, the big step towards the end of her life. You see it often enough, Father Mahon, can you get used to the cruelty of death or does the hurt come fresh each time?'

I shouldn't think I said anything he hadn't heard relatives say a thousand times before, railing at the way one person's death underlines the futility of all of us, but he showed not a flicker of impatience or boredom. After that I got on to the subject of Joe Flynn.

He said: 'Yes, she says how keenly she misses him.'

Blunt, I said: 'The way she put it to me, she wants me to find him for her before she dies.'

'Ah, did she say that?'

'She called him unfinished business, she said she suffered the ache of unfinished business, that she's an old woman and doesn't have long to finish it.' My voice was high, challenging his God who was letting her time run out. Then I turned to him in supplication: 'Tell me how to find him. Tell me what you know.'

He cleared his throat and we stopped at a red light. Danger again. For Father Mahon or for me? Or just for Kitty Flynn?

Father Mahon said: 'What I know, Laura, is . . .' He repeated the throat-clearing and I thought that if he gives me that line about being bound by the secrets of the confessional I shall surely scream.

Instead he said: 'What I know is mostly second-hand because your father disappeared before I came to the parish.'

'How long before?'

'A year or two. Perhaps three. I knew the story from your mother, and from Kitty herself.'

'And from a lot of other people too, no doubt. Very well. Apart from Gran and my mother, who else seemed informed about it?'

'Well in truth I find it hard to say that anyone did. The point was that Joe Flynn's disappearance was a great mystery.'

'Any names at all,' I pleaded. 'I've got to start somewhere and you know I haven't long.'

But he was less precise than old Gerry MacGuire who I'd disturbed over his pint in the Irish pub. I cut in and offered Father Mahon the name of Cotton, a Mrs Cotton who'd left her publican husband the same time Joe Flynn ran off.

The three-year gap was too long, he didn't know about Mrs Cotton. Never mind, let him tell me about the people he did remember from those days and where they might be now. Knowledgeable people, I meant, not people of my generation who were too busy growing up to take notice.

I sat in my flat that night, on the expensive thick carpet that was the best seat in the room, and I took a fresh notebook and wrote into it all the things I remembered Father Mahon saying. This helped me to cope with the worry of Gran's illness by attempting to do something practical.

Far too early next morning I rang the hospital and learned she'd spent a quiet night and was 'comfortable', lying there among strangers and with peculiar things stuck into her and taped on to her.

Then I went round to the square to tell Ada Carey about Gran being comfortable. Ada blinked vaguely at me and I saw she hadn't slept any more than I had. I made a pot of tea and I sat her down, just as she was, in her plaid Viyella dressing gown and asked her to tell me how much she remembered about Joe Flynn and the way he went.

Without Gran to interrupt and argue, Ada was illuminating. 'The eighteenth of December it was, a Tuesday. I was living with my sister and the great brood she had in the house. Your mother came by with you in your push chair and she saw me by the front step and she stopped for a word. There was a keen wind but you were asleep and didn't care, so she stayed talking a minute. Then she said she had to hurry on, she had the hem to do on a dress she wanted to wear the next evening because your father was taking her out somewhere. Home she went. And I remember my sister saying to me shortly afterwards how was it that those two – she meant your parents – were always off out somewhere together and she couldn't so much as get her man to take her to the pub for a quick drink.'

I refilled Ada's teacup and coaxed her on. She said: 'Two days after that we had a message to ask if we'd seen or heard anything of Joe because he'd gone out for ten minutes and not returned. Now it was a wild sort of night for wandering off and he'd only his jacket, not his overcoat or a macintosh on him. He went out of that front door and away, Laura, and it's a mystery and always has been.'

'Ada, what do you know about Mrs Cotton? Someone mentioned my father had gone off with a Mrs Cotton.'

Ada was nodding. 'Ellen Cotton from the Queen's Head, that's who you mean. It was a story but we never heard the truth of it. Your mother, mind, she never believed it. Nor Kitty. They both expected him to come walking back in, any day he liked, with the cigarettes in his hand and the change jingling in his pocket.'

'But Mrs Cotton, did anyone hear what became of her?'

'I never heard, and to say the truth, Laura, I had never myself known of the woman before Joe disappeared. Your mother neither. It was a story, that's all.'

We looked searchingly at one another and then I said: 'I'll try ringing my mother now to tell her about Gran. Her phone wasn't answering last night. I'm going to have to ask her about my father. I haven't any choice, have I?'

Ada twisted her hands and agreed I hadn't.

The line to Dublin was poor, as though we could hear all the waves of the Irish Sea that separated us. I shouted that Gran was in hospital after a mild heart attack and my mother shouted back that she couldn't hear. I shouted louder.

We decided she wouldn't come over just yet but wait and see what the doctors had to say later in the day. Her cousin was on holiday in the west and she was running the business on her own. Just when she thought we'd said all we had to say, I told her Gran had asked me to find my father.

There was a pause that was filled by the Irish Sea and then she said she couldn't help, there'd never been any scrap of information to point the way he'd gone and she'd accepted that there'd been another love in his life and he'd gone chasing it the way men sometimes do.

I came away from the phone dispirited. My mother had crushed her own curiosity years ago and was afraid to awaken the cruel sense of betrayal (yes, I do mean that word this time) that had wrecked her life. She'd developed into a strong and resilient woman but her voice on the line had faltered and seemed smaller once we'd moved on to this subject. To bring Joe Flynn back into her life would be to damage her.

She'd said to me: 'Laura, men can lead a double life in a way that's beyond a wife's imagining.'

Beyond imagining. It had taken a chunk of her life coming to terms with the obvious truth, that Joe had left her for another woman, that he'd never come back to her. And now, because Gran was going to die, I was demanding answers to the questions she'd buried.

I took my questions to the *Islington Gazette* instead. No, there was no missing person inquiry by the police, or if there had been it wasn't reported in the paper. But I wanted a sense of what had been going on around the family during the fateful year.

Much of it was the same as would have been going on all over the country but some aspects varied, the Irish aspect for one. I'd heard, and Gerry MacGuire had reminded me through his cigarette smoke, about the tough times. Here they were, recorded in the local paper. Not the full tale, just the legal come-uppances.

Rival Irish gangs fighting in the streets. Arson at the Irish clubs. Stabbings. And behind it all not, as you'd be forgiven for assuming, fierce Irish politics. Oh no, this was all about money.

It was about money and it was about jobs. Job fiddles, often enough. Underlying the troubles, whether the court cases revealed it or not, was the battle for contracts to rebuild London after the wartime devastation and the slum clearance. Suddenly the money was to hand and the Irish came swarming into the borough to build and to make, just as they'd done for centuries when jobs over here had outstripped labour.

Old papers have a fascination that beats anything in the papers that drop on the mat in the morning. I meandered through the backnumbers in the *Gazette*'s library off Holloway Road, not methodically and selectively as I ought to have done, because I was engrossed in the flavour of the period.

But it wasn't without profit. I wrote into the notebook names that featured in the stories, any names that might be of help when I wanted to go on asking questions. Quite a few of them were names of families I knew. I was giving myself a lesson in the history of my tribe.

Gerry MacGuire was there, for instance. He'd been on the borough council at one stage, described as a builder although I can't myself remember seeing him do anything except hang around pubs. My grandfather Flynn was in the papers too, photographed at a topping-out ceremony.

There were also interesting gaps in this public record. The Scot, Jock Currie, who'd been a power to reckon with in the building trade and whose name had become legend, was missing. If you hadn't figured in court cases or signed important contracts or been photographed on ceremonial occasions, the *Gazette* had had no use for you.

Alarmed to realize how many hours I'd spent, I abandoned the files and chased back to my office where I found a doubtful Keith Jay hovering on the stairs outside my locked door. I apologized, adjusted my mind to the matter of the stolen dress design and the fate of its designer.

'I'll level with you, Laura,' said Keith. 'There's been a break-in at Kate's place and some documents have been stolen from her desk.'

I strived to look astonished. 'What was taken?'

'Something pretty useless, actually. A folder she keeps her notes in, phone messages and what have you. Kate's wonderful, she's the most marvellously tidy person I've ever worked with. It makes it easier when she's not there, but now Kate's gone and so has the folder.'

'Could she have come and taken it herself?'

'Through a window? At night?'

'Ah.'

I let him tell me how the burglar alarm had disturbed him, in his flat at the top of the house, a couple of nights previously and how he'd discovered a window in Kate's office unbolted, her desk unlocked and her folder missing.

'Did you inform the police?'

Thank goodness he said no.

'Who else has keys? Did either of the other two who live at the house hear an intruder, or see anyone running away?'

'I'm the only one with keys and I never let them out of my sight. The others were woken by the alarm but didn't hear or see anything.' Then: 'I'd like you to investigate, Laura.'

'I see.' It was going to be the easiest case I'd ever solved.

But he went on: 'Not just the theft of the folder. I want you to look into the theft of the dress design too. It was from the collection she's doing for Bethesda.'

I caught him reading the time from my personal Big Ben on the church tower across the road, then he was on his feet saying he had another appointment and I was to keep closely in touch about the inquiry.

'Of course,' I promised. Once he'd gone I poured myself a glass of mineral water and stood at my window watching vehicles grinding up and down Upper Street and the women trailing in and out of the gym and the boutique down below, and I thought about the mess I was getting into.

Maybe I should have had the wit to own up immediately and admit to being the intruder, and then maybe Keith Jay would have explained why he'd also been creeping around in the dark and locking a previously unlocked desk after replacing the folder I subsequently took away.

Who else could it have been if he was the only one with the key, and that had never been out of his possession? And if it was Keith, why was he tiptoeing without the lights on when he could have legitimately examined the contents of the desk any time he liked? Holding back my bit of information had made it impossible to challenge him.

The hospital put me through to the ward sister who told me Gran was still comfortable and I could look in on her that afternoon if I wished. I rang Chris Ionides and asked to borrow his car again, but this time he had to say no and mean it. He was off somewhere himself. 'My motor bike, she is here,' he offered, teasing.

'Fine,' I said. 'One o'clock?'

I relished his astonished silence.

First I hurried over to the Canonbury house and went through the formality of checking what Keith Jay had said about a break-in, and I squeezed from him details about the collection Kate had intended Bethesda to make.

'No,' he said, 'she had all the stuff with her. None of it was here when the break-in occurred. She took it with her three weeks ago when she left.'

'But you've seen all the sketches?'

'Some of them. Kate isn't a *prima donna*, love. She's a super person to work with. Not secretive either. She likes to discuss what she's doing, the way she's thinking. Not with anyone else, mind, but I've worked with her a long time. We went through about twenty sketches saying what we felt would go and which ones mightn't be pitched right for Bethesda. Don't forget, this Bethesda thing's new for her. She's always aimed her ideas at the up-market woman until now.'

'That dress I was wearing, was that designed before she went away?'

'Yes, I've only seen the things she did before she went. I expect when she comes back she'll want to talk about the rest but the slightly worrying point is . . .' The freckled face puckered, emphasizing worry.

'Yes?'

'Well, in this business one can't afford to lose a month here and there. She's cutting it fine if Bethesda are going to have the range ready for the shops in the spring.'

We looked through the desk, another formality because I already knew what was kept there. Then I explored the ground floor and offered the suggestion that if anyone had broken into the house it might well have been through the unsecured cloakroom window.

Keith Jay laughingly assured me that no one could possibly squeeze through that tiny gap, and I laughingly remarked that he'd be surprised how small a gap would do.

Later I telephoned the man at the sweatshop showroom and told him the dress he'd given me had been a huge success at a party but I'd like to know how he'd come by the design. He started on a repetition of the explanation about talented sketchers being able to copy a garment from a glance at something on a catwalk, and I had to cut him off by saying that was all very fine but this particular design seemed not to have been shown anywhere.

At that he became upset, first blustering that what I was saying was impossible and then begging me to return the dress. I didn't agree to that and pushed for more information, which naturally he didn't give. As I said, I was getting into a mess.

I put it all to the back of my mind, picked up the motor bike and went to the hospital.

It was years since I'd been on a bike but, as they say, you never forget. What I'd overlooked was how much I liked it. For a while I sat beside Gran who was lying there, unaware or uninterested. I didn't know which but it was heartbreaking either way. Then I slipped out again, comforted myself by heading through the traffic, north, following the road and enjoying the easy motion. The machine was what you'd expect Chris Ionides to go for: not an up-to-the-minute piece of Japanese technology but a sporty BMW, an R100 RS.

Just beyond Barnet you get to sham countryside, the Green Belt, and there are villages and farmhouses, the occasional cow and plenty of riding schools and paddocks. I fancied seeing some of that. I had to be quick, though, because light was already fading.

Shortly before you reach the Green Belt you pass Arkley Lane where Kate Mullery had hidden herself at Knights End Farm and where Robin Digby had been less than pleased to see me. I turned into Arkley Lane, let the bike bounce over the rough road between the frost-crimped hedges.

The first time I'd been up there I'd had difficulty finding the house but now, knowing its precise position, I understood exactly when to cut the engine and conceal the bike for a quiet approach. I won't pretend I was prepared for what happened next.

Robin Digby's dog bolted from the farmhouse garden and came for me. We remembered each other well. He was the one with the teeth and I was the one with a bite out of a good wool skirt. We didn't stop to consider it. He charged at me, and I dived into the garage of a bungalow and shut the door.

The brute kicked up a fuss in the lane by the garage but nobody stirred in the bungalow and I guessed that the owners were out although there was a Vauxhall in the garage with me. Eventually – and it seemed a long time – I heard Robin Digby calling the dog off, getting nearer, cursing and shouting at the animal from a range of six yards of the garage door.

If it was my lucky day Digby would fetch his dog and go away. If not, he'd inspect the garage for burglars. I held my breath, which, like most clichés, has the benefit of being an accurate description. I like clichés. They're a shorthand way of communicating and why not? There I was, acting a cliché and waiting to find out whether my luck was in or out.

Out.

Digby came up to the garage door and I'd already learned it wouldn't lock on the inside. I hid behind the car, knowing a bit of ducking and dodging might prevent him finding me but couldn't deter the dog.

And then I climbed into the car boot and pulled the tail gate down. More breath holding, while I wondered whether Digby, who'd simultaneously opened the garage door, had noticed movement in the interior gloom. From inside the boot it was difficult to hear what was happening, except for the occasional growl of the dog. I pictured the beast circling the car, rumbling frustration at his lack of clear speech and humans' lack of comprehension.

Once the growling had stopped I began to count one hundred to give Digby and the dog time to get clear before I swung up the boot lid and emerged.

'Fifty-one, fifty-two, fifty-three, fifty-f . . .'

The car juddered, then it bounced up and down, then all movement settled to the steady pulse of an engine running. Below me an exhaust pipe hammered and I sniffed its poisoned air. The fumes had nowhere to escape, they swirled in the enclosed space and they seeped into the boot. They could kill me in minutes, damage my brain in less, make me extremely sick in seconds.

It was a relief when the car rolled forward and I felt it lurch and dive along the road. Like a lot of things relief is comparative, and while I was glad not to be poisoned in the garage or chewed by the dog, I couldn't think of many other things I wanted less than a mystery tour in the boot of a car driven by a man who disliked me.

Best not to be found though. Holding the boot lid down to prevent it jiggling and catching the driver's eye in the rear-view mirror, I tried to guess when we turned right and when we turned left, and how far we might have gone. I had the picture fairly well when there was a great surge and the car was going flat out for a long way on a smooth surface. North, or west or east then. Not south for sure, because south meant London and we were on a big empty road where Digby could put his foot down. A motorway perhaps or else a dual carriageway. Hertfordshire has lots of them.

There are 4,000 private detectives operating in Britain. I shouldn't think I'm the first who's taken an unexpected ride in the boot of a car. If you work for a big agency you take on cases such as internal pilfering in businesses, surveillance, under-cover and counter-espionage, anti-counterfeiting, computer fraud, executive and diplomatic protection, insurance claims and infringement of patents, credit checks . . . Lower down the market you can collect debts and reclaim cars and goods when hire purchase payments haven't been made. Flynn Detective Agency has handled all kinds. Some months I'm so busy I'm very picky. Other times I take whatever I can get. This Christmas was a lean period: my own burglary at Kate Mul-lery's house, the stolen dress design and Mrs Lotti's cat.

My grandmother's voice echoed in my mind: 'Will you settle to something and make a go of your life?'

Maybe Gran had a point. This was ridiculous.

Well fair enough, today was ridiculous but things weren't always like this. I take decent jobs on the whole and I charge a good rate. I like the freedom and the fun of it, and anyway Christmas was usually a quiet period unless an association found the treasurer had run off with the Christmas club money and didn't think the police were giving it their all. The New Year was usually better. I had great hopes of the New Year.

I was getting used to the speed of Digby's driving, when we

hit the traffic jam. This was Friday afternoon, I should have been prepared for it. If we'd ever come to a complete halt I might have jumped out and walked away but we didn't stop, we crawled and tootled along and Digby stamped on brakes and jabbed at the accelerator in a way that nearly convinced me he knew I was behind him and was deliberately making life hell.

Hell ended with an uphill grind and then some slow-motion wriggling about that explained he was parking. I braced myself for escape. I lifted the lid a fraction but could see nothing but a brick and flint wall, close. A thud, and the car shuddered as the driver got out. And I was all set for another glimpse of the wall when the lid came crashing down above me and my glimmer of light was switched off.

Now I dare say a mechanic knows how to unlock a car boot from the inside, and I'm pretty sure my lock-picking acquaintance who was doing five in Pentonville would have the answer. But me, not a clue. All I knew was that I had a chance of dying in the boot of a car in an unknown town. Town? Oh yes, I'd been aware of plenty of slow-moving traffic in the uphill drive and some other shunting as the car was parked. I was confident I was in a town.

In a car boot in a town in the dark. That was the position. The position was also cramped and uncomfortable. But don't say I'm not an optimist. On the plus side I had beside me a set of car tools and the car was a hatchback. Houdini would have said it was too easy.

Yes, Houdini might. Me, I struggled. Chiefly because I was too squashed to get leverage and in the pitch black I wasn't at all sure where I ought to be applying pressure. I fumbled and cursed, pushing at the shelf above my head because I guessed it was a weak point but learning that it was held rigid by the slope of the back window.

I groaned in exasperation, battering at the rear seat that I understood ought to fall away into the passenger compartment but refused. And I fought desperately for my freedom whenever I caught myself wasting time worrying that Digby might return and drive on, that he might have something to put in the boot and discover me after all.

Somehow I hit the right thing at the right point because a section of the rear seat collapsed away from me and suddenly there was lamplight and the fusty air of a vehicle in which someone smoked cigars. I crawled over the seat, unbuttoned the door, pushed the seat upright and escaped. That damp bitter air waiting for me was sheer joy.

I was in a car-park, outside a hotel. The hotel was behind a wall, off an ancient narrow street of whitewashed cottages, a good place in summer because a terrace reached down to a lawn and the lawn reached down to a garden and the garden was bordered by a stream. Lamplight told me all this, and the yellow glow from uncurtained windows told me Digby was not in the bar.

I hesitated about going inside the hotel to check. If he were there he might recognize me. In any case I'd attract attention because this was a place that didn't expect customers carrying motor-cycle helmets and I was grubby. A waiter came outside and I asked him whether there was a man of Digby's description in the bar, a big florid man in his fifties with thinning brown hair and a loud voice. He checked and said not.

'He's definitely here,' I persisted. 'He came in that car.'

'Oh, *that* man. He's in the other bar. You go along there.'

I set off to the other bar. From its doorway I could squint at Digby and a handsome silver-haired man sitting, heads close across a table, talking intently. I backed out and found the cloakroom where I washed my hands and face and titivated my hair. Then I left the helmet I'd borrowed from Chris, and my own leather jacket, in a corner. I was trying to look less like a biker.

I was in a hotel, St Michael's Manor. I still couldn't say which town.

Digby had his back to me throughout. He didn't notice when I walked in and Silver Hair didn't spare me a glance either. I bought a drink, thumbed a magazine and overheard them talking about a business deal. Deer farming wasn't mentioned, Digby was involved in some other kind of business.

A land deal, that was it. I sipped my scotch and I picked up the details. They were irrelevant to Kate Mullery and the mysteries surrounding her. A land deal. So what? Digby farmed on the tip of the Green Belt, landowners were always on the look-out for ways to convert fresh green fields into houses. It's the most profitable crop they know. Again, so what?

So all of a sudden I knew they weren't talking about Digby's farmland, they meant a plot on the south bank of the Thames, a short stretch from where Kate Mullery's body had entered the water.

Digby said: 'They're holding out. The old man is, the youngster's all for taking the money.'

'There's a limit,' said Silver Hair. 'A limit to the money and a limit to the time.'

'I've told them that.'

'Well, then.'

'Yes. Look, Reggie, there's something else.' Digby's voice had dropped but behind me I felt him shift in the seat and then he was whispering. All along he'd sounded mildly deferential, now he sounded edgy. Reluctantly the other man agreed with whatever Digby had asked. They got up and left.

I let them get to the end of the passage. They were going slowly, side by side like a couple of friends with time to chat. I knew differently. I grabbed my helmet and jacket and I made it out of the side door before they reached the car-park. Good. They weren't diving into a car to talk privately, they were going to walk. When they passed under the trees and started down a path through the grounds, they didn't spot me in the shadows and I tailed them right the way down to the stream.

I won't claim I never cracked a twig or rustled a leaf. What I will say is that Digby and his pal were so engrossed in their complicity that they were never aware of my sounds. By the stream they paused for a while, letting me edge closer.

Up until then I'd learned that a piece of land owned by two unnamed men held the key to a proposed development on the banks of the Thames; that one man was willing to sell for development but the other was waiting for a higher offer; that the developer was applying pressure to get a deal finalized. The conversation was carried on in intense murmurs and, like most eavesdroppers, I was disappointed. That changed.

'*Jesus Christ!*' Silver Hair swung to confront Digby. 'How on earth . . .'

Digby's hands flapped in a quietening gesture. 'A misunderstanding. I didn't say . . .'

But the other man exploded into recrimination. 'Some bloody misunderstanding! *God*, Robin. What the hell was she doing down there?'

'Getting herself killed.' Digby defended himself: 'I couldn't keep guard on her the whole time.'

'That's exactly what you should have been doing.'

There was a long, bitter silence. I begged them not to notice my breath staining the air nor the insistent chatter of my teeth. Finally Digby spoke again, his voice wavering, emotional, the fight gone out of him.

'I swear I don't know how she got on to it. She was supposed to stay at the farm, out of harm's way. Instead of that, she . . .'

Silver Hair talked him down. 'All right. She didn't do what you thought she'd do, but what do *you* propose to do now, Robin?'

'Do?'

'You must have thought about it. How are you going to handle this?'

'Well, I . . .' He had no answer. He let the other man take over.

'Who knows about this?'

'You and me.'

'Not . . .'

Quickly Digby said: 'No, he still thinks it was the other one. I didn't tell them he was wrong.'

A sigh. Resignation or relief, I couldn't tell. Then: 'Good.' Optimism had crept in. 'Yes, good. That's the best thing. But I'm not sure you should keep it that way much longer.'

'What then?'

Silver Hair stamped his feet on the frozen ground and began to walk on as he said the next bit. I missed it but I saw Digby trotting beside him, reduced to listening and seeking help. I heard Digby raise a couple of questions but for the rest he was content to be told what to do. I let them go. I'd run out of trees and I had no option.

There was another way out of the hotel grounds and I took it, crossing the stream and joining a path in open land where a winter lake was an expanse of grey sheen. Beyond the lake I came to a pub, the Fighting Cocks. That's when I learned I was in St Albans. I bought another scotch and coaxed a big black dog out of the way of the fire.

Kate Mullery was dead and Robin Digby knew it.

I'd been hired to do three things. To check out Bethesda, the dress manufacturer. I'd checked and they'd been clean. But Kate had hired me to look again, something had made her doubt their reliability. Then Keith Jay had hired me to find out how one of her designs had fallen into the hands of a high street copyist.

Nobody was going to hire me to find out who'd killed Kate Mullery or why she'd been killed, yet that's what I wanted to do.

Unfortunately my grandmother was in hospital and begging me for news of my runaway father, and I hadn't made much progress. And, as Silver Hair had said to Robin Digby, there was a limit to the time.

Robin Digby and I both knew that Kate Mullery was dead. Neither of us had been to the police. I finished my drink and decided that I ought to report what I knew and then retreat, abandon the muddles of the fashion trade and concentrate on serious matters like looking for my father and unimportant ones like Mrs Lotti's cat. But when I used the telephone at the Fighting Cocks it wasn't the police I called, but a cab to take me to the railway station.

Home, weary and late, I sank beneath the soothing waves of a foamy bath and I read two chapters of my detective novel before the water cooled down. They are pretty short chapters.

The hero is a typical detective story hero. He has no family, he has no friends to speak of, he has no luck except in the final reel when everything slithers into place. Fantasy. Real life, it's different. Mind you, he has hope. Oodles. Unjustifiable and largely unjustified, but still he goes right on hoping, from book to book.

I'll tell you, there are whole weeks when I do not suffer from hope. They're the kind of weeks that begin with being attacked on the Underground by steamers intent on parting me from St Lucy, the kind of weeks that see my biggest paying client killed, and my grandmother about to die, the kind that let me walk slap bang into my ex-husband who just happens to have taken up with one of my closest friends. They are not the kind of weeks I like.

I emerged from foam and fantasy and remembered to check my answering machine. It had been pretty busy while I'd been trailing out to Hertfordshire on motor bikes and in car boots.

'Laura! Isa Mrs Lotti. You remember my cat, eh? He'sa no come home.' And so forth, cheerfully chivvying me to get my snout to the ground and go scenting after Jaguar, the creature the Italian *mamma* of Nonesuch House called a cat and I'd call a monster.

'*Domani*, Mrs Lotti,' I vowed. 'I'll get on to it *domani*.'

I heard a click and a plop and then Chris Ionides was on the tape wondering what I'd done with his motor bike, me being the girl who'd promised to return it straight after she'd been to the hospital to see her dying granny. He sounded like a man who'd never again trust any story that featured a dying granny.

81

Another click and a squeak and then there was a breathy pause just long enough for my stomach to tighten like a row of french knots.

'Too many questions, Flynn. Too many questions.'

And the Whisperer let the silence that followed become as menacing as the vicious voice itself, or perhaps I did that part for myself, geared up by reading fantasy and an evening of living it.

It pleased me then to switch the machine off, deprive the Whisperer of his silence and his power, even if I hadn't been able to forestall his words spilling into the room. His capacity for frightening me was restricted tonight: the machine was at my office and I was in my flat, the one with the thick, thick carpet and not much furniture. My address was private. That was one reason I had the office. Lead a risky life and you need a bolt-hole, a sanctuary where the problems you're paid to fret over stay on the street side of your door. OK, I know your fictional detectives eat, sleep and fuck their cases. But this is different.

From the office, reached via the remote-control device that worked my answering machine down the telephone line, I jumped back to my private life. I rang the hospital and learned that Mrs Flynn was asleep.

She was Irish, the ward sister I'd spoken to. One of the clan. A Flynn, or else it was her married name. Some married women still use them. Hard to remember in Islington. So many don't.

Was Sister Flynn more patient with me, *nicer*, was there a tingle of empathy because we were both Flynns? Ada Carey had asked her where she was from and had been told Tufnell Park, but the answer was also Donegal.

I'm not posing a serious question here. She could simply have been in a good mood. Maybe a doctor had smiled at her. Maybe a patient she loathed had obediently faded away in a morphia-induced haze. How is one ever to know why a perfect stranger is kind beyond the call of duty or else inexplicably rude? And while I'm asking difficult questions, why is a stranger 'perfect'? Can people only appear perfect before you've got to know them?

I digress, and digressing I went to bed and switched on the television set for the late film. Well no, let me tell the truth. I intended to watch it but within a few minutes I found my mind wandering. It wandered through the pubs of north London, places Gran would have known about and perhaps my father had gone into. It meandered after a doubtful Mrs Cotton who did a bunk the same time Joe Flynn did, and it sauntered up to the Irish clubs where there was pitched battle in the streets most Friday and Saturday nights when I was in my high chair and before that too.

Round and round it went, like the pink elephants on the mug in Robin Digby's kitchen. Round and round and round, endlessly. Getting nowhere.

THREE

Sue Preston's curly red head ducked back into the kitchen as I walked down the passage of Anna Lee's house, early on Saturday morning.

'How's your grandmother, Laura?' Anna asked.

While I reported the hospital was stuck on comfortable, I knew Sue was listening just out of my sight. Avoiding me, because she was embarrassed to be having an affair with my ex. Poor Sue, wasting her time because it wasn't Anna I'd come to see, it was Sue. She didn't know it yet but she was going to help me out.

Anna attempted to shepherd me into a room but I pretended not to notice and ran downstairs to the basement kitchen and Sue.

'Hi, Laura.' Sue sounded a shade too bright. Her very pale skin flushed prettily. I'd never wondered what Mike saw in her. She's pretty and she's intelligent, an art teacher. She busied herself with a task that didn't need doing.

'Hello, Sue. How do you and your van fancy a trip to the country?' Why mess around? I said it straight out, the advantage of surprise.

'Today?'

'This minute.'

'Oh.'

I mentioned the calamity of a left-behind motor cycle and left out the calamity of a ride into danger in the boot of a car. Sue said oh a couple more times but she didn't say no. I'd picked the right day. School had broken up and she was free, give or take Christmas shopping.

Anna, who'd come into the kitchen behind me, hovering in case awkwardness needed to be smoothed away, now offered us both breakfast and provided it in her best motherly fashion. Life has cheated Anna of motherhood but not of motherliness. Life's often unfair that way.

Have you ever noticed that when two people have the same subject in the front of their minds, it's the very one they don't bring up? That's how Sue and I came to talk about everything from international crises to the filthy state of the London Underground and the new film at the Screen on the Green, and never once got near the topic of Mike Brenan. Not, that is, until we were in her van and going up through Archway on our way to collect Chris Ionides's bike.

'Laura, about Mike . . .' Sue said once she'd done a sequence of gear shifting and lane changing and beaten a smokey truck on to the straight. The flush began creeping up her throat again.

I struggled for a tone that relegated Mike to the role of stranger, not this time 'perfect' stranger and not that for a number of reasons. 'What about him?'

'It's just that I'm sorry if it's difficult for you. I mean me taking up with him. I mean, you and I've been friends a good long while, and I'd be sorry to think . . .' The flush had reached her hair line. Poor Sue, emotions exposed, every discomfort paraded.

'Then don't, Sue,' I said cheerfully, without expending any sympathy on her. 'Just don't think about it. OK?'

She said yes, but she said it nervously.

I wondered what she'd said to Mike on the subject, or he to her. I kept my wondering to myself. Ever since Anna Lee had told me that Mike was Sue's latest, I'd kept up a pretty good act of finding the event beneath my notice.

Mike and I had come unpaired, like socks in the wash. It didn't mean that I could feel nothing for him. Mention his name to me and you could arouse curiosity, or contempt, or regret, I'd even stretch to a wistful affection. But I couldn't feel nothing.

Chris's bike was roughly where I'd dumped it although

someone had wheeled it up to the garage in which I'd hidden. It was leaning against the wall and there was ice in the muddy puddle where the driveway joined the lane. Paying better attention to the bungalow this time, I could see what ought to have been obvious earlier. The building was on farmland, as much part of the estate as the Victorian farmhouse a few yards along the lane. Perhaps Digby lived in one and a farm manager or stockman lived in the other. Whichever it was, it explained the tiny puzzle of Robin Digby having the use of the car I'd jumped into.

I began to wheel the motor bike into the lane. Sue was a hundred yards on, gone to turn the van round. I'd warned her not to reverse into the entrance of Knights End Farm but she did. The dog didn't like it. Neither did Robin Digby who launched himself out of the farmhouse. I could hear his objections from where I stood.

Sue gave as good as she got, wound up her window and moved back down the lane towards me. I was busy discovering somebody had cut the bike's high-tension cables. Digby noticed me. I saw him too and I stuck out a hand to stop Sue driving off. She mistook it for a wave and accelerated away.

Digby and the dog came for me.

I had the feeling I'd been through this before: Digby shouting, the dog raring to attack and me attempting to placate without giving way an inch. Try it sometime. See how *you* get on.

Oh yes, I was also trying to look over my shoulder in the hope of willing Sue to come back because I knew in my heart that there was no chance of me starting that bike. Digby had seen to that.

He was blathering about trespassing and burglary and snooping but I kept my temper and thought oh boy, if you only knew, if only you realized you'd taken me all the way to St Albans and let me overhear you confessing Kate Mullery had been killed because of some crooked land deal in which you're up to your apoplectic neck.

He dived to grab me and the dog took that as a signal and leaped too. Digby got his fingers around my shoulder and the dog sank his teeth into my sleeve. Not far in but enough. Digby I might floor, but the dog? He was several hundred pounds of venom and he thought he'd found a fight.

I did what neither of them would have chosen and neither of them expected. I filled my lungs and I screamed. Extremely loud. Digby released my shoulder and dragged the dog off. I didn't let him know his pet hadn't ripped my flesh, I cradled my arm. But I was poised to defend myself if either of them came at me again.

Fortunately, the quality of my defence was never put to the test. Sue's car came reversing up the lane, bouncing red curls out of the window as she searched for me. And a sweet old lady, all lavender and Earl Grey tea, appeared at her gate nearby and did a Miss Marple act of sussing us out in the guise of gardening. Sue and I manoeuvred the bike into the back of her van while Digby and the dog glared impotently.

I watched them in the wing mirror as the van pulled away. We reached the end of the lane and the tableau hadn't changed: Digby and the dog watching us and old lady in garden watching them.

'Laura,' said Sue in an accusing voice.

'I know, I know. I should have explained.' All the awkwardness was on my side for a change. If I were the type who blushed, I'd have been blushing.

'You didn't say you were making me bring you up here to be attacked by a big man and a bigger dog. Please, Laura, what the hell was going on back there?'

'He doesn't like me. Nor does his dog.'

'Very funny. You owe me, Laura. Explain.'

I did. Of course, not much of it. Too long and complicated for that, and none of her business either. She asked a pertinent question or two and I headed her off. 'Sorry, Sue. Clients' business.'

Sue pulled on the handbrake at traffic lights in Barnet. 'If I were you, Laura, I'd think about acquiring some classier clients.'

'The kind that don't feed me to wild animals? Sure, I'll give it some thought.'

She spared me a sidelong look and might have come out with a succinct rejoinder but the lights were changing and there was a determined pick-up planning to rip the side off her van if she didn't shift fast.

Chris Ionides took the bad news about his motor bike as philosophically as any Greek who's already lost his homeland, his inheritance of three olive trees and a patch of mountain, and his taste for yoghurt. The bike was bust? A shrug. Ten minutes to fix the leads, that's all. Things could be worse. But he didn't offer to lend me the R100 again, not then and not ever.

Once more I turned down his gift of tea in a muck-streaked mug, and once more he assured me the part for my car was on its way. There it was, my car, forlorn and gathering dust. I almost said she was in the corner of his workshop but Chris's place is too cramped to have corners. There she was, a tripey mass of dusty metal taking up his meagre space and she was there because Chris loved her more than I did.

To make sure he didn't forget she was mine, I wrote my signature for a second time in the dust on her bonnet. Chris's habit of personalizing the inanimate is catching, and as *amaxi*'s neuter it has everything to do with sentimentality and nothing to do with translation from the Greek. Cutting across Highbury Fields and aiming for Upper Street and the office, I told myself I was to stop doing it even if Chris couldn't.

Nobody had rung while I'd been away, except a puzzled editor at *Time Out* who wanted me to call back and say why a Turkish clothing manufacturer had been on to them to stop publication of a piece I was allegedly writing on the garment industry. No, I wouldn't call back. I'd go to ground and pretend the answering machine had been faulty and failed to impart the message. They're a boon, these machines. This age of technology has distinct advantages.

But I couldn't settle to work. I made coffee and read the *Evening Standard* from cover to cover. Jaci Stephen's television column was one of her acerbic best, the producer would probably never work again. The small ads were cryptic as ever, abbreviations robbing them of all sense. The leader was rubbish, I usually think that. I began to write letters in my head: fan mail for Jaci Stephen, a plea for a glossary to be published along with the small ads, a demolition job on the leader. No, I didn't drag out the typewriter, those letters are best left in your head.

I tossed the paper aside and made a phone call to the pub in Canonbury where Mrs Cotton and her husband had lived. Nobody there had heard of them. Then I rang the Licensed Victuallers' Association and asked after a member called Cotton. I was given the name of a pub in south London, but it wasn't helping much. I needed the wife, not the abandoned husband. In other words, I needed a local gossip not a membership secretary with a subscription list.

That's when I took my gym kit out of the filing cabinet and ran downstairs for an hour's workout. Sharon works you hard. Glad I'd caught her class, I stretched and reached and counted press-ups before attacking the machines. I shut my ears to the chatter of the rest of the class who were there to socialize as much as keep fit, and I did a grand job with the lats and the side-bends. Throughout I thought about Mrs Cotton and who was the most accomplished gossip I knew and whether she mightn't be willing (somehow I knew it would turn out to be a she) to tell me all.

Alas and alack, the best I knew was lying in a hospital bed. Gran's funny that way. She knows everything about everyone and she succeeds in passing it on, but oh so discreetly that it's a brave woman indeed who'd declare Kitty Flynn, so quick to stand on her dignity, an outrageous gossip.

Well, then. Where did that get me? First it meant the best

gossip I knew was unavailable. Secondly it meant that Mrs Cotton wasn't the answer to why my daddy ran off, because if Mrs Cotton *had* been then Kitty Flynn would have known, and Ada Carey and the rest of the tribe too.

On the other hand, Kitty Flynn was not infallible. All right. Who was the second-best gossip?

Oh, no.

You wouldn't want me to talk to *her*.

Not after . . . *everything*.

Yes, I know it depends on how desperate this is, and it's a desperate state I'm in, but . . .'

St Lucy and I batted it back and forth. She, you'll recall, is the one in charge of finding lost things. Wallets, fathers, gossips, it's all the same to our Lucy. Or so I hoped.

Anyway, there are some things that are beyond the call of filial duty and the name that kept bobbing into my head while I heaved a controlled 30 kilograms up and down was a name I preferred not to hear.

As I'd said to Sue: 'Then don't. Just don't think of it.'

I didn't. I thought about the third best and the fourth best and by the stage I'd reached down to the fifth best, I wasn't thinking about the best at all, I was thinking about the easiest. The *very* easiest had been Ada Carey, old Gerry MacGuire and Father Mahon and I can't say they'd been a power of help.

I stood in the shower and let the quick short burst of hot water drench me. I rubbed shampoo into my hair. What was wrong with me? Obviously I could go to the second best. This was life and death we were dealing with here, not face saving and embarrassment. What was wrong?

I didn't want to lose face and I feared embarrassment, that's what. Fine, I was normal. But I could overcome that, I did most days of the week.

Ah but that's different. That's professional. I get paid for that.

Very well, treat it like a job. Pretend Gran hired you.

No.

Yes.

No.

St Lucy and I kicked this around too. Then I carefully dried her on my towel, rubbed as much damp as I could from my hair, dragged on my clothes and shoved the gym kit back into its bag. No decisions had been reached but, I tell you, I felt terrific.

I carried on feeling terrific and ignoring St Lucy's advice until I'd dribbled away the afternoon in a series of phone calls that pointed me at a pub landlord who'd once worked for a man called Cotton in Islington. To begin with I thought I'd struck gold. Yes, the man knew about Mrs Cotton. Yes, she'd lived with her husband at the Canonbury pub, so we were talking about the right Mrs Cotton. Yes, she'd left him around the time that interested me. And, he finished, hadn't she settled down to running a boarding-house with her sister in Eastbourne and hadn't she died there ten years ago?

Goodbye Mrs Cotton.

But what might I have learned if I'd gone to the second-best gossip?

I was nibbling my pen cap and mulling over this when I heard the unfamiliar sound of a client running up my stairs. That's to say a client or else somebody who thought I was an employment agency. Well, whoever came in was going to find me in jeans and a scruffy blouse (I'd expected to be motor-cycling from Arkley, remember); with my hair dried unsupervised; with a plastic cup made bendy by too-hot water on my desk; and with a litter of doodled scraps of paper in front of me. Not the way I like to meet prospective clients.

Neither was it the way I'd have chosen to meet Mike Brenan.

Mike was an astonishment I couldn't take in. He was slyly amused by that astonishment.

He said: 'It's a bad idea, Laura, and you're to give it up.'

'But I haven't . . .' Would you believe I was silly enough to think he knew what was in my mind? That's the measure of my turmoil. Part of me was registering that he was still a man I'd

91

look at twice in the street, part was cursing him for his cheek in barging in on me, and part was convinced he was the answer to a prayer.

'Look,' he said, 'it's not worth it.'

I gathered my wits. 'Life and death, that's what we're talking about.'

'Life and . . .' His assurance faded. 'I don't think we can be talking about the same thing.'

'We often weren't,' I said blithely. 'It became a bad habit with us. Remember?' Crudely I'd seized the initiative but at the cost of stirring what might have been better left unstirred.

He said: 'Sue told me about a terrifying scene involving you and a thug and a dog the size of a barn.'

'Thanks, Sue,' I said ironically.

'She was scared for you. She's afraid you're getting into something you can't handle.' As soon as he'd said it he knew it was the wrong thing. I didn't trouble to ask what business it was of Sue's or his. I managed it with one long look.

Good old me. I'd stirred and here we were heading for a row.

He said: 'You're thinking it's none of my business what you do.'

I said nothing.

He said: 'Well, all right, it isn't. Except that you'd be on my conscience if you got yourself bitten to death by that dog . . .'

'What are you planning to do? Interpose your body between me and the fangs?'

'I'm serious.'

'Me too. There isn't anything anyone can do to alter an incident that happened this morning. Well, is there?'

He didn't like me mocking but he disguised his annoyance, I'll give him that. 'I'm suggesting you drop the case that led you into that predicament. You weren't light-hearted about it when it happened, Laura. Sue heard you screaming.'

At that I threw back my head and laughed. Sue, who'd driven off after mistaking a stop signal for a farewell wave. Sue, who'd enticed Digby and his beast out of the farmhouse in the first place. Sue, who'd failed to understand the reason for the scream. Oh, who cared about Sue, anyway?

Mike Brenan, that's who.

He'd tried out the tacky chair I have for visitors but it seemed as flimsy as the Flynn Detective Agency and he gave it up and stood instead. I watched him taking in the details of the place. The inadequacy.

And I felt as exposed as when we'd had our first brief re-encounter the other evening, the wind shaping the silky material of a new dress to the curves of my body. Then it had been the physical me that was held out for scrutiny. Now it was the professional me.

I didn't want to be scrutinized, explored, made to pass or fail exams. I wanted to be private, concealed, contained. I could be all of those things if the world would let me.

There was a silence, the kind that ended with both of us speaking at once and then neither of us being willing to go on. I actually brought the impasse to an end by shouting: 'Don't do that,' because he tweaked open one of the filing cabinet drawers. Toying with it, nothing reprehensible, finding something to fiddle with while he thought about what he wanted or didn't want to say to me and what he wanted or didn't want me to say to him.

He threw up his hands in a gesture of surrender. 'OK, I wasn't going to . . . Anyway what's in there that makes you so jumpy?'

'Nothing,' I said quickly. That was pretty well true. I covered the ambiguity with the insistence that the thing was *choc à bloc* with files on cases I'd completed or was currently investigating.

'You don't keep the drink here then?' he joked, and pulled open another drawer and looked down on a mass of gym kit and umbrellas.

Immediately I was round the desk, protective and anxious, going for the key to lock the cabinet. Talk about stable doors and horses.

Mike was smiling that wicked smile of his, the one he uses to cover all manner of mischief and provocation. I chose to ignore it, regained my equilibrium and offered a choice of coffee-bags or instant, ordinary tea-bags or fancy. He looked at me in wonder and said instant would do nicely.

When the telephone interrupted me he was content to go through to the washroom and fill the kettle, and tactful enough to ignore my unlocking of the filing cabinet to liberate a jar of instant coffee.

He made a second shot at getting on terms with my rickety chair. He was politely grateful for the coffee. And he was leading up to something, I recognized the signs.

'This life-and-death thing you mentioned, Laura,' he began.

'Hmm?' This in an absent-minded manner, as though life and death weren't all that important.

'Would it be anything to do with the writing on the mirror?'

Oh no, I'd overlooked the lipstick threat left by my burglar. Now I'd have to discuss it. Or would I? What business was it of . . .

He said: 'Did you show that to the police?'

'Of course not. Somebody broke in and scrawled on the mirror, that's all.'

'My but you're tough.'

'Look, Mike,' I said, 'how about you involving yourself in one of my inquiries where you might actually be able to help?'

I received the kind of look you'd expect me to get. Incredulous.

'You see,' I went on, 'I've been working on something this afternoon that's led me into a delicate area. I know what my next step must be but it's a very hard one for me to take. You, on the other hand, would find it no trouble at all.'

His mystification was most rewarding. 'What do you want me to do?'

'Talk to your mother,' I said. 'Ask her what she recalls about the time my father disappeared and whether she knows if he'd been associating with a Mrs Cotton, or anyone else for that matter. Tell her Kitty Flynn is in hospital and dying, and she's begging for news of my father.'

'Kitty dying? Oh, Laura.' He didn't come to me, but his voice was a caress.

I swallowed and went on rapidly. 'Your mother's the best chance I have, but . . .'

'But she wouldn't speak to you.'

'Will you do it, Mike? Please?'

'Tell me exactly what you want to know.'

He made a note of the salient points. Then: 'How soon do you need this?'

My voice was a whisper, hardly audible above the sounds of traffic in the main road outside. 'How long does dying take?'

Anna Lee came round to the flat that evening and we indulged in sliced fish with black bean and chilli sauce from Chinese Chef, London's most superior take-away. We're lucky it's close to us, in Caledonian Road. The treat was a spur-of-the-moment event because I'd rung Anna to tell her about Mike's unscheduled visit, and I'd caught her suffering a bout of misery because she was stuck on her book.

I gave her some advice. 'When Raymond Chandler was stuck, he always had a man with a gun walk in.'

She said she didn't think her editor would like it if she did that.

'No,' I said, 'but I bet the children would.'

Anna said she'd think about it.

I'd like to know how it would be if she broke out and wrote a racy, raunchy adult novel. Apart from riches, I mean. She says she wouldn't do it, it's not her kind of thing. More than that, she won't confess to ever having tried. She must have done, surely. I mean, haven't we all? Even if it's only a few chapters in our heads, even if it's only one scene that we wished we'd read and nobody has written for us?

People write the books they'd like to read themselves, on the whole. That's something Anna does admit to. Not enough reading as a child, just *Girl* and *School Friend* and a swap for a friend's *Crystal*, not enough books and so now she doubles back in time and writes them for herself. Or not, on the days she's stuck.

After the fish we marvelled at the cool cheek of Mike Brenan to walk into my office, and at my opportunism in sending him to quiz his mother. Anna sprawled luxuriously on my sofa, her generous curves subdued by a loose sweater and skirt. I sat cross-legged on the carpet. She giggled. 'He was probably knocked out by the sight of you the other night – that dress is rather stunning.'

'It would have to be if it was enough to make a man pitch up three years after a divorce and open the conversation as though it had never broken off.'

She put on a funny voice: 'As I was saying when I was interrupted . . .'

We both giggled. I said: 'Well, if he imagined I'd been transformed into a svelte sophisticate, he found out this afternoon it isn't true.'

'Perhaps you'll never see him again.'

'I don't care about that, as long as he phones me and tells me what his mother has to report on the mystery of my fourth Christmas.'

Anna confessed she couldn't fathom why I'd never asked Mrs Brenan about it, during the easier times before the marriage broke down. I replied that there hadn't been easier times. Mrs Brenan had disapproved of me, she'd been guarded and unapproachable and Anna wasn't to imagine me and Mrs Brenan playing happy families. After the divorce she'd refused to speak to me, although in truth the opportunity had rarely arisen. That's why I'd recruited Mike for the Joe Flynn case. I'd been too plain scared of his mother to go to her myself.

'You?' said Anna with a hoot of disbelief. 'I've never heard of you being scared of anyone. What about this morning? Sue's told me everything, how you handled a man three times your size *and* his dog. She was impressed, kept going on about it, saying how she'd been in shock just to be a witness and there was little Laura treating it like an everyday occurrence.'

'Huh?'

'It's no good trying to brush it off, Laura, she was most impressed. Shall I tell you precisely what she said?'

I shook my head. 'No thanks.'

'The gist was that you were a match for both of them.'

I dug my fingertips into the rich pink pile of the carpet and asked myself whether one could be a liar and a blusher. Could Sue truly have told Anna one version and Mike another? Or wasn't it likelier that Mike had lied?

This led to subsidiary questions such as why he'd lied but I couldn't be bothered with any of that. He was a man I'd excised from my life, his truthfulness or otherwise no longer concerned me. All I wanted from him was that he squeezed information out of his mother.

He phoned half an hour later. I hadn't wanted to give my home number – I give it to very few people – but with Gran being ill and the matter urgent my priorities had changed. If need be, I could always change the number. What I couldn't do was buy back any time I wasted in the search for my father.

When Mike phoned he was speaking very carefully which spelled out that he was at his parents' house and believed his mother to be listening.

'She says will you come over, Laura.'

'She wants to talk to me?' There was a leap of hope, but distrust too.

'That's what she says.'

'Does that mean she has news?'

'Well, she hasn't put it as plainly as that.'

Anna let herself be shooed out of the flat and I took a cab to Highgate. The Brenans had moved up there when Mike's father became a director of the company he worked for. The house had a view over London, a pretty garden and a full complement of the right things. Mrs Brenan had set her heart on all that. She'd been ambitious for Mike too, indeed for all her children, and when Mike had turned out not to care too much for the things she cared about, she'd found a scapegoat in me.

Mrs Brenan – no, I'd never got close enough to call her Della – was looking good. I'd never known her look otherwise but it was an aspect I'd forgotten because there were many more memorable aspects to our relationship apart from the fact that she was always what used to be called well-groomed and I was, well, more relaxed.

This evening she had her hair swept up with a discreet tortoiseshell clip, and I was wearing mine long and frizzy from the shower at the gym. She was in a grape-green silk blouse and dark skirt with spindle-heeled shoes. I was in a bit of a mess.

'Sit down, Laura.'

I guessed she was hoping I'd trip up on the Chinese carpet but I made it to the chair.

She said, clipped and irritated: 'You should have come yourself in the first place, fancy dragging Mike into it. What would he know?'

I'd decided to appeal, and to do it appealingly. 'What do *you* know, Mrs Brenan? Anything at all would be helpful. I'm short of time and I'll be grateful for whatever help I can get.'

She had a way of challenging with a raised eyebrow. 'Even mine?'

I let it go. I said: 'Did Mike mention the name of Mrs Cotton to you?'

'He did but that rumour was laid to rest years ago when the woman was heard of living on the south coast with her sister.'

'It was definitely only a rumour then?'

'Oh yes, and there were no other rumours and no other women's names. Wherever he went, your father, he didn't mean to be followed.'

I said, a shade apologetically I fear, that I wouldn't have tried for myself but it was Gran who needed the answers. I owed Gran a lot, I owed her at least an attempt.

Mrs Brenan smoothed one delicate hand over the other

before she said: 'He covered his tracks, Laura. No one saw him after he left the house. He had a plan and he went high-tailing out of our lives.'

'Just a minute.' I was on the edge of my chair, leaning out at her. 'What makes you say no one saw him?'

'That's the way it was.'

'You mean none of the family saw him. Somebody else, several people probably, must have done.'

'I mean no one who knew him. Obviously he didn't turn into the Invisible Man. Even oh-so-clever Joe Flynn wasn't quite as smart as that.'

With an effort I stopped my face reacting to her sarcasm, but she'd let out that she hadn't admired my father any more than she admired me. People generally referred to him with affection, he'd been a likeable personality. His photographs showed a happy man who'd made people happy. Here was Mrs Brenan inferring something other.

I cautioned myself not to make much of it. She'd disliked it when Mike had fallen for me, resisted the marriage, been antagonistic to me for the duration of it, and hated me more when it ended in divorce. Why should I be surprised if her objection extended beyond me and encompassed the rest of the family?

Yet I was, because I hadn't experienced this before. Mrs Brenan had preserved a cordial politeness to the rest of my family, letting it be clear only to me that while the Flynns were very well in their way, it didn't do for any of her children to marry them.

'*Was* he clever?' I asked, smiling and misleading her into thinking this was a total change of direction.

'Oh, a very quick mind,' she conceded. 'Not one to have the wool pulled over his eyes, you know.'

'Like Gran?'

'Yes, I'd say he took after Kitty Flynn in lots of ways. Always had to know what was going on. An inquiring mind, if you care to put it like that.'

I coaxed her to say what kind of thing he'd inquired about, decking it out with a joke about Gran needing to know everybody's business. I knew it wouldn't offend Mrs Brenan, because gossips seldom recognize that in themselves.

No good. The answers were vague, except that we seemed to have shunted from personal matters to business. Joe Flynn, if I read the subtext correctly, had been nosey about other people's business affairs.

This I could shrug off. Hadn't I spent the previous morning reading the backnumbers of the *Islington Gazette* and boning up on the troubles in the days when getting contracts for building jobs was nasty work? Who, in the midst of it, wouldn't have been interested to know what was going on or likely to?

At last I winkled from her what I hadn't heard before: Joe had been upset at the death of a friend of his on a construction site, had made accusations of unsafe practices. The man was called Laughton.

Then Mrs Brenan was on her feet, indicating in a queenly manner that my audience was over. I kept her there a moment, rejecting the signal, and tried for more.

'What construction site? And who was Laughton working for when he died?'

She laughed but without warmth. 'No, Laura, I can't remember. Probably I never knew.'

But of course she had. Wasn't she the second best?

Reluctantly I made the return journey across the carpet. She said: 'Give Kitty Flynn my regards, Laura. But don't hold out any hope that she'll discover what became of her Joe.'

As I started to reply, Mike came in. Until then I'd assumed he'd left the house before I got there. His car hadn't been outside. We went out together, leaving Mrs Brenan thin-lipped and displeased.

Neither of us spoke until we were out of the front door. Mike's car was in the street and we were walking towards it. I held back. He stopped and waited, making me catch up.

'Laura, I'm going into town. I'll drop you off.'

'You mean you want to talk to me, to know what she said.'

'That too.'

He opened the car door and I got in. It was far too cold an evening for grand gestures like walking to Underground stations or praying for taxis.

There are a lot of unkind things I have it in my heart to say about Mike Brenan, but I cannot criticize his taste and I cannot fault his choice of cars. Unlike mine, his murmured seductively and movement was barely perceptible.

Below us lay a swathe of London although everything was concealed except the bright glow of its night. Lights of office blocks clambered up the sky. I switched on the car radio and got a brief burst of Shakespeare's Sister singing *You're History* before Mike switched it off and said: 'All right. Tell me.'

'You first. How did she react when you explained I was asking after my father? I want it word for word, if you can.'

Mike didn't do that. He claimed she hadn't shown surprise and that she'd already heard that Gran was seriously ill, and then she'd said that if I wanted to hear anything from her I was to put in an appearance myself. He added his own comment that she never expected I'd turn up.

I didn't blame him for editing it down, but I was fairer. I repeated everything she'd said to me. He wasn't able to add anything to it, at any rate he didn't.

'Why don't we stop for a drink?' he said, slowing towards the pub car-park.

Saturday night, Christmas, and I was walking into a Highgate pub with my ex-husband. I opted for bitter lemon and wariness.

The pub was festooned with paper streamers and balloons. It was crowded with people bubbling with that peculiar will to be demonstrably happy that Christmas inspires. I found a place to sit and Mike went to the bar.

I jotted into a notebook the things Mrs Brenan had said and then I took from my shoulder bag the photograph. I held it in the palm of my hand and stared down at the soft dark hair, the wide-apart grey eyes, the light of a smile. Joe Flynn's face. Mine too.

The picture dissolved into a memory.

Eight years old and I'm tiptoeing across the rugs in my mother's bedroom. I can hear her voice in the hall below and I think I have time, just. On my knees by her dressing table I'm teasing open the drawers. Hand-knitted cardigans in the new double wool that's cosy and quick to knit because you go up a few sizes on the needles. Underwear, thrown in anyhow, the stockings rolled into balls but then lobbed in among the panties and the petticoats of greying nylon. A drawer for scarves and gloves, unmarried pairs of white crocheted or lace gloves that are a few years out of style but not to be discarded because mightn't they come hurrying back in any summer you care to think of? Handkerchiefs, lace-edged or ragged-hemmed, embroidered sometimes with a lopsided initial (my work) or done with exquisite drawn-thread work (Ada Carey's work), and the prettiest of them twisted round a pinch of lavender to make the drawer smell nice.

Beneath the handkerchief is an envelope, big and white and stiffened with a sheet of card dropped in. My fingers slip inside and touch the sharpish edges and satiny surfaces of photographs.

Her voice comes from the lowest flight. I haven't time to shake everything out on the floor as I want to. But why trouble? Don't I know what it is I'll be choosing?

Unsighted I feel within the deep envelope and sort out the photograph by the size. He comes up head first, born into the wintry afternoon, recreated in my life. Thick dark hair, a smile in the eyes, a good open face. Joseph Flynn. My father.

My mother's saying goodbye. In a moment I'll know whether she's coming up to her bedroom. Ah, the bathroom, so that's it. I shoot the photographs out over the rug.

They're all there. The old-fashioned wedding photograph, the pair of them looking fools right enough. I'm never going to get married. At a party they make the perfect couple. Danny joins them, a yawning bundle. Then the others. Often it's just the kids and their father. I expect she was shopping or cooking or cleaning while the fun and the photos were going on.

Then I hear her step on the landing below and I scrabble the photographs into the envelope and bury them under the hankies. Would you believe I'm standing by the window, as if nothing whatsoever had happened, two seconds before she walks into the room?

'Goodness, Laura, is it you there? What are you doing?'

'Nothing.' The way a child says it, meaning plenty but it's not for telling grown-ups.

'Why don't you away now and help your gran check the shopping?'

The shop sends the groceries in a cardboard box once a week, but you never know with the shop. Or maybe it's the delivery boy who's the cause of anxiety. The contents of the box have to be checked off against the list to be certain it's all there. It rarely is.

My mother's cajoling me: 'You know it was you who spotted the Bourbons were missing last week, Laura.'

I slouch out of the room. I'm happy to go. The view of a crumbly row of white houses across the square was boring. It's worse since we all came to live in Gran's house, at least there was traffic to watch when we had a place of our own. I wonder why we can't live in the country and ride horses and keep dogs that lead us merry chases along the clifftops and through the woods? That's how the children in the books I read spend their lives. London's so DULL!

Gran and I check the shopping and sure enough there's an item short.

'The divils!' cries Gran, throwing down her pencil.

I pluck it up before it rolls off the kitchen table.

Her shriek brings Ada Carey. 'Bless us and save us, Kitty, what's all the noise about?'

'A Viota cake mix, Ada. That's their trick this week. They've connived to deprive me of the pleasure of it.' Gran, indignant, always sounds comical to me. I begin to giggle. I'm known in the family as an awful giggler.

Ada says: 'Kitty I've told you there's no call to be sending out for such fandangles. I crossed off that cake mix myself.'

Gran rounds on her. 'Ada Carey, will you leave my shopping alone!'

Ada gets her teeth into the cake mix. 'Where's the necessity for a "convenience food" when you have the convenience of me to make your cakes for you and always have had?'

Gran draws herself up yet another inch. 'You wouldn't care to understand, Ada Carey.'

In a flash Ada does. She flounces out of the kitchen, convulsed with a rage she dare not speak for fear of finding herself homeless.

I purse my lips, in conscious imitation of my mother, and give Gran a look of the now-look-what-you've-done variety.

Gran says, still haughty: 'That Ada Carey has betrayed my trust, Laura.'

And then she subsides and chuckles, betrayal being altogether too large a word for the circumstances. She opens a packet of biscuits and she offers it to me. I take one and bite into it.

'Take another, for later,' says Gran.

But I have to say no thank you. If I put a Bourbon biscuit into my dress pocket for later then I'll be sure to get chocolate on the photograph, and it's too precious to risk that.

A man comes to stand in front of me, he's putting a bitter lemon on a table . . .

I jerked back from childhood memory to the present: a Highgate pub with Mike Brenan. He sat next to me, ready to remark on the photograph. He'd seen it once or twice in the past. I put it into my bag, with care. I didn't want to discuss it. It influences me, that glossy smile from more than twenty-five years ago. Because of it, I always think of Joe Flynn as happy.

I said to Mike: 'Are you still living in Blackheath?' He'd

bought a house down there after we'd split, crossing the river, getting well away.

He answered the unasked question. 'Sally isn't there any longer.'

'I'm sorry.' Automatic, I didn't know whether I was or not.

'She went to work in Italy.'

'Oh.'

'Quite a while ago.'

'I see.' I stepped up my wariness a degree. It was unlikely, possible but unlikely, that Mike was lonely, dejected and wanting sympathy. Sympathy can be dangerous in a woman.

But I was overdoing it. He changed the subject himself. 'That dress designer who was drowned, didn't you know her, Laura?'

They'd identified her then. 'I did some work for her.'

'Well I hope she paid you before she jumped in the Thames.'

'She paid,' I said. Or Keith Jay had done, handing me the cheque from the drawer.

The drinks went quickly. Sipping saved talking and we were finding it difficult to talk. Too much noise around us and too many things not to say.

In a few minutes he gestured at my empty glass. I shook my head and we got up to leave.

Downhill to Islington. Downhill in various ways. More poor people, more mean lives. But I didn't begrudge the Brenans their house on the hilltop by the woods. For myself I love the crowded Georgian and Victorian streets, the mix of nationalities that shoulder for cultural space and give the area its vivacity.

Again I switched on the car radio. Shakespeare's Sister had given way to the Eurythmics.

'Mike, how would it be if we dropped by the hospital?'

For answer he swung from one lane to another, annoying a taxi driver, and set off in the direction of the hospital. We were coming downhill fast, the chains of street lights rushing to meet us.

I hesitated at the entrance to the wrong ward. There was a flap on with several pairs of feet visible in the gap beneath a screen around one of the beds. A nurse appeared from another direction, recognized me and swept both me and Mike along to Gran's bedside. Neither of us had intended him to be there but his attempts to hold back were thwarted by the nurse who mistook his whispered reluctance.

Gran was asleep, her hands on the bedcover limp and stained with old age, the knuckles gleaming white beneath bluish flesh.

I sat and took one of her hands in mine. 'Gran?' I couldn't hear my voice myself, it was so faint. With my thumb I stroked the back of her hand. 'Where's the rest of the family,' I thought, abruptly angry that none had come. My mother had chosen to wait because she was coping alone with the Dublin shop until her cousin returned from the west. My scattered aunts and uncles had stayed scattered. No cosy gathering around the deathbed for Kitty Flynn.

'Oh Gran, what have you done to deserve this?' I thought. 'Couldn't just one of them have troubled?' And yet I had the answer in a recess of my mind all along. Gran was tough, they had trouble grasping that her heart might give out at the first sign of weakness. She'd complained of nothing, with the result that they found it hard to believe her. She was a resilient old woman, and she'd been hard on them. There was only one of them she'd actually asked for, and he was the one who'd left her years ago. Poor Gran.

A rush of emotion sent a tear sparkling on to the bedcover and I used my free hand to rub at my eyes. Mike rested a hand on my shoulder, consoling, and Gran opened her eyes a slit and looked at me. Then they closed and she lay without movement, without expression, enduring.

The nurse came back and checked the paraphernalia that was keeping Kitty Flynn in this world. She said Mrs Flynn was having a nice quiet night, and I accepted this as a hint that it would be best if I left.

The nurse was blurred through my tears. I dabbed my eyes again, and Mike and I left the bedside. Behind the screens in the other place there were no longer any visible feet. Two grim-faced nurses and a doctor were walking wordlessly away.

Back at the car the Eurythmics had stepped down in favour of jangly stuff from one of north London's Turkish pirate stations. We turned it off and talked about Gran and the urgency and the impossibility of finding my father.

I asked Mike to drop me at the office in Upper Street, not that I had anything specific to do there at that time on a Saturday night. He knew it too and made confidently towards the street where I live, demonstrating that it was pointless to hide my home address from him. He had the street right but had to ask: 'What number?'

'This will do fine,' I said and opened the car door and was half out before he could persist. Silly of me really because he could find the number simply enough if he wanted to, but it was my way of underlining that I wasn't willing to have him at my flat. After the break I'd fought hard for what I have now. He'd put me through a lot of anguish and I wasn't about to forget that.

I walked away down the street, and opened an iron gate above a basement entrance. Mike's car was moving off, but slowly. I ran down the area steps, far enough for my head to be below pavement level. When I heard the car change gear for the turning and then accelerate up Thornhill Road, I reappeared, shut the gate behind me and went home. I made some coffee and curled up on the sofa to think. Someone, then, had identified the body from the river as that of Kate Mullery. Mike had heard it on the radio news. I twiddled with the knob of my radio until I caught a news bulletin: The Irish fashion designer Kate Mullery had been taken dead from the Thames below Tower Bridge. That was about all it said.

Yawning I decided I'd leave Detective Sergeant Donnelly in peace on Sunday, delay until Monday before keeping my promise to myself and telling him the things I knew would interest the team investigating Kate's death. There was one question I wanted answered before then, though: I wanted to know who'd identified the body.

I have a friend who works as a casual sub on the news pages of a Sunday paper. I rang him.

'A man called Robin Digby,' he said. 'Described as a friend of hers. Why, Laura? What's it to you?'

I promised to explain sometime.

The last call I made that night was to the hospital. No change, but keep hoping.

Sunday and I was hanging around outside Father Mahon's church and waiting for an attractive thirty-seven-year-old man I knew would wish to dodge me. People trickled out after the service and I caught him.

'Peter, I need to talk to you.'

'Talking? Is that all you want?'

Once we'd wanted more of each other, but once was a long time ago.

'It won't take long.'

'I can't talk now, it isn't a good time.' He flicked a glance behind him, afraid of being seen with me.

'And when would a good time be?'

He wasn't going to be pinned. He shuffled. I pinned him. 'Kate Mullery's dead, Peter. We have to talk. Jack's bar, in half an hour?'

'No, Laura.'

'Yes.'

I walked away.

In half an hour I looked in at Jack's place but Peter wasn't there. A ten-minute wait and then I went to where they'd know his movements. His fault if he didn't like being followed around. I'd given him the chance to come to me. I pushed open the door, there he was at the bar.

Carol, the barmaid, nodded a greeting at me but Peter didn't see me as he was giving his order. '. . . and a gin the way Lacey takes it.'

'And another with tonic,' I tacked on the end.

'And another with . . .' He started to echo before discovering me. Then: 'Oh no, not you again.'

Deliberately ingenuous I asked: 'Is this a good time and place to talk, would you say?'

He was rattled. 'It is not! Look, Laura . . .' And then the fight went out of him. He sighed. 'OK. Four o'clock by the deer pens. Will that suit you?'

'That'll suit me fine.'

I didn't linger to see whether I got the gin and tonic. I went through the door marked Ladies and from that into the street.

Four o'clock and I was tramping across the rimed acres of Clissold Park to the deer pens. I could see Peter from some way off, and I could see his three expensively dressed small children too. Peter kept peering round but stopped once he'd seen me coming.

I covered the last hundred yards wondering what on earth we'd ever seen in each other and how I could have minded so much when he'd backed away. He was still quite attractive but now he was greying and careworn. Marriage and fatherhood had brought anxieties and the anxieties made him seem older than his true age. I decided Peter didn't laugh much any more.

He disentangled a twin girl from his leg and sent her to see the deer in the next pen. Then he strolled to where I was standing watching some hinds nibbling. I felt absurdly like a character in a spy story, keeping the clandestine rendezvous in a park lest the other side bug the conversation.

'You told Kate Mullery to hire me,' I began. 'She was your cousin, wasn't she?' That was what I'd heard, but on the grapevine, not from Kate.

'A distant one. I hardly knew her, and I had nothing whatsoever to do with her business.'

The little girl ran up to him. She had his look, when she was older she'd have the same determined jaw-line. Proprietorial, she put a tiny gloved hand on his arm. He brushed her off, suggesting a closer look at the animals. She attached herself to me instead. She swung on my hand while I pushed him for information.

'Did Kate say why she needed a detective's help?'

'Sure, she was being pestered with phone calls and her cat was killed.'

'Peter, do you have any idea who was making those calls or who shot the cat?'

'Me?' He rolled his eyes at the preposterous question.

'Kate was under pressure ever since she came over to London. Perhaps somebody didn't want her here.'

He drew the child away from me. 'There's no way I can help you with this.'

The child squirmed free and came to me, cold white face staring up at me from beneath a red woolly hat. I said: 'Peter, she's dead. There are going to be a great many questions asked.'

'They're questions for the police. Why don't you stick to looking for cats, Laura? It's more your style.' He dragged at the girl and she sulkily obeyed and left me. Peter was turning away, insisting he had nothing to tell me about Kate Mullery or anything else.

I blocked him, saying I hadn't finished.

'Laura, you and I finished a long time ago. Now I've got to take these three for their walk.'

I didn't block him a second time. He'd told me a lot in his rebuttals, although I doubted he realized it.

Peter's name was on the piece of paper with mine in the folder I'd taken away from Kate Mullery's desk. It appeared to be the note of a telephone conversation they'd had and it included my name and office address. The way it looked, she'd spoken to him about her threatening calls and dead cat and he'd suggested she hired me to look into it.

But when Kate had come to me first it was to ask me to investigate Bethesda, to make sure they were sound enough for her to entrust them with her high street range. Peter hadn't mentioned that, and as I watched him walking away over the frosty grass with the children eddying about him, I wished I'd asked outright. It wasn't stupidity that had held me back, it was conviction that the client's business is private. Even a dead client's? I thought so, although I'd never had a dead one before.

Why had I gone to Peter? Because in that morning's papers, searching through for reports of Kate's death, I'd come upon something else that concerned me. In the business sections there was a story about Shirlands the developers which, ultimately, owned Bethesda and a string of odd little companies. Shirlands were tipped to develop a Thames-side site. The copy was accompanied by photographs of a director of Shirlands, a man I recognized as Robin Digby's silver-haired companion from the hotel in St Albans. Silver Hair wasn't alone in the photograph in one of the papers. A group of Shirlands management people appeared, and one of those people was Peter.

Walking back from the park I thought I saw a woman I knew. I was wrong but the similarity triggered a memory. The woman I was thinking of would be in her seventies and I'd been misled by a likeness of her in her fifties. Maudie had been a familiar face in the streets where I'd grown up. The wife of a man who ran a corner pub, she was a timid woman not cut out for pub life and only venturing behind the bar early evenings before it grew rowdy. In those days if you wanted a packet of cigarettes in the evening you went to either the off licence in the main street or you called in at the pub.

I knew what had happened to Maudie. Her husband had retired and died and she'd gone to live with her daughter who was married to a man who owned a shoe shop. Pulling my scarf tighter against the wind, I turned in the direction of the shop.

Maudie saw me in her untidy sitting room in the flat above the shop. I doubted she got out much. Her legs were bad and the stairs were steep. She seemed smaller, partly the effects of childhood memory and partly that she'd caved in on herself. Habits hadn't changed though. She still chain-smoked, still had the same nervous gestures.

To begin with I pretended I was there to talk about Kate Mullery, and once the daughter had drifted away I twisted the conversation round to reminiscence about the old days when Maudie and I were neighbours.

'You're Joe Flynn's girl,' she said, and I thought she was wandering because we'd established who I was before we'd begun.

'You remember me, do you, Maudie?'

'I knew them all, all the Flynns. Kitty Flynn, I remember her. She and her husband took one of those big houses in Gibson Square. A bit of a queen I'd say. A number of us discovered we weren't good enough for Kitty Flynn. Mind you, those houses weren't the way they are now.'

I let her remind me how there'd been several flats squashed into each building and too many people squashed into each flat, how tin baths and communal toilets were the norm. How families could wait ten years on the council housing list to fulfil the dream of a nice modern purpose-built flat somewhere like the palaces estate, somewhere like Nonesuch House.

'He was clever, your grandfather,' she said, rubbing the side of her nose with a finger to indicate she meant he was crooked. 'Got that old house and suddenly all the tenants were top of the housing list and out of it. He made it a palace, fit for Kitty to queen it.'

Her hint didn't wound me, I'd heard it before and suppose it to be true. Tenants didn't have effective legal protection, it took Rachmanism in the sixties to change the law about tenure. I don't doubt my grandfather knew a builder on the council who was adept at pulling strings, but I refuse to think of him as dishonest. To me he's the white-haired cheery man who always had a joke with me and who, to Gran's disgust, would break out into Fenian songs when he'd downed a few Guinnesses.

I asked Maudie: 'Tell me about the evening Joe Flynn left. Didn't he call at your pub?' This had never been suggested, family lore being that he vanished as soon as he'd crossed our doorstep.

'A packet of twenty Players he had, and a half pint. It was unusual, the half, but he said he was going out again later. I never saw him again.'

'Who else was there when he looked in?'

Her cigarette had gone out and she played around with a lighter and filled her lungs before she went on. 'The MacGuire brothers for sure . . .'

'Gerry MacGuire?'

'And the brother they called Ginger, although why I never knew because all those MacGuires were red-haired, there was nothing to choose between them.'

'Was my father talking to them?'

'For five minutes, no more because he had to be home and then off out again. There was a man had been killed, an accident on a building site, and they were speaking about that. Oh sure, I remember like it was yesterday.'

'Did you tell people, when they came asking for Joe?'

'Me? Why would I be telling anyone anything? We had our custom to think of. "Not a word of it, Maudie," my husband, God rest his soul, said to me when word got out that Joe Flynn had run off. I kept out of the bar for a time and nobody thought to inquire whether Maudie had a thing or two worth telling. It suited them to make it up for themselves if it was details they wanted, no one ever came troubling Maudie about it.'

'Did he leave the pub alone?' I wondered.

'He did. The MacGuires stayed on – or perhaps only Gerry stayed, I can't say for certain. But there were two or three in the bar when I went out the back to listen to the radio and my husband took over. I didn't like the pub, that's the truth of it. I never worked into the evening although lunchtimes and the early evenings were all right. The noise and the fuss, you see. My nerves were no good for that life.'

And I had to learn a lot I didn't care to know about Maudie's nerves.

Then she moved on to the MacGuires. This was better, because it was Gerry MacGuire who'd tried to send me on a wild goose chase after Mrs Cotton, Gerry MacGuire who'd been quick to say that Joe Flynn had gone off with a woman but slow to come up with a name and couldn't say where they might have gone. If he'd ever believed it was Mrs Cotton, then he'd years since discovered that was untrue. Others knew about her fetching up in Eastbourne running a boarding-house, the MacGuires would surely have heard it too.

Maudie ground out her cigarette in a layer of black muck that concealed the pattern in her ashtray. 'Laughton, he was called, the young fellow who died. Joe was saying he was going up there.'

'Up where, Maudie? Where did you hear Joe say he was going?'

'Up there. That's all I heard him say, Laura. Up there. "Something has to be done about this. I'll be going up there." It was something like that he said.'

'Did the MacGuires say they were going with him?'

She laughed. No, she cackled. She said: 'Oh, you've a lot to learn about the MacGuires, Laura Flynn. They did *not* say they'd be going up there with him. "Leave it alone," they told him. "What's the use of causing trouble," they said. Oh, it was a wee bit of an argument for the few minutes he was in the bar with them.'

Maudie was already lighting her next smoke. 'I expect he went wherever it was. They never agreed, Joe Flynn and those MacGuires. Not on any mortal thing at all.'

She coughed while trying to inhale and laugh simulta-neously. 'Except for one thing,' she got out, 'that he was always asking questions.'

You ask too many questions, Flynn.

We were both accused, my father and I. I was paid for

asking, made a business of it, but he'd been goaded at the death of a young man on an unsafe building site. Whose site?

Maudie shook her head through a cloud of smoke. 'I couldn't say who owned it, but that doesn't matter. The MacGuires were doing work up there but they didn't employ this Laughton who fell. And the MacGuires had got the work when your grandfather thought it was to be his, so Joe was mad about it all anyway. It was like that then, too many men chasing the work, too many frictions and undercutting. That's one reason I hated being in the pub in the evening. A few drinks and the suspicions would surface, about who'd bribed his way on to a site and who'd undercut to get a contract, and who was skimping and bodging the job.'

'Or making the conditions dangerous.'

Through the smoke she added: 'Unhappy times, Laura. All right for the few who prospered but most of them didn't. This place wasn't paved with gold, not for everybody. Droves of them stuck it a while and went home not a penny the richer for it.'

Listening to Maudie was like having the backnumbers of the local paper brought to life. A washed-out sort of woman people ignored, she'd been no more to them than the yellowing paper on the walls of the pub bar. They hadn't troubled about what she heard and what she didn't because her husband's policy had been absolute discretion about his customers' conversation, impermeable loyalty to them. He hadn't wanted his pub burned down in the way the factions were burning each others' clubs, had he?

She was happy to reminisce, old Maudie, and I let her wander all over the subject so that by the time her daughter interrupted to offer a cup of tea, and Maudie said yes and I said no, we'd travelled a long way from Joe Flynn.

December. Darkness. A sting in the wind that said snow on the way. No time to be tramping alone through the streets of north London to a cold and empty flat. Instead I tramped to my cold and empty office. Detective Sergeant Ray Donnelly had tramped there first. I saw his lean figure prodding the street doorbell.

Cut and run? No, I had to face him sometime and I'd promised myself I'd come clean about Kate Mullery as soon as she'd been identified.

'Nice day for a walk, Laura,' said Donnelly looking me up and down: the blue face with the raw red nose, the roly-poly bundle of clothes, the uncomfortableness of it all.

'Hi, Ray. Your luck's in. I know of no good reason why I should be here on a Sunday afternoon, and neither do you. Coming inside?' I felt for my key.

'Unless you feel like coming to my place instead.'

I got the door open fast. Threats of taking me to the police station have that effect on me. I was once kept for hours in a police station because a twitchy inspector thought my inquiries were hampering the case he was working on.

'Bloody cold,' Donnelly said, getting as close as prudence dared to the electric fire.

'You should take more exercise, Ray. Keeps you fitter, warmer.'

'Oh yeah?' He was watching me unravel scarves and peel away gloves. 'Any chance of a hot drink?'

'I'll put the kettle on.'

I went straight to the washroom to do it, not wanting a repetition of a visitor helpfully filling the kettle and discovering the writing on the mirror. Once out there, I pretty well decided to clean it off, but I was dithering over it with a wad of paper in my hand when Donnelly came into the washroom anyway. Visitors sometimes need to seek out the loo.

He read aloud what was left: 'Any questions Flynn.'

And he asked me: 'What's this supposed to be, Laura? An advertisement for the agency?'

'Ha, ha.'

By then he'd taken in the red-smeared wad in my hand and he said: 'Go on, tell me the rest.'

'It wasn't much.'

'Let me guess. You were burgled and the burglar daubed the mirror. They frequently do.'

'I know that.'

'So all right, tell me what he wrote.'

'Originally it said "Too many questions Flynn". I've rubbed off the "Too m".'

The kettle boiled and I got out the mugs and the coffee from the filing cabinet while he was out of the room.

When he returned I said: 'You came here to talk about Kate Mullery, right?'

'No, to listen. But I'll tell you this much. She was dead when she hit the water.'

He sat on the fragile chair. It swayed and he redistributed his weight to steady it. He never took his eyes off me and I said everything there was to say, except that I'd seen the body brought ashore and that Robin Digby had given me a ride to St Albans in the boot of his car. Yet I couldn't fairly conceal my knowledge that Digby and Silver Hair had discussed Kate's death before her body was identified. I was working out a way to introduce that information when Donnelly said: 'The fiancé. Digby. Did you run across him?'

'Fiancé? Unlikely, this.

'He reckons he'd heard wedding bells. Kate, she isn't saying.'

I gave him a look that said I didn't like sick jokes about my clients. Then: 'Who else says she was his fiancée?'

'Who apart from Digby needed to know?'

'Yes. Well.'

'But you don't believe him?'

I screwed up my eyes, demonstrating solemn contemplation. 'It's your job, murder. Mine's stray cats and dead cats, or threatening voices on the telephone.'

'Or threatening writing on the mirror. Sure. Solved any good cases lately, Laura?'

He was getting to his feet, setting his mug on the corner of my stained desk. Finished with me. Poor little Laura Flynn, caught up in a murder case and not knowing who or what to believe. I said: 'What motive would Digby have for murdering her, if she was his fiancée? I mean, the murder of a fiancée is less probable than the murder of a non-fiancée, unless you uncover a huge life-insurance claim.'

He shook his head, despairing at my logic.

I said: 'I was only thinking . . .'

'Keep looking for the cats, Laura.' And he blew me a kiss and left.

Alone, I took out the file on my inquiry into Bethesda. By now I knew most of those pages of notes by heart but there were bits I'd skipped over before as they hadn't seemed relevant. Now I wanted one of those bits.

I found it on a page of information about which company owned what. You remember, when I was wading through a morass of detail about take-overs and mergers and name-changes. Here it was, then. Among the things Shirlands acquired when it acquired Bethesda was an address in Bermondsey.

Over the road my Big Ben warned me it was getting late. My conscience warned that I ought to have handed over the information about Bermondsey along with the rest. The other side of me objected that Donnelly wouldn't have wanted it, especially as it was vague and unconnected.

My *London A-Z* was no use. I'd have to go and see for myself. I traced a finger over the Underground map on my wall. It meant changing trains, getting out at London Bridge station and taking a lamplit walk down Tooley Street as far as Jamaica Road. Just the kind of treat to look forward to on a wretched December evening.

The riverside has changed. I think of the old and therefore the new always comes as a surprise. It's hard to get one's bearings, hard to keep on a track now that offices have sprung up across your route. I overshot and had to walk back and take stock.

Over there was the river, a new block cutting it off from me although the evening was quiet enough for me to hear water swaying on the shoreline after a boat passed. Next to the block were flats with a landing stage. Then there was a conglomeration of businesses around an atrium fronting the water, and after that came a dark emptiness partly surrounded by hoarding. Possibly the rest of it was boarded up too, but I couldn't see and neither could I see how to approach the site from inland. I prowled the road but didn't find an access.

I became aware of a car, parked along with others, without lights but with movement inside. I hurried away from it, then darted a backward glance and was in time to catch the door moving. People had been watching me, waiting for me to go so that they could get out and do whatever they'd come to do, covertly. I left them to it, and dived into the comforting warmth of a pub.

They've done wonderful things with old buildings along the river front. Putting a pub right there is one of them. I ordered a scotch and wrapped myself around a radiator. Outside, the river was viscous.

My fingers stroked St Lucy. I wondered whether she was any good with missing accesses or whether that was asking too much of her. In a few minutes I was going to have to go back into the cold, find what I needed and then return here and telephone for a taxi home. The parked car had deterred me from walking to the station. Oh, I could probably handle any man who attacks me, but he won't know that until he tries and I prefer not to chance it. New developments have improved the face of the district, but it retains some of its traditional roughness.

Out, then. Right and along the river front until I met the hoarding and squinted through a gap into a nothingness. Back, then. Left and eventually inland and along the road again, watching all the while and counting steps until I was sure I was parallel with the point where I'd been brought up short by the hoarding.

A small brick building fronted the road. Small, that is, by

comparison with the gigantic warehouses and modern blocks in the area. Actually, the brick building was about 35 feet long, with two rows of windows heavily meshed for protection. There was no name on it, but I guessed it was occupied. Locks on the door looked newish and the letterbox and doorway were clean. Butting up to the building at one end was a modernized warehouse, on the other end a row of buildings under construction.

The brick factory looked rather odd, squeezed in between one massive new development and another. Odd and significant.

I peered through the letterbox but could make out nothing. The windows were no use either. So I walked on and noted the name of the adjoining business before circling and getting down to the river. The low railing I met was designed to dissuade rather than prohibit. I climbed over and crossed a private river front to reach the empty plot.

The way ahead was blocked by a corrugated fence, too high to climb, too awkward to scale. I didn't go up, I went down. I located the iron rungs in the river wall and I let myself down to the patch of gravel and mud that passes for a beach when the tide's out.

My walk to the next set of rungs qualifies as one of the least pleasant I've ever had. Dark, stinking, footing unsure, and an underlying uncertainty about whether there was another set of rungs waiting for me. Worse, I felt the first flakes of snow on my skin.

The rungs up were slimy with algae and green-black weed. Progress was slow and treacherous. I slipped and banged my knee but my arms gripped firmly and I rescued myself, drew breath and climbed again. It wasn't brave and it wasn't far. It was foolhardy and much too long.

At the top I wriggled forward on my stomach, exhausted but safe. I hadn't mustered much confidence that it was going to work out that way. Above the level of slime, rungs had been rusted and insecure. One near the top was missing altogether.

Briefly I sat there and brushed at the mess on my clothes, but it was hopeless. I simply rubbed the stuff further into the fabric, and it was foul.

I was nicely positioned inside the boarded-off area that was awaiting redevelopment. There was a certain amount of rubble but no buildings, a certain amount of vegetation but the site hadn't been left derelict very long or that standby of London's unused corners, buddleia, would have taken hold. Someone had cleared the land and before long someone would build afresh. That someone was Shirlands.

With the river behind me I moved inland, aiming for a wall beyond which I assumed I'd find the small factory. My jacket was starred with snowflakes.

I didn't get over the wall because a rubble bank allowed me a good enough view. Another row of meshed windows and a rear door into a small yard. No access to the development site, and therefore probably no connection with it.

At last I had something to substantiate my suspicion. Shirlands had acquired a valuable plot of development land on the riverside but they had no direct inland access. They were cut off by a tatty old factory about 35 feet long. Roughly the width of a road. They could make no move until they'd bought up and flattened that factory. Then they'd be set to reap millions. Well they'd bought Bethesda, and Bethesda owned the address where the factory stood. And yet there was every evidence that the factory was still operating. If Shirlands had acquired Bethesda as a means of increasing the potential of its riverside plot, then something had misfired.

What was it Silver Hair, the Shirlands chief, had said to Digby in the hotel in St Albans? Digby had reported: 'They're holding out. The old man is, the young one's all for taking the money.' And Silver Hair had replied: 'There's a limit to the money, a limit to the time.'

My hunch was that they'd been talking about this. What was to happen when the limit was reached?

I found the answer to that too because right then I heard the sound of a wooden panel giving way to pressure, the creaking and tearing noises as part of the hoarding was forced back. I was no longer alone.

Automatically I dropped down, scuttled away from the rubble mound and went for the cover of tangled weeds. Remember those old films about jungle warfare? It was like that, only this time it was *my* face blinking apprehensively through the greenery and watching the enemy slink by.

The enemy? OK, so I dramatize. But the two men who ran up the plot and bunked over the wall into the rear yard of the little old factory didn't look like the sort I'd choose as friends.

Time to be going. They were out of sight, there was a nice big gap in the hoarding and I didn't face the iron rungs and the pong of the shore a second time.

A third man appeared in the nice big gap when I was within 100 feet of it.

I saw him in profile and dropped again, going crabwise for a darker patch. Too bad, he'd seen me too. I heard the intake of breath and he lumbered round and filled the gap. I guess he was 8 feet tall and maybe 9 wide. Well, anyhow he was bigger and tougher than me and there was no getting past him.

How long the others would give me I couldn't guess, but for now it was only Big Boy and me. A few minutes, seconds possibly, and then it would be three to one. Big Boy was the lookout and he wouldn't be tempted to leave his post because, unless he knew about those iron rungs, he'd believe I was trapped. But when the others came back they'd have plenty of time to spare for me.

The corrugated fence looked no better on the dangerous side than it had on the safe one. I ran along beside it, seeking a section where bolts created a rough ladder. My shoes were wrong, they wouldn't grip on the smooth surface. And my hands were never going to reach the top. For one thing, the snow was making my gloves wet and . . .

Damn!

I fell back, into nettles although I hardly knew it, too cold and too well wrapped up for easy movement and for pain. Landing, I curled round and caught Big Boy watching, hands on hips. I'd been wrong. He was easily 10 feet wide.

I brushed snowflakes off my eyelashes. It was coming down thick now. All right, then. The rusty rungs and the disgusting beach it would have to be. I ran to the edge of the wall, wishing I knew exactly where I'd tumbled ashore. Somewhere in the middle of the stretch? No good. To the left?

That's when the factory went up in flames.

They'd done a thorough job. They hadn't even cleared the wall before a whiff of smoke reached me and the old building was painted orange in flames.

I registered Big Boy beginning his move forward and I raced along the river wall, hectic, locating those rungs. I know they're there, somewhere. But where? Think! *Think!*

No time for thought. Big Boy was waving, the two arsonists were veering from their dash to the gate to hunt me down. I saw them all, silhouettes racing in the snow. The flames were that high, that good. The men saw me.

I zigged and zagged, praying Big Boy would be lured away from the gap and allow me a chance of freedom. I had seconds, that's all. The other two were closing, spread out and ensuring my opportunity of escape was negligible.

Inside the factory something inflammable exploded. A column of fire several feet high rose from one end. It might as well have been floodlight. Damn again.

When the three of them were near enough for us to speak, if we'd had anything to say, I realized the full danger. It was worse than the news that I might be hurt by three men who understood I was a witness to arson. Arson's a serious business, it rates penalties as severe as murder does. Suddenly I'd grasped that they had nothing to lose if they killed me.

When you are faced with oblivion you find extraordinary reserves. I went for the one with the slightest build, the one who was nearest to the gap. I went for him with my head cracking his jaw and my knee going for his groin. Why not?

Hadn't I practised only days before on a thief on the Underground?

I winded him, I grounded him. I regained my balance and I would have been through that gap if, frailty of frailties, I hadn't tripped.

I know what you do when you trip.

I rolled.

I dodged lashing boots and I rolled. A boot caught me on the leg and I lurched forward, half on hands and knees and half flat-face. I won my freedom from the boots. Doubled over, almost falling again, I ran beyond their reach. Three cheers for the ladies' gym. I outpaced them.

Unfortunately, I was nowhere near the gap. They forced me back up the plot. I thought of nothing but getting away from them but in truth I wasn't getting away at all. I was the hare and they were the dogs flying after me. You know what happens, either the hare gets lucky and gets free or one of the dogs stops it happening. You know too what doesn't happen. Animals don't run into fire.

I ran into fire.

I cleared the bank of rubble at a step, my toe touched the wall and I jumped down into the rear yard.

I remember looking back, looking up and seeing one, then two faces peering over the wall at me. At the time all I felt was relief that they'd stayed there, given up the chase. Then the faces moved away and I let the adrenalin subside a fraction and I took in the reality of what I'd achieved.

The realization was accompanied by another explosion in the building. This one sent three of the rear windows high into the air, steel mesh guards and all. Burning fragments mingled with the starlight snowflakes covering me. I beat them out with gloved hands. And I drew into my lungs something deeply noxious.

Many people who die in fires are long dead from fumes before ever the flames come within singeing distance. I decided not to wait for the fire brigade. There was only one way out and that was the way I'd come in. People give you a better chance than noxious fumes. Back over the wall then.

This wasn't very easy. The wall wasn't as impossible as corrugated iron but it was fairly high and I needed something to stand on. The box that would have been ideal otherwise was well alight. I dragged one of the mangled mesh grills across and leaned it rakishly against the wall. The metal burned into the palm of my glove. Then I ran at it, hitting the grill and bounding up to get a handhold on the top of the wall.

I was up and astride the wall before I knew the men were hanging around the plot and wondering. Firelight allowed none of us to hide. I waited on the wall of death while we all tossed up what to do. Behind me another window blew out.

Perhaps they'd decided their best option was to chase me back into the flames because Big Boy and one of the others thundered towards me. I didn't move, I braced myself and when the first one arrived and a hand went for my foot, my foot went for his face. After that he left my foot alone. Did he expect Big Boy to have a better idea than tipping me backwards into the flames? Like pulling me forwards off the wall and making mincemeat of me? Quite probably.

I didn't find out because I was saved by a keening fire engine. Big Boy slewed to a halt, slithered round and went back the way he'd come. The one who'd have a black eye in the morning went after him. Me, I sat on the wall and laughed. Relief, not amusement. Not truly a good time to be laughing. But I sat there and listened to a second fire engine chiming in, then a third. Then I couldn't count because the sounds merged but it seemed half the London fire brigade was on its way. Factories with inflammables qualify for that sort of attention.

Big Boy and Co. had made an effort to close the gap in the wooden boarding but with additional effort on my part I got it open again and wriggled through. The end of an all too exciting episode.

I was thinking phew and inarticulate rubbish like that, when a figure stepped from a shadow, an arm went across my mouth and I was lifted clean off the ground and carried away into the night. He was tall, dark and ugly. He was around 9 feet high and 11 wide and I knew him as Big Boy.

Fay Wray may have formed an attachment for King Kong, but I reckoned I wasn't going to live long enough to do likewise with Big Boy. I'd never had reason to believe in gentle giants and I saw no reason to begin.

I recognized the car, the men in it too. The one I'd floored grabbed my hair as Big Boy thrust me in, like a housewife presenting her Christmas turkey to her oven. The one awaiting the black eye smashed a cushion over my face. One of them slammed the door. One of them started the engine. I don't know who did what, I was engaged fighting feathers and suffocation.

Maybe it was only fifteen minutes before the car stopped. All I could be sure of was that we passed fire engines and commotion, and after a while there was a change of feel about the ride which made me suspect we were going over one of the bridges. Not Tower Bridge, if we'd crossed that we'd have done it sooner. We travelled a good way and then I heard Big Ben. Not my own personal version in Upper Street, but everybody's Big Ben. Close.

My mental map of London unrolled in my head. Over the river from the Bermondsey side, then left – which it must have been to get Big Ben so near – and down the Embankment. Therefore we were now either branching inland up Victoria Street or else we were going along Millbank towards Pimlico. Whichever it was we were on long empty roads, main ones. There was no jiggling round corners.

How did the ride compare with being in the boot of Robin Digby's car two days earlier? Yes, I considered that. I'd say this was worse. On this occasion I was in the company of three criminals who knew I was there and, I imagined, had planned to dispose of me. As they'd been content to let me be found as charred remains in the rear yard of a factory, then they wouldn't have qualms about my remains being found else-where.

The cushion shifted as the car jolted. I gasped air, stuffy tobacco-laden air. The man beside me was smoking. Nobody was speaking. I'd hoped for a snatch of tell-tale conversation, a revelation about my future and the extent of it. I got nil.

When we stopped we did so in an unlit alley flanked by shuttered factories. I didn't protest as they dragged me out of the car and through a metal door into one of the lock-ups. They communicated with grunts and gestures, near telepathy. No clues.

Big Boy lashed me to a chair. Black Eye made a phone call. 'Yeah,' he said, 'the job's done. Witness, though. Yeah. Got her here. That's right: *her*. Yeah. OK.'

There was a longer pause while he was asked a longer question. He replied with a description of me. Then he said: 'It's definitely her this time.' Then: 'Yeah.' Then 'OK.'

That sort of phone call. Not encouraging.

There was a gag but it didn't rate much. When they left I squirmed until it slid over my chin. If anybody ever wanted help I did but it was no good shouting for it. An alley of lock-ups late on a Sunday evening in December is not a place where Galahads go wand'ring by on the lookout for damsels to rescue and good deeds to perform.

Apart from which I don't see myself as the kind of damsel that needs rescuing. I can take care of myself. Yes, I was too proud to start bawling for help on the offchance of being heard.

You can waste an abundance of energy attempting the impossible. I saved energy and quietly worked out the options. I was in a small empty workshop with well-oiled machinery at the far end and an office partitioned off to one side. One of the men had brought the chair from the office and another had used the phone. The conversation suggested they'd make no decision about my future themselves but were awaiting orders from the man Black Eye had called.

They'd done their training by reading the wrong thrillers

because the gag had been amateurish and they'd allowed me a fair degree of movement with the chair. This was an ordinary upright kitchen chair. My ankles were each tied to a front leg and the cord from my hands, which were behind me, was anchored to the strut that braced the back legs. I could walk, after a fashion. An ungainly kind of walking if you like, but it got me up the room as far as the door to the office.

The phone? Wonderful, if it had been the push-button type but it was an old model and I know no way of dialling with my nose. There was another drawback to using the phone. Who was I to ring and where was I to say I was?

I eyed the machinery speculatively. The string on my wrists was thin and strong, it would resist any but the sharpest implement. I saw nothing approaching a blade on the machinery.

The desk then. I staggered into the office but got it wrong and had to back out and reverse in. The office was minute and the desk bare except for the telephone, but there were two drawers. Backing up, setting the chair down sideways to the desk, I set about opening the drawers.

I couldn't. My teeth would have preferred a wooden knob but were offered a mere indent in the drawer front.

After several minutes I shuffled out again, came in sideways and performed contortions until I gripped the indent with two of my fingers. The drawer slid and, squinting round at the contents, I spotted my rescue kit. Scissors and a razor blade.

They were out of reach. Once more I went out, came in frontwards, dipped my head into the drawer and with my teeth took up the scissors.

I lay them on the desk top. I was thinking that if I were careful I could lick up the razor blade without slicing my tongue, when the phone rang. I flicked my head and knocked the receiver off and pressed my ear to it. A loud male voice said: 'Ron? Is that you?'

I grunted what I hoped was a deep enough grunt to pass for a preoccupied Ron. The voice said: 'Look, I've had an idea. About the girl . . .'

I tried another grunt, a querying one. Apparently Ron didn't carry on in this Neanderthal way. The voice on the line changed. 'Who *is* that?'

And when I didn't make a sound, it swore violently and hung up.

For a few seconds I stayed exactly as I was, head resting on the desk by the phone, body exhausted by the fight to manoeuvre with the chair snail-like above me. My muscles screamed for release. I didn't listen to them. I was hearing that voice on the phone, his words over and over.

It was a revealing call. It told me one of my captors was called Ron, and that Ron was probably Black Eye who'd made the call from the factory. I'd heard the voice on the phone before, enough times to be sure. The caller was Robin Digby.

Robin Digby, who'd had a hand in Kate Mullery's death, had now had an idea about me. I was convinced I'd hate it.

I scrabbled at the scissors, tried to open them because *I'd* had an idea too. I hoped to jam them in the desk drawer and rub the string on my wrists against their cutting edge. Useless. The scissors fell through into the drawer and I was back where I'd been minutes before the phone rang.

Not exactly. My position was considerably worse because Robin Digby could be on his way to the lock-up. Where he went, that dog of his went too.

I had a sounder idea. I blundered out of the office, making for the machinery. Overbalancing in my hurry, I stopped myself falling by butting into a wall. But I shut my mind to the pain and the nausea and I swung the back of the chair at the machinery, hard. Once. Twice. Five times before I was re-warded by the staves cracking, loosening and ultimately the back of the chair disintegrating.

My arms, tied, swung free of what was left of the chair, and when I'd forced out the cross-piece there was enough slackness in the cord for them to become useful to me. I staggered back for the scissors, sliced string between my wrists and the knots on the fetters around my ankles.

The door to the lock-up was fastened with a padlock on the outside. I could go nowhere.

I rifled the desk drawers, found a few sheets of headed writing paper with a company name and an address in the Pimlico area. Robin Digby could be on his way. I rang the police.

'A joker locked me in for a prank,' I said. Nothing serious. Nothing they'd feel obliged to look into. I wanted to get home, I didn't want a trip to a police station.

In a few minutes I heard a car grind over the rubbly street to the door. Robin Digby came in.

He closed the door behind him and leaned against it. His leather jacket was wide on the shoulders. It made him seem hard but I'd seen worse. I'd spent my evening in the company of Big Boy. Digby, though, didn't have the blank expression of Big Boy. There was intelligence in Digby's eyes. Big Boy responded to situations but Digby created them.

He hadn't brought his dog. I was still being grateful for that when I discovered a possible reason. Digby took a gun from his pocket.

I goggled in disbelief. No one had ever pointed a gun at me.

Digby did. He ordered me into the office. I didn't move. I was halfway up the room, where I'd been when the door had swung and he'd come in instead of the law.

'Move,' he shouted. The gun jerked in the direction he wanted me to go.

My incredulity was at a peak. I couldn't move. I was asking myself how I could have so misjudged him as to classify him as a man whose sin was to indulge in selfishness and too many large whiskies. I tried to say something.

He shouted me down, like he'd done before at Knights End when he'd caught me halfway through his kitchen window and again when he'd met me in the lane collecting the motor cycle he'd rendered immobile. He was a bulky, florid man with a big angry voice. The gun, by contrast, seemed pathetic.

It's a mistake to underestimate the average handgun. It isn't the firepower that counts, it's the power it conveys in the imagination of the person holding it. Digby believed himself invincible. You can't argue with invincibility. He insisted on the office and I began to believe in it too. I took the first tentative step towards it.

Digby came closer. I hesitated. He shouted at me to hurry up. I turned round, mouth open with a question. He wagged the gun again. I wondered about the odds on getting it off him. I went another step towards the office.

The doorway appeared the most reliable opportunity. If I could wheel and kick the gun away at the confusing moment of us passing through the narrow space . . .

Once more I turned to him, trying out a question that he bit off and spat away. There wasn't much distance to cover. Another two steps and I'd be in the doorway.

But why the office? If he was going to shoot me what did it matter if he made a noise and spilt blood in the workshop? I couldn't appreciate the difference.

In the doorway I side-stepped suddenly, whirled round, got a leg high and my foot in contact with his wrist. The gun arced out of his hand, behind him. Out of his reach and well out of mine. I was set to chase after it, beat him to it, but he didn't move the way I anticipated. Robin Digby came for me instead.

I didn't understand. He was playing according to rules I'd never heard of. If there's a weapon you go for possession of it, you don't discard it.

The office was the worst imaginable place for hand-to-hand fighting, and he wanted to force me in there. *Of course.* If he wasn't committed to shooting me down then he wanted me in a space where I couldn't manoeuvre and my guile could be crushed by his sheer weight.

With a surge of energy I defeated his attempts to corner me in the office. I lashed at him and I ducked and raced for the gun.

There it was, within my grasp. I dived on it, my hand clamped around steel and I straightened to see Digby coming full steam. Hopping aside I let him career past.

'All right,' I yelled. 'That's enough. Now stay right where you are.'

He took no notice. He'd fetched up against a wall and once he'd snatched a breath he came at me again. I levelled the gun at him. 'Stop right there.'

He didn't. I swung the gun to the right, pointed it at the centre of an empty wall and tested a theory.

Click.

Nothing. No bullets.

I jumped out of his way but he jumped too and skidded on a patch of machine oil. Down he went, legs scooting from under him and a foot catching hard against one of mine so that I fell on top of him.

For a big man he was quick. If I hadn't cracked the side of my head on one of the machines, I wouldn't have proved such easy prey. But while I was woozy he was throwing me around, pressing me to the floor with his body in a grotesquerie of love-making. My wits reassembled in time to notice the pad in his hand.

And as I arched my head back in a feeble bid to dodge the chloroform, I saw the light alter down at the end of the workshop as the street door opened. Sir Galahad, 6 foot something in navy-blue serge, stood there.

The police constable called: 'Anybody supposed to be locked in here?'

Digby was away from me. I sat up. 'I was, but I got unlocked.'

Digby was endeavouring not to look like a man who's been discovered on the floor of a workshop with a young woman. The policeman was deeply puzzled about what was going on. He had a go at me first about hoax calls.

I lost control then. 'If you'd come when I called for you it would have been true. And if you'd left it two seconds later I'd have been dead. You arrive at the scene of an attempted murder and all you can do is criticize me because someone who knew I was locked in here came to kill me.'

At last he took it in, especially when I told him that Digby was a man who'd already been questioned about the Kate Mullery murder.

From the squad car the constable's colleague radioed a message and then another vehicle came and took Digby away. Sir Galahad himself drove me to a police station.

Later, after I'd spilled out everything I knew about Mullery–Digby–Shirlands and arson on the bank of the Thames, I was allowed a taxi home. The snow had settled, muffling the streets.

Emotionally and physically drained, stinking from river sludge and sweat, and every inch of my flesh battered, I was desperate for a hot shower and bed. Instead I got a message from the couple in the flat downstairs: an old woman who lived at my grandmother's house had been round to say we were wanted at the hospital.

Ada Carey. Poor old Ada Carey who'd rung and concluded my phone was out of order, and had trudged up from the square to say the hospital thought Gran wouldn't survive the night. I called the hospital. Ada Carey was there, the nurse said, and yes, please, would I like to come? I booked another taxi, showered while it raced round, and I set off for the hospital.

Gran didn't know me. She slept, disappearing by degrees each time I looked in on her. The lines that gave her face character were being smoothed away, but it wasn't the smoothness of a young woman's skin that I saw, it was the pale imitation of death. Feather-light against her pillow, her head made barely an impression on its surface.

Ada Carey and I took turns at the bedside and occasionally held whispered conferences in corridors. Should we contact the rest of the family again? Ada had done so. Should we send for Father Mahon? He'd been in earlier. What could we do, then? Nothing.

Ada choked over a cigarette. Gran had banned her from

smoking in the house years back but Ada's response to this crisis was to scrounge a couple from a nurse. I didn't need any detective skills to know Ada was threatened with more than the loss of a lifelong sparring partner, she was also threatened with the loss of her home. When Gran went the family would swoop and the house would change hands. Everything in Ada Carey's life would change as a result of Gran's death.

'Laura,' said Ada, between chokes. 'You know that nice Irish nurse who was here earlier?'

'She's another Flynn. What about her?'

'She says Kitty was asking.'

My father again. 'What am I supposed to do?'

I hadn't intended to sound irritated. It was frustration at being so ineffective, and I had a headache from my conflict with the side of a machine during the brawl with Digby and another from the hour of questioning (that promised to be the first of several) I'd endured at the police station. I patted Ada's arm, an apology for sounding cross.

She screwed up her mouth in distaste and stubbed out her cigarette on the sole of her shoe because there wasn't anywhere else to do it. As there wasn't anywhere to throw it away, either, she absent-mindedly handed the hot stub to me.

She said: 'I've been thinking hard about this, Laura, ever since you asked me what I knew of the night he went.'

I forgot about the discomfort of the gritty trash in my hand. 'What have you thought, Ada?'

'That there's a woman you could speak to who'd have more answers for you than I could hope to have.'

My pulse quickened. 'Who, Ada?'

'Well, now, I didn't say you'd like to go near her, Laura, but you see her family was closer to things than ever I was myself.'

'Who?'

'And I can't vouch that she'd know, only that, with things the way they used to be, she wouldn't have been passing anything on to the Flynns if it had been in her power to do so.'

'*Please*, Ada. Her name.'

Ada avoided my eye as she muttered. 'Her name was Deirdre MacGuire.'

I knew only one family of MacGuires in the area and I'd started with old Gerry in the pub. He had no daughters and his wife, who'd grown eccentric and was more often in hospital than out of it, was called Bridie. The MacGuires were a big family but I still couldn't pin down a Deirdre.

Ada slanted her face to look up at me. 'You wouldn't know her by that name Laura. She got married and changed it. You know her as Della Brenan.'

Now this was like a scene from one of those frightful old detective stories where someone rips off a wig and false moustache and reveals himself to be another character entirely. Anthony Shaffer sent it up beautifully in *Sleuth*. Della Brenan proving to be none other than Deirdre MacGuire was definitely in that league.

Ada filled in some explanatory details for me. 'A second cousin she is to Gerry MacGuire but one of his brothers took her into his family for a time when her own parents had some trouble, sickness and so on. She got well away from the MacGuires, transformed herself into Della and a mighty snob she's been ever after. There's none of us worth the corner of her eye. Wouldn't you say so yourself now, Laura?'

What I said was spluttering nonsense. Then I made a grab for some facts. 'Which of the MacGuire brothers did she live with?'

'The one they called Ginger. He died far back, fell off some scaffolding when they were building those flats with fancy names off Holloway Road. You know the ones I mean. Palaces, they're called.'

'Nonesuch House. Windsor. Hampton. Hatfield. Those, you mean?'

'The very ones. The scaffolding went up and Ginger came down. Oh that kind of thing was always going on. Somebody ought to have tightened a bolt and didn't trouble, or there weren't enough bits and bolts on site in the first place so it wasn't as safe as the regulations said it should have been.'

She raised a hand to quash my next questions. 'Don't be pestering me for details. I really don't remember. I'm only telling you that what happened to Ginger MacGuire was nothing entirely rare, more's the pity.'

I questioned her all the same. 'Do you know of a man called Laughton being killed?'

'Laughton is it?'

'Yes, Laughton. My father is said to have been angry about the way the man died.'

She shook her head, wisps of grey hair floating like cloud.

I said: 'This Laughton was someone he knew.'

Another shake.

I said: 'Well, can you say what sort of work the MacGuires were doing back then?'

'They do all sorts,' said Ada. 'Now the sons have the business they run up extensions and build patios, anything people want.'

Anything small, I noted. I said: 'But in the past, Ada, at the time we're talking about. What were they likely to have been doing if they were employed on a big site?'

'They turned their hand to anything, always did. Jacks of all trades, if you like. Cheap, you see. They could always get the work. Not that they necessarily did it well, but the bigger people who were awarded the contracts would let the MacGuires on to the site and save a few pounds that way.'

We'd talked too long. Gran was dying alone in the ward a few yards away. Ada stayed in the corridor and I sat beside Gran. No movement. No sign of life except the tiny feathering breaths.

When I came out again Ada Carey's stooped figure was choking over the second of her cadged cigarettes, hastening her own end.

FOUR

Circles. Round and round. Like the pink elephants on the mug in Knights End farmhouse. Often my life's like that, recycling ideas, repeating actions. It gives me no sense of achievement and doesn't make for progress.

Monday found me walking through slushy melting snow to the *Islington Gazette*'s library in Fieldway Crescent, settling down with the backnumbers as I'd done the previous week. This time I wasn't looking up Flynn, as in Joseph Flynn. This time I was after Ginger MacGuire and Mr Laughton.

In death Laughton had been reduced to a couple of paragraphs, his inquest a distillation of facts. He was a self-employed bricklayer who had an address in a lodging house in Liverpool Road and a proper home somewhere unspecific in Ireland, and he'd been climbing up to his work one December morning when he'd fallen off the scaffolding. Verdict: Accidental death. End of inquiry.

No hint of unsafe practices or dodgy scaffolding or any contributing factor. If I wanted details then I'd have to look elsewhere. The *Gazette* that week had made greater play of the inquest on a cyclist who'd been crushed by a bus, but then he'd been a *real* local.

Ginger MacGuire, six months later, had been treated to six paragraphs for an accident which, from the bones of it, sounded similar to the one that had put an end to Mr Laughton. There was a salient difference though. Ginger had been dismantling the scaffolding because on that occasion the MacGuires had been scaffolders for the project. The project? It was one of the walk-ups on the palaces estate. Verdict: Accidental death.

Then I looked up the MacGuires in general. Deirdre, or

Della, or Mrs Brenan, wasn't there, naturally, and a good thing too because most of the mentions were snippets of court cases. Petty things like dumping rubbish where they shouldn't have, not coughing up vehicle tax on the dot, going down Essex Road with an insecure load and up Holloway Road without vehicle-licence plates. There'd been a flurry of court appearances over speed limits, parking without lights, and failing to pay off fines. Also there'd been one small matter of being drunk and disorderly and another case resulting from fighting in the street. None of it was seriously criminal but it was consistent. They were people who bucked whatever rules applied and now and again they'd been caught.

I was quite content sitting there with the files. The police had asked me to go to Rochester Row police station to talk to them again about the events of Sunday evening: the fire and the confrontation with Robin Digby in the lock-up. I didn't want to. I'd told them everything I had to say. Let them chase around to my office if they liked, I was keeping my head down.

This kind of thinking led to me catching a bus from near the library in Highbury to Islington Green, so that I could indulge in an hour at the Dôme café-bar reading newspapers and listening to their Mozart tapes and, quite possibly, meeting like-minded friends who also couldn't get to grips with the start of another working week.

I was just raising a chocolate-sprayed *cappuccino* to my lips when a slim pale young man walked in. Keith Jay, Kate Mullery's assistant who ought to have been holding the fort down in Canonbury. He'd have learned the previous day that she was dead. If he was lucky he'd have had a sympathetic call from someone who knew him. If not, he'd have heard it on the radio news.

He'd heard it on the news.

I ordered him a coffee and he unbuttoned a thick black overcoat and set his hat on the spare chair beside us. 'I've told the others I've had to go out and see somebody about buttons,' he said, his voice wavering. 'I just had to get out. They're all standing around talking about her . . .' The remark ended with a sigh. He pulled the sugar bowl towards him.

I pictured the Canonbury workshop. Long faces and bewilderment, gossip but not enough information to make *good* gossip, fear about what happened to their jobs now the boss was dead. A fashion house isn't like a conventional business where someone can always move up and replace the boss. If the designer went, what was the business worth?

Distracted, he poured too much sugar into his coffee. His freckles were standing out darkly. I suspected he'd been crying, but the wind whipping the street could make anybody look like that if they'd prowled all the way from Canonbury to Islington Green.

'Bethesda were on the phone first thing,' he said. 'Wanted to know what the hell was supposed to happen about their contract for the high street range. Honestly, Laura, some people. There's Kate, in a morgue, and all they can think of is next year's profits.'

He was looking fragile, too much emotion too near the surface. I took advantage of him. 'Tell me the rest,' I said.

He hid his face in his cup before murmuring: 'What rest?'

'You know, about the dress I was wearing and how the Turkish dress manufacturer got hold of that design.'

Distrait, he'd forgotten he'd asked me to investigate that. I was depending on him forgetting. He said: 'Oh I don't know. I mean, it doesn't matter now, does it?'

No, I thought, but it would be nice to know. 'Yes,' I said. 'We could clear it up right now instead of it being dragged out in the police inquiry along with everything else to do with Kate.'

He plonked the cup down and bent his head. Another sigh. Then: 'How did you know it was me?'

'There wasn't anybody else, you'd virtually confirmed that. She showed the designs to no one but you. Also there was no evidence of the desk being broken into and you were the only person with keys.'

He said: 'It was true about the burglar getting in and the folder being stolen.'

I looked disbelieving.

He shrugged. He'd told so many lies he assumed he didn't have a hope of convincing me.

I waited for him to say something about the dress. When he didn't I said: 'Why, Keith? Why ever did you do it?'

He shrugged, weighed up what to tell me. 'It's Bethesda, Laura. I know you'll understand this. I didn't want her doing business with them. They're not right for her. She felt it too. You know she did, she hired you to look into them.'

'Only their financial security to begin with.'

'Yes, but later she was still unsure. I couldn't persuade her to follow her instinct and turn them and their money away. She said it was a good deal, her advisers were all for it. I said: "Kate, you're a designer, love, not a business tycoon. It isn't the bottom line that counts, it's whether you feel happy." '

I murmured agreement.

He said: 'Kate wasn't a happy person, you know. There was always one thing or another to agonize over. This situation with Bethesda was classic Kate. She couldn't make up her mind what to do. I thought up a way of dissuading her from going ahead with them. I mean, there are dozens of other companies out there who'd do a better job for her. She was being – *perverse.*'

He'd finished. He bent over his coffee again and awaited my reaction. Simple, loyal Keith Jay, who'd always spoken of Kate Mullery in superlatives of admiration, had done to her the worst thing in his power.

I asked him: 'What would she have said if she'd found out?'

'She never would have. Mind you, it was a fluke you walking into a party wearing the dress before it reached the shop rails. All that flowery floaty stuff before Christmas, it's quite wrong.'

'Oh?' I'd thought it delightful and it had certainly made an impact.

'Yes,' he said, lapsing into professional concern. 'This

140

season's feel is for tailored jewel colours. Flowers are being held over until spring.'

'As usual.'

'What? Oh, yes. Ha, ha.'

'Well, I'm sorry if I've pre-empted the fashion industry's salute to spring but how was I to know?'

He looked hard to see whether I was joking but never decided. He said: 'You, er, you won't . . .'

'Tell anyone? No, I don't see the need to tell anyone. Especially if we forget about the nocturnal burglar alarm too.'

His face was wonderful. Gratitude coupled with half-formed suspicion.

I said: 'And we could ignore night-time prowling, popping folders in and out of desks.'

'Laura?'

I said: 'The dress is what interests me. How was it done? And don't say you walked into the place in Islington Park Street and handed over a drawing because I mightn't fall for that.'

Keith said it hadn't been as straightforward, it had been done through a friend of a friend and he'd had no information about which company's hands it had finally fallen into. What he'd hoped was that a manufacturer would run up a model to show buyers. He'd have been able to alert Kate Mullery to the fact that one of her designs had been leaked and she'd have blamed Bethesda's laxity, and that would have been the end of her involvement with them.

'I was really shocked you'd seen a rail full of the stuff ready to go out to the shops,' he said.

'That's the risk you ran.' And I left him to work out that if Bethesda had denied that they'd ever been shown that design then Kate Mullery might indeed have realized who was the traitor. He'd be very stupid if that didn't occur to him, and I didn't believe he was stupid at all.

I said: 'You weren't the funny phone calls and the dead cat, were you?'

Indignation. 'No!'

I cocked my head on one side, smiled sympathetically and said I'd never thought he was. Then I switched the subject to Robin Digby. Another of my Monday tasks was to flesh out what I knew about him and as Keith was with me he might as well hear the questions first. 'What exactly was Robin Digby to Kate Mullery?'

Keith said he was amazed to read in the newspapers that Digby was her fiancé. 'Kate never said that. He was a friend, that's all. He helped her with her business and he knew her family in Dublin.'

Robin Digby was being held for questioning about Kate's murder. I guessed they'd hold him for as long as they could legally do so because certain questions were going unanswered. His story about Kate leaving the farm at Arkley while he was out was unswerving, but the police wanted to know who'd called to collect Kate. I'd given them the version Digby had given me but it hadn't tallied with the one he'd given them himself, and he was being asked to explain away the discrepancies. The police officer who'd phoned to ask me to return to Rochester Row had divulged that much.

Discrepancies are not invariably sinister. Digby had explained to me after he'd caught me getting through his window, while we were both heated. His statement to the police came when he was a very worried man. He'd identified Kate's body, he'd had to excuse the delay between her leaving Arkley and his reporting her missing. All in all, he was having the bad time he deserved.

I knew one way of finding information about Robin Digby. Perhaps I should have shut off my inquisitiveness and let matters take their legal course, but Digby and I were tied in a way that intrigued me. All I'd ever done was respond to the instructions Kate had given me. And this had repeatedly led to vehement attacks by that man.

That it had culminated in attempted murder, the police chose to ignore. At any rate, that's the impression they'd given me when Sir Galahad had taken me to meet the senior knights.

Doubtless Digby, in another part of the forest, had produced reasonable excuses for being in possession of both a gun and a chloroform-soaked pad and for being discovered about to clamp the pad over my face. Offhand I couldn't fathom what those reasonable excuses might be.

My critics don't generally try to kill me, deep down they aren't that bothered by me. Digby was.

At our first meeting I'd guessed at his nature and I'd been misled. I'd taken his clothing and his physique and I'd turned him into a stereotype. All the bits that didn't fit the picture, I ignored. And so I'd got it dangerously wrong.

To Anna Lees's next, for lunch, parting on a street corner from Keith Jay who sloshed back through the slush to what was left of his job. He'd made one or two pathetic attempts to clarify whether I was his burglar but I was better at changing the subject than he was. When we separated, though, I said I'd see he got the folder back. He had to be satisfied with that.

Anna was heating soup and stodgy brown bread when I arrived. She was pushing on with her book, sluggishly, but at least working on it again after her slump at the weekend. I didn't press her for details about the story. She's usually shy about discussing stories, saying they sound silly until they're finished because it isn't easy to see where the bits fit in. I tell her my cases are like that too.

Sue was at an art exhibition, Jennie was doing a task up at the college, the other women had scattered either to jobs or women's rights groups. It was only Anna and me, the way I preferred it.

Anna said: 'Sue spent a very bad-tempered evening on Saturday, because the man she was due to go out with telephoned and put her off.'

I did one of my non-committal ohs.

'Yes,' Anna continued, maliciously gleeful. 'I've had a difficult Sunday, I can tell you. Sue's been stamping around in her room and brooding over Mike Brenan and saying nothing's the matter; and Jennie's been lecturing us all on the perfidy of men. Well, the second bit's normal of course, but Sue's quite out of countenance and that isn't. You know, she isn't a tiny bit pretty when she's cross.'

I laughed. 'Don't you ever think of evicting them all and moving more cats in instead?'

One of her cats heard this and came to stroke a tail around my ankles.

'Frequently,' said Anna. 'Especially on Monday mornings. Although it has to be said that cats don't pay their way.'

She asked then what she'd been too tactful to ask when I appeared on her doorstep: why did I look such a wreck? I mentioned half a night spent at Gran's bedside until the nurse said Gran's condition was stable and Ada and I could go home. I admitted to a scrap or two with assorted villains and a collision with a hunk of cast-iron machinery. I confessed to feeling half dead and aching from tip to toe. Yet the alternative would have been worse. A dose of chloroform and endless sleep.

Anna said: 'Well, it must be a relief that it's all handed over to the police and you can forget it.' Then she became suspicious. 'Oh, Laura, you *must*. If you go on poking around in this Kate Mullery business you'll . . .' She wouldn't finish it, she was worried with nameless worries.

'I'll what? There you are, you see? Nothing can happen to me. Robin Digby's enmeshed in the legal system, whether he's behind bars or on the streets he won't dare touch me. And I need to understand why he's been violent towards me, right from the first time we crossed each others' paths.'

I could say it to Anna without risking being side-tracked into a dissertation on the classic violence of male towards female. Good. It wouldn't have explained anything in this particular case and it would have wasted time. The soup was reviving me, the bread filling the corners that were achingly empty. I'd felt too sore to want breakfast and I had difficulty recalling the previous time I'd eaten.

'I'm coming to your place tonight,' Anna said.

'Are you?' I couldn't remember an arrangement.

'Yes,' she said firmly. 'I think a nice quiet evening in front of the television's called for. A proper supper and a relaxing evening followed by an early night.'

'You're being bossy,' I accused. She wasn't. She was being motherly.

'Unbearably bossy,' she said. 'I'll bring the food. All you have to do is be there and do as you're told.'

There wasn't any point arguing.

I quite liked the idea of being looked after to the extent of not having to lug food from the shops and find the energy to cook and eat it. I rarely get like this but Anna's the perfect friend to have around when I do. I just hoped she wouldn't catch a glimpse of my developing bruises or she'd have me locked in the flat on an invalid diet for a week.

If she assumed I was going to catch up on some sleep when I went home after lunch, it was because I didn't bother to object when she suggested it. In fact, I raced home, rang the hospital, heard there was no change, dressed in my smartest rig and ordered a taxi. I'd also put my hair up because I was going to have to talk my way past a secretary or two and I wanted to look like business.

The Flynn power dressing worked a charm and by early afternoon I was in Peter's office. He'd had no opportunity to dodge me as he'd tried to do on Sunday, making me hop from church to pub to pub and eventually to a rendezvous at the deer pens. And he was without children to hide behind. I walked right in and cornered him in his office.

This office is in one of those high-and-mighty blocks in the centre of London, its lights among those I'd seen as Mike and I drove down from Highgate on Saturday evening. Peter himself wasn't all that high and mighty at Shirlands Development Ltd, but I'd had to bulldoze a series of doormen and secretaries out of the way to get to him. No, I didn't use a false name. That would have been a sight less effective than my own.

'I've never known anybody so tenacious, independent and

confident of their rights in this world,' he said, and it was no compliment. The secretary had been sent away, the door had been shut.

'If I were a man you'd probably hire me on the strength of those qualities.' I rushed straight on. 'Give me answers, Peter, and I'll go out as smoothly as I came in.' I left him to remember how troublesome I could be if I didn't.

He looked despairing. Probably nothing to do with me at all, probably everything to do with the memo he'd been dictating when I hove to by his desk.

I said: 'Peter, I'd like to know what connection a man called Robin Digby has with Shirlands. He lives at a deer farm at Arkley and I know he's in contact with your MD.'

'Digby? I've heard that name.'

Good. He wasn't going to quibble, he was going to hear me. I said: 'Probably in connection with Kate Mullery's death. He says he was her fiancé.'

'She was a distant cousin of mine.'

'I know. Distant and you hardly knew her. But when she wanted a detective to look into some funny phone calls and a dead cat, you gave her my name. You involved me, Peter. She's dead and the case nearly cost me my life.'

The subtext was plain. *You owe me. Time to pay up.*

He said: 'Look, what is this? I did you both what I thought was a good turn. I met her at a friend's dinner party. I hadn't seen her since we were kids. She was upset. She got there late, rather upset. Funny phone calls and so on. You know more about this than I do, Laura. She asked if anyone knew a detective who'd help her, someone who'd take it seriously and not laugh it off. Nobody else had any ideas so I named you.'

He was pacing about the room, safely the other side of his acreage of desk. I said: 'Who else was present at this dinner party?'

He rattled off seven names, including Kate's and his own. I didn't recognize any of them except his wife's. I tried another tack: 'Who was Kate with?'

'She came alone. I saw her briefly a couple of times more but I never saw her with a man.'

'But Digby claims he was her fiancé.'

'Laura, I don't care if he claims he's Father Christmas, I still didn't see her with a man.'

That was definitive. 'All right, Peter. I'll tell you about Digby. Kate went to stay at his farm because those phone calls got to her. So did a bullet through the skull of her cat.'

Mention of the bullet held his attention just fine. I had him for the rest of the tale. Naturally I filleted it, sticking to the Shirlands connection but saying only that I knew Digby had spoken to the MD about a property they were desperate to get hold of.

He held up a hand. 'Wait, Laura. You're losing me. You say that access to one of our sites is blocked by a garment manufacturer's factory?'

'Not exactly. The old factory isn't used by Bethesda. In fact, it won't be used by anyone again because last night I watched two men set fire to it.'

'You didn't think of stopping them, by any chance?' Peter could be acid.

'No, I didn't have my gamma-ray gun with me. Listen, Peter, what I need to know is . . .'

'You'd be well advised to let the police take care of this.'

'So my friends tell me. I'm here because you're in a position to get the information I'd like. If you do, it'll save me more risk.'

'There's no hope you'll stay at home and avoid the risk?'

'None.'

'No, I thought not.' He drew out his chair and dropped into it. It was a fat, padded thing, an executive's chair. He mightn't be in the top echelon at Shirlands but he was doing all right. He said: 'Suppose you tell me what you overheard between your Robin Digby and my MD?'

'Did I say I'd overheard anything?'

'Not precisely.'

'Then let's keep it nice and imprecise, shall we?' I said.

'As long as you repeat it verbatim I don't give a damn how imprecise we make your methods.'

I told him.

It's hard to gauge how much to tell someone when the only purpose of spilling anything at all is to entice information out of them. They need sufficient to become interested, not enough to confuse, and certainly not enough to ruin the case, because how is one to know how reliable that person is going to be?

Peter and I knew each other from way back. I'd misjudged him then, and misjudged myself too. But I was young. The young are excused crass errors of judgement. It's called learning from experience.

What we'd been left with was a bundle of uncomfortable memories: Peter trying to extricate himself and lacking the skill to do it with grace; me not willing to let go, not prepared to admit the relationship promised nothing for either of us. I'd had better loves since and so had he. We were both glad of that, but the gladness wasn't sufficient to banish a residual awkwardness.

Yes, I knew Peter well and I was relying on that knowledge to steer the conversation in his tower-block office that Monday afternoon. For the memory of the good times, I was trusting him not to let me down.

He ran a finger along the glossy edge of his walnut desk, one elegant finger with a neat square nail. He was looking extremely thoughtful but not careworn as he'd been in the park. For the first time I was seeing him in his milieu, and I grasped a truth that had eluded me. At work he was more the man I remembered. It was the personal things – the marriage, the children, the petty private considerations – that burdened him. For Peter life in a big company, a job with responsibility and pressure, was a respite from the emotional round of family life he wasn't equipped to enjoy.

Revelation helped. It enabled me to feel better about the me that used to be. I'd matured carrying the blame for an emotional disaster I'd attributed solely to my own girlish mistakes.

Peter watched his finger glide along the wood in what I took to be a habitual gesture marking concentration. Then he raised his eyes to mine. 'OK, Laura. I'll find out about Robin Digby and Shirlands. I'll *try*, I'm not going to put it any higher than that.'

I was nodding encouragement.

He said: 'But I'll do it only on condition that you don't discuss this with anyone else.'

I sought beyond the words for a deeper meaning. 'You don't mean in the meantime, you mean ever, don't you?'

'That's right. I'll get your questions answered, if possible. I'll give you the answers I get. But then it stops. You must promise me you won't go to anyone, inside Shirlands or out of it, with information I provide. Or, indeed, with the information you already have.'

I said I thought this was a bit steep.

He said in that case he'd forget it.

I said oh no he wouldn't, he'd find out for himself anyway.

He shrugged and said if I didn't accept the terms I'd never know whether he had or not.

Ruefully I gave in. 'They're lousy conditions,' I grumbled.

'You've promised,' he said.

And there was the echo of long-ago promises, and betrayal.

He reached for a buzzer and the secretary appeared, ready to take up her memo where she'd left off. I departed with a display of confidence and good humour that was three parts sham.

If I hadn't been too tired, too injured, I might have handled it better. Yes, definitely I would have done. With more intelligence anyhow. But human beings don't bounce back unscathed from the experience I'd suffered the previous day. Only my detective-fiction heroes do that. For the rest of us a clout on the head is a headache, a strained muscle is a pain. I ached, I was in pain.

On the Underground, going home, I chivvied myself into believing I was pleased to have an excuse to do nothing further to tease apart the puzzles surrounding Robin Digby and Kate Mullery. The police were looking into Kate's death and Peter was looking into Digby's life. Laura Flynn could relax and turn her attention to other matters.

Between the Tube station and home, I called in at the office. The music from the gym downstairs was loud. A door had been left open. I winced, imagining my stiffening limbs forced to join the workout or heave at the machines. On the other hand a sauna could be just the treatment I needed. I opened the filing cabinet and hooked out a towelling robe.

And then I saw the red eye on the telephone answering machine. The Turkish man from the sweatshop had rung.

'Laura, I believe I have news of your cat,' he said, and there was a smile in his voice.

My what? Oh, er, yes. Mrs Lottie's cat. The monster she called Jaguar.

'Telephone me and I'll explain.'

My hand went to the phone before I remembered my ruse about writing an article for *Time Out* and his approach to the magazine. Tricky. Did I really want to talk to him?

No.

But then I pictured the *mamma* of Nonesuch House, and I wanted her to have her cat back.

'*Sí.*'

I dialled. A cat lover, the man was more interested in Jaguar's fate than my dishonesty and didn't mention *Time Out*. He said the cat had been seen on open land in Laycock Street.

Laycock Street's very close to the office. One side is a field, a relic from the days when Islington was a dairy supplying milk to London. I immediately went round there. All I found was a cringeing mongrel, three Jamaican boys playing with an old bicycle, and the beginnings of a snow shower.

The boys stuck sticky fingers on the picture of Jaguar and said sure they'd seen a cat like it but not as big and glossy. I figured that a stray Jaguar would be less juicy than when it was being pampered by Mrs Lotti.

'When did you see him?' I asked, hoping the creature kept regular hours.

'Friday,' said the most talkative of the trio. 'In the afternoon. An old lady comes and feeds the cats.'

They couldn't say what time of afternoon but I narrowed it down somewhat by establishing roughly when they'd come to play there and that it wasn't getting dark by the time the old lady showed up to do her act of animal charity. In late December dusk falls early, I calculated the incident probably took place around 2.30 p.m. to 3 p.m.

'Do you know where the old lady lives?'

They didn't but knew she appeared from the direction of a pub. They'd often seen her feeding the cats but seldom paid attention. On Friday though a dog had run over the field, scattering the cats and causing such a squealing and a squalling that the boys had been unable to help noticing.

The kids had enjoyed the disaster. They giggled happily through the retelling of it.

From Laycock Street I went to the nearest pub and asked after an old woman who fed cats. My Jamaican informants had done well. The old woman actually called in at the pub and collected scraps for the cats.

'Where does she live?' I asked.

The landlord pointed. 'Up that way.'

His wife named a street but not a number. I called at three houses before I found a neighbour who knew the woman's name and number. The house was the only unmodernized one in the street, the brickwork blackened from the days of London smogs and the paintwork not touched for half a lifetime. Cobwebs and dirty net curtains hung in the windows.

Mrs Daniel was in. If she'd eaten all the goodies she fed the cats she'd still have been thin. She made even Ada Carey appear robust. Angular beneath a muffle of smelly unravelling cardigans, she jutted her chin in challenge when I asked whether she was the lady who fed the cats in Laycock Street.

'All God's creatures,' she cried in a high rasping voice.

'True. So you're Mrs Daniel?'

'Don't tell me that council wants to put me in prison for feeding the cats?'

'Good heavens no. I'm looking for a lost cat.'

'Godless lot, that council. Used to have a red flag on the town hall, you know. They'd do away with cats if I'd let 'em. Catch 'em and turn 'em into gloves and sell the rest to the Chinese. What do you want with a cat? Not from the council are you?'

'No, nothing like that. I know someone whose cat's run off. I wondered whether you'd seen it.'

'I didn't think you were from the council. They push their bits of card in your face, council people. Authorization, they call it. Allows 'em to ask questions.'

'Well,' I said, 'I haven't got anything like that. I wanted to ask whether you'd seen this cat?'

And I showed the photograph of Jaguar.

She sniffed. 'Funny sort of cat, that is.'

'Yes. He *is* unusual. His name's Jaguar.'

'Hmm. Funny sort of name too.'

I said: 'Did he turn up when you were feeding the cats on Friday?'

She chewed her lower lip, false teeth sliding. 'A dog sent 'em all flying. But . . . I think he might have been there. Let me look at that again.'

She took the photograph close to her sharp nose and her bleary reddened eyes. She sniffed again. 'It could have been him. There are often new cats and there were a couple last week. Skinny, scrawny things. I'll be there half-past two tomorrow. Come and see then. He might be there again.'

I thanked her and left her, a skinny, scrawny thing herself. She stayed on the doorstep to make sure I went, called after me that I wasn't to go to the council about her, that it was her

Christian duty to feed God's creatures, and then she slammed the door.

I'm not much of a hand with cats. Not like Anna Lee. I thought about enlisting her the next afternoon to trap the putative Jaguar, but it wasn't ideal. We might trundle off with the wrong moggy. Better by far to enlist Mrs Lotti herself.

That's why I walked from Mrs Daniel's house to Nonesuch and rapped on Mrs Lotti's door.

'Ah, Laura. My cat he isa found, *sì*?' She beamed wide as her letterbox.

'No,' I said, 'but he might be soon.'

She agreed to be at Laycock Street next afternoon, babysitters permitting. I retreated before she thought of hiring me for an hour's babysitting.

On the way back, the snow set in in earnest. It splattered and splodged, churned grey underfoot and was thoroughly unpleasant, demonstrating the gulf between fantasy and reality.

Once I thought a car driver had taken pity on me and was offering a lift but when he'd taken a good look at me he pulled away. No, I was being unkind. He'd probably stopped for something quite different, though why anyone should stop near Nonesuch House and linger exactly long enough to raise my hopes I don't know. It was a new car, a red Peugeot, and it was driven by a face I couldn't identify what with the snow and the wind driving into my eyes.

I kept to the lighted streets and main road the rest of the way. Nervous, perhaps, but I'd already had two unscheduled rides in cars with men who wished me no good whatsoever.

Then in Holloway Road I noticed the same car, parked badly while a passenger, half in and half out, spoke to the driver. As I neared, the passenger emerged fully. He was old Gerry MacGuire. Strange to think he was a second cousin to my former mother-in-law. The news put both of them in a curious new light.

He was between me and a pub door, the red car was moving off, when he recognized me.

'Is it Laura Flynn you are?'

'The very same, Gerry. Cold enough for you today?'

'Ah it's a miserable time I'm having of it, Laura. Up at the hospital again.'

'Bridie?'

'Isn't it always Bridie in the hospital?'

'I'm sorry to hear it,' I said.

'Mind, it's not so much the old trouble this time. She's a divil of a toenail on her and they're to perform a wee operation to set it right.'

All this as he was backing into the bar and I was backing away down Holloway Road. And both of us thinking more about my search for Joe Flynn than about his dotty wife and her toenail. Anyhow, the meeting gave the answer to one minor puzzle: I knew full well who'd seen me leaving the palaces estate and had chosen to let me plod through the snow rather than give me a ride part of the way home.

At Highbury Corner I ran into the carol singers and it cost me a pound to get by them and their greetings of comfort and joy.

No more messages in the office. I telephoned the Turkish cat lover and let him know how the Jaguar hunt was progressing. He was so keen he said he'd stroll through Laycock Street himself now and then, it was on his way home.

Time for that sauna. I had it to myself. Ideal for thinking. Ideal for *not* thinking but I couldn't manage that. I tried, quite hard, but the pink elephants started going round. Robin Digby and Kate Mullery. The MacGuires and Joe Flynn. Peter and Shirlands. Too many loose ends flapping around in my mind.

The sauna eased the aches, made me feel I'd made an attempt at recovery. A woman I didn't know joined me and pretended not to notice the extent of my bruising. I left her to cope with her fantasies and went to enjoy my shower.

As I put my towelling robe to dry on a hanger behind the washroom door, the telephone rang. A heavily accented voice asked: 'Laura Flynn?'

'That's me.' I was running a hand through my tousled hair,

trying to smooth it before it dried in wild curls again. I dread the day we all have phones that let the caller see you.

'Is it true you were at Badlocks last night?'

'Badlocks?' I was placing the accent. Possibly Pakistani.

'The factory that was burned.'

'I might have been. Who wants to know?' I'd never noticed a name on the place.

'The owner. My name's Patel.'

'Who told you I . . .?'

'The police said you were there. Look, I want to talk to you. I want you to tell me what you saw.'

I ought to have insisted I was too busy, that I'd already made an exhaustive report to the police. Instead I said all right.

He said: 'Can you come down here, please?' He named the pub on the river front, the one I'd been in before I fell into a trap and the trap caught fire.

Again I ought to have said no.

Home, briefly, I shed the outfit that had fought its way past secretaries, and I changed into warm trousers, tied back my hair, slipped on my titanium ear-rings and touched St Lucy for luck. I took a cab to Bermondsey.

Monday evening. The pub was quieter than it had been the evening before. A head count might have revealed an identical number of people but these were quieter office types winding down after a day's work in the new blocks around us. I waited on my own for twenty minutes, sitting by the window where I'd been asked to sit, the river hard to distinguish from reflections in the window pane of the Victorian-style room. A group of young men and women came purposefully through and up stairs to a gallery where they turned on the laughter and *bonhomie* of an office Christmas outing. But still no Pakistani factory owner.

After half an hour I finished my drink and went out. The wind off the water nipped my ankles in the gap below my trousers, and sneaked a way round my scarf as I wandered towards the ruins of the factory. A short thickset man came round the corner, leaning into the wind, head down. He was level when he noticed me. 'Laura Flynn?' This time I was sure. Pakistani.

'Sorry to keep you waiting,' he said. 'I will buy you a drink, perhaps, or we can go back to the factory.'

'I've had the drink. Let's see the factory.'

I let him lead, the path was narrow all the way to the road and then we had to fight the wind along Jamaica Road. He apologized again, saying someone had come and he hadn't been able to leave. Absurdly he was carrying a key for a building that was open to the skies. Habit, refusal to accept the extent of the change in his life. He shoved back the wreckage of the unlocked door.

'You see what they did to my business.'

I saw.

I saw nothing. What the flames hadn't achieved, the firemen had. Ashes, wet ashes. No business. Nothing to buy or sell or to make things with.

I said: 'This looks dangerous.' Nice British understatement.

'There's an iron stairway. That's intact, but the rest . . .' He made a sound that was a sigh and a moan and a protest. 'I wanted you to see this, what they have done to me. Now will you tell me, please, what you saw yesterday?'

'First you explain what the police told you.'

This was uncomplicated. They'd said there'd been a witness to the arson and they'd told him it was me.

I ran through Sunday evening, starting at the stage where I noticed three men on the vacant lot behind the factory and ending where I saw flames shooting up. I described Big Boy and the other two.

He brushed ash off a sleeve where it had touched a cindered spar. 'You didn't say why you were out there.' He said this without meeting my eye. I withheld my reply until he stopped fiddling with his sleeve and was forced to look at me.

'And you didn't say why you want to know. The police are investigating the arson, why do you think I can be of use?'

He was a man who used his hands, to underline words or replace them. Now he replaced them with a gesture, palms uppermost showing openness, resignation.

I said: 'It doesn't matter why I was here.'

He laughed ironically. 'Oh no, no, no. That doesn't matter. Twice you are here and now the factory is burned out.'

'Twice?'

'You were seen the other time. Ha, you didn't know that? Well, yes, you were seen. You were taking a deep interest in my factory, or was it in the land behind it? The police officer told me there was a witness, a woman, and I thought now that is an odd thing because there was a woman once before. So I said to him, please, what does she look like, this woman witness of yours? And he told me. Long black hair, he said. Well, I thought, I recognize that. So I said to him, please, what is her name? And when he told me it I looked in the telephone book, to see if there would be a very easy answer to my question. And yes, it was extremely easy. Flynn Detective Agency, it said. And I rang it and, goodness me, Laura Flynn herself answered me.'

I smiled wryly. 'You had the kind of luck I wish I had more often when I'm tracing someone.'

But he wasn't smiling. 'Don't let us play games, Miss Flynn. Please say why you have been hanging around this place.'

I matched him for solemnity. 'I haven't. I came once only, and that was yesterday.'

He contradicted me with a shake of his head. 'You are asking me to believe in two young women with long black hair in a space of days?'

'I've been here once. Supposing you tell me what happened the other time.'

He said it was the previous week. He and his nephew, his partner in the business, stayed on one evening because they were having a meeting with a man. During the meeting they became aware of someone entering the building but when the nephew went to investigate the person ran off.

'He described a dark-haired woman, Miss Flynn. After the meeting was over, we went outside, the three of us and we all saw her. She was peering round the corner of the alley up there, the one you and I walked down from the pub. Well, she darted away. I was going to drive off but I thought I would make absolutely certain the premises were secure. I came back in, and I checked the windows and the doors. I don't know why but before I left I ran right upstairs to the top floor and I looked out over the empty land between us and the river. Do you know what I saw, Miss Flynn?'

'The black-haired woman.'

'Indeed, Miss Flynn. There she was, walking across the site towards my factory.'

'And what did you do?'

Here he hesitated. 'What could I do? Keep watch here all night?'

'You went home.'

'I telephoned my nephew who was already on his way home. He has a car phone, you see. I told him there was somebody lurking near the factory. Well, why not? He's a young man, Miss Flynn. Tackling intruders is more in his line than mine.'

'And did he? Tackle her?'

'No. He came back here but found nobody.'

We watched each other cautiously, each convinced of duplicity. I repeated that I'd visited the site only once before.

He shrugged. 'Very well, Miss Flynn. But why did you come here even once?'

The wind swirled down from the open roof and stirred the ashes of his business, spattering his hair with its dust. I worried again that it wasn't safe where we were.

'Then let me have answers, Miss Flynn, and we can go to our homes.'

He was short and thickset and he was between me and the way out. A tangled heap of metal that might once have been clothes racks blocked the way into a further room. Behind him rose the iron staircase, sturdy beneath its encrustation of burned muck. Another pinch of dust drifted down.

I mentioned Bethesda, inquiries for a client and so on. Good. So far I was making sense to him. I asked: 'Who's trying to get you out of this factory?'

He was scornful. 'You're not such a very fine detective, Miss Flynn, or you would know that Bethesda has been offering us a very good price to move out. They own the freehold but we have a lease on the building. However, offering a very good price is a far cry from burning us to the ground.'

I reached an opinion about the falling ash. Someone was upstairs. Beyond the muddle of blackened spars and charred slabs of ceiling over our heads, someone was listening to us.

I returned Patel's thin smile. 'Yes. But who have you been discussing this with at Bethesda?'

And while he was objecting that it was none of my business, I fired off a series of questions. How much money had he and his nephew been offered? If it was a very good offer why hadn't they accepted it? Were he and his nephew in agreement about rejecting the offer? And who did he think had fired the building?

The detritus of his business was cold and wet around my shoes. A lorry went up the road and its vibrations sent cinders rattling down from a joist. The whole place could come down at any minute. I was sure we oughtn't to be in there. Not if we valued our lives. I was beginning to doubt that he did.

I made my move towards the door. 'Let's talk about this in the pub. It's too cold in here.'

'No, no.' He moved an inch, a blocking move. 'Please, I am waiting for explanations.'

'You too?' I said sarcastically. My battery of questions had elicited no replies either. I *couldn't* answer, he *wouldn't*.

Ignoring his intimidation I strode to the door, obliging him to side-step unless he chose to use physical force. He didn't choose. He stumbled after me, a hand out in supplication. 'Please, Miss Flynn, I beg you to help me.'

In the doorway I paused, seeing him afresh. The assurance had wilted. He looked like a man desperate for help, not a man putting pressure on a suspect.

I sighed. 'All right. Let's start again. And let's do it on the basis that I'm telling the truth. I don't know why those men fired your factory and I don't know their names.'

'Yes, yes. I believe you. But, you see, the coincidence of two dark-haired women is very odd, very odd indeed.'

I dismissed that, saying the other woman might not have been as dark as me, she'd been seen in poor light on a winter evening. I wanted to get him away from that and back to the offer Bethesda had made. Then he said something peculiar.

'My nephew was positive she was dark.'

That's when it surfaced that the older man hadn't seen the woman clearly from the top floor, that the description of her long dark hair had come from the nephew. The two Patels had glimpsed her peering round the end of the adjacent building and later the nephew had come face to face with her on the empty lot.

I asked what he'd done with her.

'He told her to go away, sent her packing and nailed a board over a gap she'd used to go on to the site.'

'But what did she say she wanted there?'

'He says she didn't say anything. She left, then he left.'

Just like that. I didn't think so.

'The money,' I said. 'How much?'

He quoted a figure that was high enough to be a considerable inducement to get out.

'So why not?' I wondered.

'Oh for my nephew yes, it is indeed an acceptable sum. It would buy another lease in London I've no doubt. But very good isn't always good enough, Miss Flynn. Bethesda wants to knock down this factory to give the Shirlands site behind it a decent access to the road. Did you know that Shirlands owns Bethesda, Miss Flynn?'

From his tone he didn't dream I knew. I said: 'I'd worked out that this building was in their way.'

'And it still is. Damaged but still here. My price remains high, Miss Flynn, and I expect Bethesda to meet it.'

For the second time I asked the name of the person he'd been negotiating with at Bethesda. I don't know why it was important to me. Maybe it was a gut feeling. Maybe it was my hoover mentality, wanting to suck up whatever information was around.

He said: 'They were crafty, Miss Flynn. Bethesda didn't come direct to us and say they wanted the premises to knock them down and add millions to the value of the Shirlands site. Oh no, they sent a man to us pretending he wanted it for his own business. You could say he was acting as their agent in this matter, but I would say he was a liar. My nephew's a bright boy. He nosed around and he found out the man was really representing Bethesda. And then he nosed around further and found out that Shirlands owns Bethesda. We saw through their trick, and we upped the price, Miss Flynn. But we didn't reveal we knew the man was working for them. We decided we would have our secrets too.'

'The man's name?'

'The name,' he said, 'is John Manson.'

This Manson had been with the Patels on the evening the dark-haired woman appeared. I got a description of sorts but there was nothing distinctive about the man.

'When,' I asked, 'will you see him again?'

Patel made one of his gestures. 'It should have been today but . . .'

'But he didn't turn up and the factory burned down instead?'

This time I got the gesture without any words. After a pause he added: 'I hoped perhaps you would know something about this Manson.'

'Never heard the name.'

I pitied Patel his predicament. He'd lost his chance of a good price by holding out for a better one. And the nephew? How did he feel about it now? I asked whether either of the Patels had told Manson of the fate of the factory.

'No,' he said. 'We have a telephone number but he isn't answering it.' He drew a Filofax from his inside pocket and held it out to me open at a page where he'd written down the man's name and telephone number. He didn't read the number himself, he recited it from memory. He'd dialled it regularly all that day.

I chanted the number in my head, fixing it, not knowing whether I'd ever need it. Actually it seemed familiar, but I come across a great many north London numbers so I didn't attach importance to the familiarity.

'Does your nephew know you're meeting me?' I was sure the answer would be no.

'No, no, no. My nephew says that now we must take the money from Mr Manson, quick as you like. He says we shouldn't ask questions about the fire, we should leave that to the police and the insurance company and we should get Mr Manson to give us his money. I tell him his uncle is a fellow who likes to ask questions.'

We went out into the street, me first, Patel drawing the broken door after us. Surprising him, I stuck out a hand and held the door against his pressure. 'Wait,' I whispered.

He gave me the classic round-eyed look but he kept quiet.

From within came a shuffling. I thrust the door and bounded back inside. A shoe, a trouser leg, appeared at the top of the flight of iron stairs. They withdrew. I ran at the stairs, taking them two at a time, grabbing at the filthy caked handrail and feeling it shake uncertainly in my hand.

A young man was up there. Above him was the sky where there used to be the second storey. All around him were fallen joists and girders. Beneath him was the unreliable remnant of a floor. He was backing away over the rubble, scared. I went after him.

From down below came his uncle's anxious voice. 'Please, Miss Flynn, what is happening up there?'

I said to young Patel: 'If this fire was your way of persuading your uncle to sell the lease, you've gone too far.'

Second generation, he had as good an East End accent as I've heard. 'You can't put this down to me! The first I knew was when the police rang and said the place had gone up.' His heel caught on a hunk of something and he staggered back.

From below his uncle called again: 'Please, what is going on up there? Who is it with you, Miss Flynn?'

'Tell him,' I said to the nephew. 'Tell him you were snooping while he talked to me. Tell him why you were desperate to know what he was going to say.'

'Look, it's none of your business, is it? Why don't you clear out and leave us alone?' He glanced behind him, picked a route, moved backwards again.

'Watch out!'

The floor that was trembling with every step had begun to slide. He threw himself at an iron pillar, hugged it while the floor he'd been standing on a second before fell away in a blizzard of ash.

From below the older man cried: 'Oh my God.'

Young Patel was wrapped around the pillar, his face turned away from me. I addressed the back of his head. 'This is much too dangerous. We've got to get outside, all of us.'

But he'd picked out another pathway through danger. His arms slackened, he gave up the pillar and he edged away.

'For heaven's sake,' I said. 'You'll kill yourself.'

A strut of grey-black wood crashed down through the hole where the floor had been. And then, mingling with the flakes of ash, came the snow.

'I'm getting out of this,' I said. Why not? I could talk to him when he came down, and he was inevitably going to come down sometime.

Young Patel, I realized, hadn't stirred. He was out in the middle of the floor, beyond reach of the solid pillar, and he was poised awkwardly. I opened my mouth to tell him to get away from that area but my words went unspoken as the floor beneath him whipped and buckled. He withdrew his foot. Another section of the floor smashed down.

He was in very serious trouble. The floor ahead had gone and below was a treacherous mess of fallen wood and metal. Jumping down would mean certain injury. He stood on a narrow strip of firm support but to put a foot to either side of it would be to dislodge more of the floor. To turn round was virtually impossible.

'Hold on,' I said. 'Don't move.'

Against all my inclination I ventured out over the wreckage a second time. Now whether this was attempted in a spirit of helpfulness or heroism, I can't tell you. I hadn't time to consider it. The elder Patel was beating his breast downstairs and the younger one was dicing with self-destruction ahead of me. Out I went.

I had two advantages over the young man teetering on the brink of disaster. I was fit and I could see where I was going. I intended to play my advantages to the full.

I mounted the beam on which he stood, praying it would bear the weight of both of us. The snow was whirling about, making me brush it off my eyelashes when my hands were needed to ensure balance. I crept right up behind Patel and spoke quietly and decisively.

He was petrified. He was so taken with fear that he was physically incapable of movement except, that is, for a nervous quivering.

I said: 'For the first 20 feet the only safe way is along the beam we're standing on. There isn't room to turn round, we've got to go backwards. I'll guide you.'

No answer.

I said: 'Are you listening?'

A tiny grunt. He was staring down into the void, transfixed by the drop and the snowflakes dancing in the blackness down there.

I touched his shoulder. 'Come on. Let's go.'

He moved away from my touch, almost tipped over. I

gripped his upper arm, trying to convey security and assurance. 'Come on.' I drew him back slightly.

After what felt an age he responded. The spell was broken. He took a tentative step backwards, trusting me. I sensed my own way back and watched his every move, waiting until his foot was positioned in the centre of the beam before promising him it was safe to transfer his weight to it.

Halfway through our tightrope act we needed a break and I distracted him from dwelling on the danger by asking about the black-haired woman and the men who'd set fire to the factory.

'She went away,' he said. 'Like my uncle told you.'

'Did she say why she was here?'

'Yes, she was asking about Bethesda. Wanted to know if we were part of their business. I told her we weren't.'

And he said that after she'd gone he'd telephoned John Manson about the incident. Young Patel was apparently so keen to do business with Manson that they'd combined to persuade his uncle.

He said: 'I want the money. I came into the business after my father died, but it's not a business I want to spend the rest of my life running. This Manson offer – whether he's acting for Bethesda and Shirlands or as an individual – it's the best chance I'll ever have to get my hands on a heap of money.'

'But your uncle wants a bigger pile of money.'

'Yeah, but it's not realistic. Manson's keen but he's not rash. I mean, there's got to be a limit, hasn't there? A limit to the money and a limit to the time he's prepared to spend on this. It isn't as though Shirlands don't have an access at all, it's only that they'd have a better one through here.'

A limit to the time and the money. I knew where I'd heard that before.

I led young Patel back two more steps before I asked: 'How did Manson react to the news of the black-haired young woman?'

'Bloody annoyed about her. Said he recognized her.'

165

'Would *you* recognize her again?'

'Well I know it wasn't you. She was shorter. She was very pale and she had an accent. Irish, I think. My uncle was convinced it was you, he wanted to talk to you alone and he thought I'd left when he went to the pub to meet you.'

We tried another step but this was a bad one. He shifted his weight too soon, and his foot slid off the edge of the beam on to a tender surface. It crumbled. I hung on to him tightly and steadied him.

Too many questions Flynn.

Why couldn't I shut up and get us both to safety, not quiz him in this death trap? Because I was more likely to get answers when he was dependent on my approval, that's why.

I asked another one: 'Did Manson give a deadline for a decision about his offer for the lease?'

'He wanted it all wrapped up by the New Year. I talked to him last week. He said he was under pressure, time was running out. If we didn't say yes by the New Year then we could forget it.'

We tottered to the safer area and walked gingerly across to the iron ladder. Young Patel was shaken and distressed. He didn't thank me. I left him and his uncle at the factory together. They had a lot to discuss.

Anna Lee and my ex-husband were in my flat. She had the sofa and he sat on a chair from the other room. I sat on the floor, there wasn't anywhere else. Memories flooded in explaining Anna's presence but not Mike Brenan's.

'You've been out, Laura,' Anna said, accusing and hurt. I could smell food. She'd promised me some. Oh yes, and I'd promised her I'd stay in and watch television and recover from my adventures on the Shirlands site and in the lock-up. So much for promises.

I dug my fingers into the rich pile of the carpet. 'Something came up. Sorry, Anna.'

I queried Mike's presence, his unwelcome presence, with a look. He echoed me: 'Something came up.'

Anna gave an explanation that counted as an apology. 'Mike drove up the street as I was letting myself in here.'

He said: 'It's about Joe Flynn. I was passing and I wanted to let you know straightaway. We didn't realize you'd be out so long.' He looked at Anna for confirmation but she avoided his eye.

I invented the difficult time they'd spent *not* talking about this and that while they'd waited for me. They'd never met until Sue Preston had taken up with Mike and he and Anna had seen each other fleetingly when he'd called at the house to collect Sue. But she'd detested him for years, purely on my behalf because she'd seen me through a hellish divorce.

I asked Mike: 'What about my father?' The carpet was warm and soft, I wanted to stretch out on it and sleep right through to the New Year.

'Really it's more to do with Laughton. You know, the man who was killed on the site shortly before your father did a flit.'

I tried not to look disappointed. 'I read the newspaper report of the inquest. Accidental death, nothing about unsafe practices.'

'Your father wasn't the only person upset at what was happening. There was a union man called Dave Tanner, he made a protest about it.'

'Specifically about Laughton's accident?'

'I think so.'

I stayed disappointed. I wasn't investigating the death of Laughton, I was attempting to find Joe Flynn. But Mike said: 'This Tanner knew your father. It might be worth your while tracking him down.'

Inquisitive, Mike had raised the subject with his parents and although Mrs Brenan had added nothing to what she'd told me, his father had remembered about Tanner. I agreed the man was a line worth pursuing.

Mike got up to go but naturally I had to ask him to stay on

and naturally Anna had to feed him. This wasn't the most relaxed social gathering I've ever taken part in. I spent it guessing which of them would leave first, not caring much as I wanted them both to go. Mental and physical tiredness made me dull company and I wasn't up to tackling the tension that had developed between them in the hours of waiting for me to arrive.

You know that frightful small talk that happens when everyone is waiting for someone else to leave before they feel able to speak freely? Well, we got an awful lot of that small talk.

In the end they left together because Mike offered Anna a lift and it was too dark and wintry for independence. Going out he flashed me a smile that said we'd laugh together about all this later, and she gave me a look that threatened she'd be on the phone first thing next morning and there wouldn't be much to laugh about. I shut the door on them and flopped on my carpet and laughed alone.

Afterwards I made my routine check of my office answering machine. Just once in a while there'd be a message I'd rather not wait for until morning.

I heard an excitable Patel senior. 'Miss Flynn, I have seen this Mr Manson who is making us offers for the lease. He was on the television tonight. It was definitely the same man, Miss Flynn, but they were using another name. They said he was called Robin Digby.'

Digby.

The jumble of information the two Patels had given me about their dealings with Manson and Bethesda rearranged itself in a different pattern. It was no longer a sideshow to the Kate Mullery-Bethesda story. If Manson genuinely was Digby, then he was involved with Bethesda on his own account and not merely through his personal interest in Kate's business deal.

I snatched up my shoulder bag and scrabbled through its contents. There it was, the scrap of paper on which I'd noted the telephone number of Knights End Farm. And yes, it was identical to the number the Patels had for their Mr Manson.

Time, I thought, to stop fussing around at dead of night when tomorrow would do perfectly well. The people I intended to tackle would be sweeter for a good night's sleep, and so would I.

I got into bed with my detective novel. The cover line said it was unputdownable, but it dropped from my hand before I'd read a full page.

Gran had a good night too. I rang the hospital early next day and detected cautious optimism in the standard description of her condition. With a light heart I set out for the gym and an early workout and circuit of the weights.

I followed my steamy breath through almost deserted streets. The snow had stopped falling but a cold night had frozen what lay around and frost had doodled over window panes. It was Anne Stevenson's exquisite 'scriptural cold'. With the toe of my boot I scraped snow from the street doorway and let myself into the gym. I was having a wonderful start to the day and wouldn't have believed any crystal-ball gazer who'd warned me it could only get worse.

First there was the post. Kate Mullery's cheque had bounced. I telephoned Keith Jay to say what the hell, and he said: 'Oh dear, Laura, you're not the only one.' And I said I couldn't care less about the others but I was very *very* cross about mine.

He practically whimpered, saying he should never have given it to me; and I said rubbish, I should have been sent it three months earlier. Every word was a waste of breath, of course. There was no money and the bank was returning cheques. Why was there no money? Because, Keith said, that trusty old family friend and business adviser Robin Digby had been bank-rolling Kate during a difficult patch and now she was dead he'd withdrawn his favours.

We didn't wrangle about the timing but it seemed likely that Digby's resistance stretched back several months. Putting pressure on her, I guessed, to go ahead with the Bethesda deal. Brilliant, stupid Kate Mullery, with Digby urging one thing and Keith Jay urging the opposite, and Kate havering in the centre, never entirely making up her own mind but waiting for one or other of the men around her to help her decide.

After that I tried to reach Peter at Shirlands to see whether he'd yet discovered anything about Digby's connection with the company and, if he hadn't, to provide the pointer I'd been given by the Patels. A secretary informed me that Peter was unavailable and was going to stay that way all day.

Next, Dave Tanner, the one-time union official who'd known my father. This took several phone calls to union offices, starting with one where I knew a man and then I was passed along a line of people at different unions who might know people who knew. Dave Tanner was a long time ago but eventually I was speaking to a man who not only remembered him but was able to seek out an address.

The address was disastrously out of date and I squandered hours chasing up people who might know where the occupant of Flat 7 had moved to but didn't. Eventually I walked into a seedy pub in mid-afternoon, to be greeted with the surliest resistance by a group of men who could have passed for an underworld gang. As it turned out, that's probably what they were.

'Who wants Tanner?' A swarthy man in a torn anorak snarled without removing the dog end stuck to his lower lip.

'An old friend of his is looking for him,' I lied.

'Tanner don't have old friends.' The man earned a laugh for this.

'Pity,' I said. 'This old friend might have some money for him.' I knew they'd respond to the sound of money.

It wasn't the response I expected.

The man said: 'Tanner has everything he needs. Money's no good to him.'

He won another laugh.

One of the others said: 'He's doing five. In Pentonville.'

End of search for Dave Tanner. But I'd come this far, I might as well see him.

You don't, though, walk up to a prison, knock on the door

and ask if Dave's in. The initiative has to come from him. You have to write asking to visit him, if he wants to see you he requests a visiting order which is posted back to you, and you turn up at the appointed time and present the order.

Dave Tanner had all the time in the world, I didn't. I wrote my plea to him and I delivered it by hand. Not only are we lucky enough to have the city's best Chinese take-away in Caledonian Road, we've got Pentonville there too.

Five minutes later I was calling on a friend whose husband's in the prison service. All I wanted was that Tanner got my request quickly and I got the visiting order quickly. I needed someone to see I'd be at the top of the pile when it mattered.

Jill's on the borough council, and that can be useful too. This time I wanted nothing from her and we drank a couple of cups of tea while she brought me up to date on a number of local issues, purely for the pleasure of the gossip.

Back at the office gloom set in. I sat at my desk, my baggy cardigan dragged on over my other clothes and a scarf round my neck. I considered the rickety chair and the scarred desk, the futile electric fire, the filing cabinet stuffed with gym clothes and fancy tea and coffee-bags in case I ever got a fancy client.

It would have to go, all of it. I'd have to give it up and work from the flat, precisely what I didn't want to do. Kate Mullery's cheque bouncing, and there being no use submitting a bill for the work I'd subsequently done for her, made all the difference between a main road office and a desk in the corner of my flat. Good Lord, I couldn't even afford to buy a desk.

A shame I hadn't hired myself out to Peter to poke into the Digby affair, instead of asking him to tell things to me but it was easy to say that with hindsight. The inquiries I was currently making wouldn't bring in any cash. I needed a new client, a big new case, the promise of a decent-sized cheque. Oh well, something might turn up.

I heard footsteps on the stairs. Could this be the answer, on cue? No, it was Mrs Lotti. Her face told me the result of her trip to Laycock Street long before she'd caught her breath. She wobbled across to the chair. It was my turn to catch my breath as she lowered herself on to it, but it held firm.

'No,' she was saying, shaking her head. 'No, Laura, this cat isa no Jaguar. The lady she feeds him, she say he come Friday. Today, no. A cat like so, but today no Jaguar.' The 'like so' was demonstrated by a tiny space trapped between finger and thumb. And then, plaintively: 'Please, Laura, where isa my Jaguar?'

She didn't hope for a location, only commiseration. I provided it and cosseted her with a cup of coffee, made with one of my expensive coffee-bags as there didn't seem any reason to hang on to them any longer. Soon she waddled back into the weather, a mite happier but her lament for the missing Jaguar unabated.

Sporadic snowflakes were falling between me and my Big Ben. A double-decker bus pulled into the bus stop below and a few swaddled figures alighted and scattered in the mid-afternoon dimness. The thrum thrum thrum of music from the gym had become a medley of disco-style carols. I could have done with some Good News.

Chris Ionides answered my call, his voice thick with a head cold. But yes, he was working on the car. Tomorrow, maybe, the day after definitely. 'A beautiful Christmas present for you, eh, Laura?'

I said it would be wonderful. I was scared his bill would be too.

Bleak midwinter. I don't understand why it matters when a year slips away. A day is just a day, they spend themselves with unerring rhythm. But the media encourages us to guess the future and pick over the past. Without the year's round-ups on the radio or the backward glances of the colour supplements, how much would I care about the change of date? How much would you?

My friend, the one who works on a Sunday paper, says the emphasis is necessary to fill fattish papers over a long holiday period when governments and bureaucracies are on holiday, the usual sources of news have gone fishing. 'Quiet news days,' he says they are called.

The season for retrospection had arrived, and I was looking over my shoulder at 1990 and, on the business front, I was seeing defeat. A promising year had grown bad. I didn't face the workhouse but I faced crawling to one of the big agencies which was equally humbling. The one I'd left when I set up on my own wanted me back, and I'd already stooped to taking on work for it in fallow patches.

Well, there's only one thing a girl can do when she's broke and fed up about it, she has to buy something to cheer herself up. I rattled downstairs to the boutique and chose a sweater.

Coming up again, I saw the door ajar and was sure I'd closed it. I ran softly the rest of the way and surprised a motor-cycle messenger in my office.

'Something for me?' I asked.

He had his helmet on and didn't hear until I was closer. 'On the desk,' he said, rushing out.

But there was nothing on the desk which hadn't been there before, which is to say it was bare apart from the *Independent*. I grabbed my leather jacket and flew after him. Women coming in from the street on their way to the gym hampered him giving me a chance to get closer.

He had a Kawasaki GT 750, a typical London messenger's bike, but it wasn't directly outside because of the bus stop. He had to go a few yards for it. I was right with him but he wouldn't stop or speak. Then he was astride the machine, kicking life into it and leaping out into the traffic. Damn! I'd lost him.

Or had I? Traffic was congested at Highbury Corner roundabout, he couldn't wriggle through as motor-cyclists often can. No, he had to wait his turn like the cars and lorries. From his position in the road I guessed which exit he'd aim for and I raced over a pedestrian crossing, hoping to get ahead of him. I had the mad idea that if he was held up again before he was clear of the roundabout I could jump on the pillion.

Instead I stole a bike. Chris Ionides was on his way home from his garage when suddenly there I was hauling him off his BMW, begging his helmet and tearing away after the receding shape of the intruder who'd claimed to be a messenger but who I'd convinced myself was my Whisperer. He'd spoken like a man disguising his voice.

I had the bigger machine and I knew what the BMW could do. For a good part of the way east my quarry didn't know I was following him. When he tumbled to it, the Kawasaki surged forward and I snaked after it. We went fast. Often very fast. We squirmed through traffic jams and we sliced a path through speeding vehicles on major roads. Then the Kawasaki skidded badly at a junction and I decided it was wiser to hold back and keep him in sight, if I could.

Snow had been replaced by rain but the surface was far from ideal. He had leathers, I had only a leather jacket and no gloves. My boots and jeans were drenched. And yet I knew I was a match for him. Where he went I could go, whatever tricks he tried, Chris's sporty old R100 RS was up to it.

He turned off the road altogether and went across a park, a winter park with snow settled on the grass and no one around. I pursued him. He'd know for sure now, if he'd ever doubted it, that I hadn't given up the chase.

He stared over his shoulder and checked I was there. Slowing he headed for a pavilion, the kind of wooden place that old men sit in on summer afternoons and teenagers deface on summer evenings. He rode behind it and didn't come out the other side. With caution I followed.

I pulled up a shade to the side of the pavilion, ready to wheel away if need be. There was no need. He was straddling the Kawasaki, one foot on the ground and waiting for me. He threw up his visor.

Young Patel.

'You're a good rider,' he said.

'I don't get the practice. What were you looking for in my office?'

It was drearily predictable, or ought to have been if I'd stopped to give it two minutes' thought. He'd decided to see whether I'd gathered any information that connected him with the factory fire. He'd intended to ask but as I wasn't there he'd nosed around and when I startled him he'd panicked.

'Manson did it,' he said. 'No, I don't mean he came round with a box of matches. He'll have sent some heavies to do it, the three guys you saw. He'd been threatening it, not spelling it out but making it obvious something would happen if we didn't cave in and sign. I didn't tell my uncle, he doesn't like pressure. He'd have been on to the police and all sorts.'

'Perhaps he'd have been right.'

'Look, I didn't know Manson meant it. Right? I thought he was just laying it on a bit, trying to get me to push my uncle harder. Manson's the sort who says things. I didn't take that much notice.'

'What other things has he said that you didn't believe?'

'Oh I don't know. He said . . . Well, when I rang him about the woman who'd been hanging round the site he said something like: "Leave it to me, I'll fix her." He said she was an interfering bitch and the time had come to put a stop to her. That sort of thing.'

I rubbed whitened fingers, hoping for warmth. What dark-haired interfering bitches did Robin Digby know? Me, for one.

Yet it hadn't been me at the factory that first time. Who then? And what had Manson done about it? I asked: 'Where was the woman when you rang Manson?'

Patel smiled at his own cunning. 'She was on the empty site. I nailed the bit of wood back in place while she was in there and I phoned him. Manson said I was to go home and forget her, he'd deal with it.'

Young Patel had trapped her on the site and left her to be dealt with by Robin Digby. I presumed Digby hadn't arrived in person, that he'd sent in the men Patel called the heavies. If he'd been there himself he'd have realized the woman wasn't me. She was a smaller woman with an Irish accent and a keen interest in Bethesda and all its doings.

I'd known a woman like that. She'd been fished out of the Thames the day after Patel had left a nosey woman to be dealt with by Digby. I couldn't dream up an explanation for the black hair, other than the banal one of disguise, but I had a sickening version of the rest of it.

I persuaded Patel that there was nothing in my office or my flat or my head that linked him and his uncle to the factory fire, that he knew vastly more than I did about the episode and that my inquiry into Bethesda and all its ramifications was over. I flung a leg over the BMW and wheeled away. When I looked back the Kawasaki was a black dart moving over the grass. We'd gone our separate ways, not fully trusting each other but having no alternative.

A doleful Chris Ionides was waiting at the garage for my return, tinkering with my car. 'The bike, is she all right?'

I hadn't even got through the door. 'Yes, and I'm fine too, thanks.' Funny how Chris invariably cares more about machines than people. Does the kind of life where everything gets ripped apart do that to a man?

He didn't take my word, he inspected the bike for damage and somewhat surprised pronounced her sound. He said my car should be ready the next afternoon, as I'd forced him to put in an extra unscheduled hour on her. I didn't take *his* word for that, but withheld my judgement. He's thorough but he's not fast.

A bus took me up to the hospital to see Gran. Nobody had bothered to replace the defunct green lights on the Christmas tree. I went up to the ward and then I hesitated.

Although visitors were being restricted to close family (me) and similar (Ada Carey) and the clergy (Father Mahon), there was an old crone sitting beside her. I studied the back view of a round-shouldered creature with a snaggle of thinning grey hair caught back in a child's pony-tail grip. Who in the world was this? Gran wasn't going to say, she was fast asleep.

Sister Flynn, the nice nurse from Donegal and Tufnell Park, appeared beside me, all objection, and stormed into the ward. 'Will you come away now, please. What do you think you're doing, forever coming in here and troubling my patient?'

The old woman grumbled. 'You ask too many questions, Flynn.'

'Do I so? Out, please. Will you let my patient alone now. Come along now.' The nurse had the woman's arm and drew her up, allowing no scope for disobedience, and manoeuvred her towards the doorway. I was rooted there.

Too many questions, Flynn. The words on my answering machine. The words in lipstick on my mirror.

The woman swung her gaze up and saw me. 'Is it Laura Flynn you are?'

The growling voice of an old woman with a lifetime's cigarettes down her. The voice on my machine, not a whispering man after all, a husky old woman.

'Hush now,' said Sister Flynn. She was behind the woman and pushing her decisively towards the corridor.

I said: 'Hello, Bridie.' And my voice sounded a long way off.

Bridie MacGuire. Old Gerry MacGuire's wife, the one who was in and out of hospital because she was odd in the head and this time in a different hospital because of a toenail.

I stared at her feet but both were clad in amorphous slippers with fluff around them. She was teased and urged away from Gran's ward and deposited into the care of another nurse who'd been searching the place for her. Bridie was developing a habit of wandering off, it seemed.

'Gran?' I approached the bedside.

Gran opened one eye. A wicked eye, blue and clear as the flowers hand-painted on her favourite porcelain teacups. 'Has she gone, then, Laura? The old fool that she is.'

'You're better!' It was days since we'd been able to have a conversation.

'Sure and I'll be fine and away from here soon if they'll keep that old biddy well away from me. Is it a toenail she's in here for? I'd say it's her manners need fixing.'

I took her hand in mine. 'How are you feeling?'

'With all these pipes and gadgets jammed into me? How would you think it feels? Ask yourself now, Laura, would a body be comfortable this way?'

They say a patient's improving when she starts to grumble. I dared to hope Gran was going to be all right.

Sister Flynn returned, apologizing that Gran had been disturbed by the troublesome creature MacGuire. Gran said she'd been playing dead and Sister Flynn said Gran had made a fine job of it.

Gran said: 'That Bridie MacGuire's mind was turned, she was never the same after her youngest was born. It's a great trial for a family to have a woman talking nonsense at them.'

'Rude nonsense, I dare say,' said the nurse, twiddling about with the pipes and gadgets. 'Didn't she accuse me of asking too many questions?'

Gran said: 'With the name the same it could have been any of us she meant. In Bridie's mind we're all guilty.'

She shut her eyes. I waited a few minutes and then the steady breath of sleep began. For five minutes or so I remained there, thinking about Gran, thinking about Bridie and how she'd badgered and frightened me with her telephoned messages.

One thing continued to bother me about that. Bridie was without doubt the voice on the machine, but there had been other messages apart from the refrain about asking questions. There had been warnings to mind my own business and there had been a threat to kill me.

Well, all right, she was an eccentric old woman whose behaviour and words frequently made no sense. But even so, what had put it into her head that I deserved to die for my nosiness? I scarcely knew her. She wasn't someone I'd had contact with, none of the MacGuires were. Sorry to sound as snobbish as my former mother-in-law, but the MacGuires weren't our kind of people. Bridie wasn't one of the women I'd have bumped into in the normal course of the week. Yet she'd got a hang-up about me.

I turned Gran's hand over and peered at the creases on her palm. How much of this Cheiro stuff did she know and how much did she intuit or make up?

The day Gran told me she'd love to read Mozart's hand was the day that my eldest brother, Danny, was married. My mother had pinched me and sent me smartly down the room to stop Gran because, even with the throng and the distance, she'd spotted what Gran was up to.

'Laura, you're to tell her I say she's an old witch and we want none of her hocus pocus at a Christian wedding.'

'She won't take notice of me, you know what she's like.'

'She'll take every bit of notice if you tell her I'll be down there myself if she doesn't put that man's hand away and give us no more of her nonsense.'

Cross behind a public smile, I went. 'Gran, I'm a messenger from Frances,' I said, 'but you don't really need the message.'

'Will you and your mother interrupt me now,' said Gran, 'when this gentleman and I have found a favourable Line of Fate?'

'Would you go on, Mrs Flynn?' said her subject, happy with her, annoyed with me.

'I will,' said Gran. 'You have a long life and a good time ahead of you.'

'Ah, isn't that what we all wish to hear?' he replied.

I don't recall his name. He died in a car crash two weeks later. Gran said nothing directly to me about it, mentioning only, in a rather pointed way, that when one who practises the art of Cheiro foresees disaster she is honour bound to speak nothing of it.

This didn't tally with her declaration that if she'd read the young Mozart's hand, she'd have steered him towards a smoother path in life, with the result that we'd be richer by many thousands of the genius's works. From what I'd seen of it, a Line of fate was a *fait accompli*.

The sister reappeared. I unravelled my fingers from Gran's, let her hand settle again, and I went outside. 'Where's Mrs MacGuire?' I asked.

The nurse on Bridie's ward didn't want her disturbed. I laughed. 'That one? She never knows whether she's disturbed or not.'

The nurse giggled. 'Well, all right, but don't let her upset the others. There are some of them dozing.'

I fed Bridie jelly babies. I don't know whether they were hers or not, but they were on a locker and they might have belonged to her. I fed them to her in reward for answering my questions. Too many questions, I don't doubt.

'What do Flynns ask too many questions about?' 'What happens to Flynns who ask questions?' 'Who says Flynns ask too many questions?'

So on, round and round like those elephants, until I wearied of it and the jelly babies were depleted. The answers didn't amount to much. I squeezed from her a repetition of one of the threats of violence, word for word as she'd said it in the phone call. But I couldn't tell how much I'd coaxed her and how much was spontaneous. Giving up, I shoved the box of jelly babies back on the locker.

'That's it, Bridie. The end. I'm going now.'

Her vague eyes suddenly focused keenly on me. 'Joe Flynn's gone,' she said, sing-song like a child.

As casually as I could manage I asked: 'Where's he gone?'

'He won't come back. He's gone.'

I battled with my urge to shake it out of her. If I could keep calm, and keep her calm, I might do better. 'Where, Bridie? Please tell me. It's important.'

She sniggered and wiped her hand across her mouth. Her eyes went to the jelly babies.

'You don't get another one,' I bribed, 'until you tell me where he's gone.'

Predictably she gave me an answer and equally predictably it was nonsense. 'Nowhere,' she said. And I repeated it but when I looked at her with tight-lipped doubt, her face puckered and she rubbed at it with her knuckles. 'Nowhere,' she said once more, but by this time she was unconvinced herself.

I stood up. 'I'm off now.' I reached for the jelly babies and mischievously, before I handed her the packet, I said: 'I might come again and ask about Mr Laughton and Mr Tanner.'

I gabbled a bit more twaddle but Bridie had crumpled at the mention of those names. She drew away from me and put her hands over her face. I was frightened. I'd sparked off something I didn't understand. Getting out of the ward fast I left Bridie moaning and rocking herself, hands over her face to hide from the world.

'Tell me everything that you know about Bridie MacGuire,' I said to Ada Carey when I walked into Gran's house half an hour later.

'That's a tall order, even from you,' said Ada. She stood, arched over as usual, a cigarette between her fingers. I hoped she'd be able to get the smell of tobacco out of the house before Gran came home.

'I'll pour us both some of Gran's booze, if I can find any,' I offered, bribing again.

'It's in that cupboard,' said Ada with engaging rapidity.

'Whiskey?'

'Yes, but without the hot milk if you please. It suits Kitty to take it that way in the evening, but it suits me without.'

'Me too.'

I poured tots into two glasses and we sat either side of the fire. 'Go on, Ada,' I pleaded. 'Just start at the beginning and keep going.'

Ada demurred. 'Bridie MacGuire's an old lady. I mightn't live long enough to get to the end of it.'

'Then the sooner you start . . .'

Off she went. Things I knew. Things I couldn't find any

importance in. Things that might have made my hair stand on end if I hadn't been briefed by the files of the local paper and already gathered a certain impression of how the MacGuires behaved in the old days.

Ada had nothing special to say about Bridie herself, the woman had led a quiet life in a sometimes turbulent family. And she'd been odd since the birth of her youngest child, as Gran had said. Bridie's oddness was patchy. She had periods when she was quite well and was at home and busying herself with an undemanding job here and there.

'They say it's good for her to keep herself occupied and not brood,' Ada said.

'Brood on what?'

'Oh, the business of being married into the MacGuires would be enough, I should think. What else might it be?'

I refilled her glass. 'What are these little jobs then?'

'They're nothing,' said Ada, sipping. 'She does cleaning, offices and places like that, for one of those agencies. Well, the people who run it have known Gerry for years and I suppose they give Bridie the work as a favour to him as much as anything. I can't think she's the most reliable body to have . . . Whatever is it, Laura?'

'This agency, what's it called?'

Ada named it. I knew the name. In the morning I'd check but I was already sure of the answer. The agency cleaned the gym. I imagined Bridie MacGuire employed to wash down the floor at the gym. She couldn't have got in there without passing my Flynn Detective Agency sign by the street door. Crazy as she was, I could well believe she'd ventured upstairs and left me a lipsticked message on my mirror.

Ada was nursing her second whiskey in front of the fire when I set off home via Anna Lee's house. We went down to the kitchen.

'Sue's out,' said Anna. 'Jenny's taken her to an event at the Sisterwrite bookshop, an ethnic poetry reading by women of colour. I think the idea is to cheer her up after the hard time she's been giving herself because the man who put her off on Saturday hasn't called her yet.'

'Name no names,' I begged. 'I don't want to hear this.'

'OK. Come and sit by the Aga, it's the only hotspot in the entire house.'

I flung my jacket over a knob near the stove so it would be warm and dry when I went out again, and I pulled up a kitchen chair. I said: 'Where's the rest of the mob?'

'Scattered to the four winds. Drink?'

'Provided it's yours and not Sue's. I'd hate to upset Sue.'

She caught my ironic tone. 'Oh yes, I know you, Laura, you hate to upset anybody.'

I got through my apology rapidly. 'Anna, I'm sorry about last night.'

She brushed it aside with a wave of the hand and filled two wine glasses.

I said: 'I expected you to ring today and tell me what a delightful time you had with Mike until I came home and everything got worse.'

She laughed, remembering. 'Ye-es. It wasn't the easiest couple of hours. Laura, you ought to face it, you've got a problem brewing.'

'Another one?'

'He's come rushing back into your life. If I were you I'd be very sceptical.'

'I'm not the one who let him into my flat.'

'That was an accident of extraordinarily bad timing. I couldn't literally shut the door in his face, now could I?'

'Forgiven,' I said.

'What makes me nervous is that I'm not sure you can either, metaphorically I mean.'

'Anna, it's all right, honestly. I'm making use of him, that's all.'

'Hmm.'

Her concern was laughable. I laughed. 'What do you want me to do? Ask him whether his intentions are honourable?'

'You didn't have an easy time. I wouldn't like to see you risking a repetition.'

'Impossible,' I said, still laughing at her. 'I'm different now, anyway. Tougher. More independent.'

'I know,' said Anna. 'He admires that.'

I stopped laughing. 'Oh dear.'

Anna's seldom wrong about people, except for that blind spot that leaves her oblivious that the women who stay at her house are unashamedly using her. From time to time I throw the odd spotlight on it but I can't make her see it. I did, though, make her understand that I couldn't freeze Mike out at a time when he'd twice helped in the search for my father and might help again. That's life, compromise all the way.

Compromising, I splashed home. Rain was becoming snow again. I kicked hunks of it off my boots on the doorstep and carried my soaking boots upstairs. I needed a new pair but until a new client entered my life I was going to do without. I'd been home around fifteen minutes, I'd showered and was rubbing my hair dry when Mike phoned again.

'Did you meet Tanner?' he began.

'I met a little difficulty instead. He's serving five years for assault and robbery. But it could be worse: he's only up the road in Pentonville and I'm going to drop in for a chat about old times.'

Because Mike had seen the writing on the mirror, I shared with him the news that the mystery had been cleared up.

'Bridie?' He was puzzled.

'Don't be defensive, I know she's a relation of yours.'

'Don't exaggerate, Laura.' Then he *did* become defensive, insisting on getting it right: Bridie was the wife of his mother's second cousin. I was glad again that we don't have phones that let the caller see me, because I couldn't help smiling. Mike was as keen as Della Brenan herself to disclaim any meaningful connection with the dreadful MacGuires.

'And while we're on this tack,' he said, 'will you be going to Polly's party tomorrow night?'

This Polly was another of his distant relations, a friend from my schooldays and a giver of memorable parties.

'I won't if you want to,' I said.

We'd saved our friends embarrassment by avoiding the same events. Not that we'd had amicable discussions about who went where, we'd left people to decide which of us to invite to what. Polly had slipped up because this year we'd apparently both received invitations.

'And I won't if you want to.' Then he broke the deadlock, adding: 'There's something else on tomorrow. I'd more or less decided to go to that instead.'

'Fine.'

We went on to talk about Gran's state of health and what else I might attempt to trace my father. I admitted I had no other leads, apart from the criminal Dave Tanner.

After he'd rung off I switched on the television and saw a version of the news that had excited the elder Patel. Robin Digby was filmed outside Knights End Farm, fielding questions about the disappearance and death of Kate Mullery. He looked appropriately wretched, although I could have imagined that his tension increased when reporters badgered him about Kate's reasons for leaving her business in limbo and running off to the farm, and about his exact relationship with her, and particularly about the evening he came back from tending the deer and found a note saying she'd gone.

None of the questions were new to him. The police would have taken him over the course before their time had run out and they'd had to let him go. But the police have other methods. One of them is to let the press have a free run.

I own up. I have a vivid imagination, I could have been reading more into the situation than was genuinely there and I was severely prejudiced, but he looked a very guilty man to me. Unlike the journalists on the screen, I knew what it was to face Robin Digby when he had a gun in his hand.

FIVE

The quiet married couple who lived in the flat below mine gave me what used to be called an old-fashioned look as I let the policeman into the house. It was only Detective Sergeant Ray Donnelly but they weren't to know that.

Like police detectives the world over Donnelly assumes he passes for the average man in the street, and like the rest of them he looks like a plain-clothes policeman.

I said: 'You'll get me a bad name dropping in here.'

'I've been trying the office but you were never there.'

'I know. I was expecting a call from the police so I kept away.'

'I thought so.'

'How did you find this address?' I'd been hoping to keep it from him.

'A sweet young redhead called Sue gave it to me when I called at Anna Lee's house in the mistaken belief you were still one of her hen party. What happened? Female company get too much for you?'

We said all that going up the stairs, then we were in the flat. I hate the way people's eyes flash over the place, looking for faults and finding them. All I see is a succouring corner that's mine and no one else's, a place to shut out the world when I want to. Alas, the world was invading. First Mike Brenan and now Ray Donnelly. I dreaded to think who might be next.

He stood there, either waiting to be offered a seat or else rejecting the sofa. I couldn't blame him. His contact with the gimcrack chair in my office hadn't been pleasant.

'Laura, there's a dashing young inspector at Rochester Row who wants you. To do with certain events on Sunday evening.'

I mocked the jargon. 'Certain events? Don't you mean an attempt on my life, an abduction, arson, a spot of . . .'

'Can you go and see them this morning?'

'Is this telling or asking, Ray?'

'You're the only witness to some of it and the chief witness to the rest.'

I was afraid of that. The threat of court again, the probability of unwelcome publicity.

I said: 'It'll make me ridiculous. Can't you see the headlines? "Girl Detective Tells Court of Fight for Life with Arsonists and Gunman"?'

The prospect of me looking foolish in court amused him. He waited but I didn't return his grin. He said: 'Well, regard it as free publicity for the agency. Think what newspapers would charge you for that sort of advertising.'

'Oh, *honestly!* I'd appear completely incompetent. It would finish me.'

'With your looks? Come on, Laura, you'd have a queue of rich male clients paying you to look for their lost youth.'

And before I could challenge him about that remark he hurried on to ask whether there was any special reason why I suspected Robin Digby guilty of being involved in a murder.

'Yes,' I admitted. 'And I'd have told you earlier if you hadn't been so damned patronizing.'

Belatedly I described how Digby and Silver Hair met in St Albans and Digby reported that a woman had died because of a mistake.

'I think,' I said, 'it was a case of mistaken identity. The timing tallies too. Kate Mullery died because she was mistaken for me.'

Donnelly sat on the sofa and I sat on the floor and we went through the whole complicated thing. I ended by saying I was waiting to hear what connection Digby had with Bethesda or Shirlands.

'Ring him now,' suggested Donnelly.

I dialled Peter's number. The secretary said he was unavailable and would be unable to call me back that day.

I shrugged, more concerned with my impending visit to

187

Pentonville that afternoon than with any residual puzzles about the Kate Mullery affair. Regrettable, but understandable, how my enthusiasm had tailed off once I'd discovered I wasn't going to be paid for any of it.

Donnelly said: 'You talked your way in once.'

'That's what I was thinking.' I looked at my watch. 'There's just time, if I'm lucky and he's there and not truly hooked up in meetings all day. But I do have to be back here this afternoon. I've got something very important on.'

'Another stray cat?' asked Donnelly getting up.

'A stray, that's right.' I touched St Lucy for luck. Stray pets, stray fathers, what wouldn't she do if one had the faith?

Donnelly said: 'Don't forget to talk to Rochester Row about arson and attempted murder, will you, Laura?'

'*Mañana*,' I replied.

He sketched a wave and let himself out.

I rummaged through my wardrobe for an outfit that would look respectable and be warm. Power dressing was called for again. Would the charm work a second time?

The secretaries were valiant but I employed all the tenacity of which Peter had accused me. No, I didn't barge into his office but I contrived to learn which other one his meeting was in. I lurked in a passage to trip him up as he came out.

The secretary caught me there and cuttingly remarked that it would do no good, that he was a very busy man and would be unwilling to see me.

I said: 'Never mind, I'll have a word with him at lunchtime.'

'I'm afraid not,' she said, taking pleasure in crisp refusal. 'He has a working lunch today.'

At that she let herself into the room where the meeting was taking place. I heard the bumble of men's voices as the door opened. I didn't wait for it to shut. I skipped into her office and spun her desk diary round. That's how I knew where to find him at lunchtime.

The restaurant was one of those that delights in the description 'discreet'. Plenty of space between the tables, privacy ensured. I arrived early and asked for Peter's table, then ordered a glass of Perrier to soothe me while I waited. I guessed that was the only item on the menu to which my budget would stretch.

The table was set for three. I was gambling on Peter getting there first, but had no reason to suppose the odds were good. With nothing else to read, I pretended to be absorbed by my pocket diary, and tried not to look at my Spiro Agnew watch too often. Down the room the head waiter was being solicitous to a foreign woman in a sable coat. All the fur coats in London are worn by foreign women these days.

In my head I carried on an argument.

'I shouldn't be here at all, this is Ray Donnelly's doing.'

'Ah but you've got a better chance of success than he has. A policeman walks in and the thing's blown.'

'How come then, if I'm so valuable to the Met., Ray's always putting me down?'

'Historical reasons. Didn't you once say no when he wanted you to say yes.'

'But that's crazy. We were both at school then.'

'So what?'

'No, I refuse to believe Ray Donnelly's eaten up with teenage rancour.'

'No, you're right. But what is it then?'

'I don't know.'

'Nor me.'

Peter came in. The head waiter did his pandering-to-favourite-customers act, and presumably mentioned that Peter's guest was already ensconced because my quarry advanced eagerly. Me, I shrank into the wallpaper.

I won't claim he recoiled in horror, that would be overstating it. Slightly.

'*You!* What the hell are you doing here?' This in a head-turning whisper.

I said: 'Trying everything I know to get two minutes' conversation with you, Peter. Sit down. People are looking.'

189

He sat down. Fuming.

'Laura, I'm expecting guests. They'll be here any moment and I want you gone. Understood?'

'Perfectly. And I'll be on my way immediately we've discussed what I've come about.'

'You're to go now.'

I looked at my watch. 'You're wasting time.'

His hands, on the tablecloth, were clenched. I didn't expect him to lay hold of me and propel me through the door, but I'm sure he wanted to. That determined jaw I mentioned earlier, well it was more so.

I said, spelling it out to deprive him of possible loopholes of ambiguity: 'What inquiries have you made following our talk on Monday about Robin Digby and Shirlands and Bethesda?'

'You agreed to drop this, Laura.'

'No, I agreed not to pursue my own inquiries on condition you provided me with certain answers.'

'I'm not going to be bullied by you.'

My watch hand had moved on a minute. 'You've wasted a whole minute.'

He took a deep breath, ran a finger over the smoothness of the damask, made a decision, kept the finger stroking the linen as he spoke. 'Digby has many business interests and Bethesda is one of them. He used to be active in a company called Larches but that was linked with Bethesda and a few years ago . . . God, you won't follow this, I don't know why I'm bothering.'

I said: 'The companies were in financial difficulties, the accountants played games and the companies swapped names and carried on in business. I know the background. Concentrate on Digby.'

'Well that's his Bethesda connection.' He swivelled his head to the door.

'I'll let you know when they arrive,' I said. 'Now what about Shirlands and the boss man with the silver hair?'

He hesitated. 'That's more difficult, Laura.'

'Oh no it's not. It's nearer you. I can't believe you've had time to dig up the old news about Digby but not the new.'

'*Easy*, did you say?' He rolled his eyes seeking heavenly confirmation of my stupidity.

My watch had knocked off another minute.

'Please, Peter.'

The door was opening. A man and a woman were entering. I don't know why but I'd assumed he was expecting two men. Silly sexist assumption, no doubt.

Peter took up a knife and sketched patterns with it on the linen. He said: 'Digby had a hand in the sale of Bethesda to Shirlands.'

'And Shirlands's interest wasn't in the clothing business but in the land Bethesda owned, parcels like the riverside site?'

This time it was a sensible assumption.

'Yes. Bethesda owned the freehold of an old factory. Digby understood he could get the leaseholders out but they proved intractable. He'd done a deal and he couldn't deliver.'

The head waiter was fawning over the couple near the door.

I said: 'In that case somebody at Shirlands equally misunderstood the position about that factory lease.'

'And you know who.' He flopped the knife down on to the tablecloth. 'So there you are.'

'It surprises me that Shirlands's top man should be involved with Digby in a rather petty thing like that.'

'He wasn't so senior when it happened. There've been changes since.'

That look we exchanged clearly stated that there could be more changes yet. Behind Peter's back I could see the waiter leading the man and woman forward.

'Congratulations,' I said.

Peter cocked an eyebrow at me.

I said: 'On whatever advantages you've gained from all this.'

'Oh . . . er.' He was nicely flustered.

I rose to leave. 'There's no need to thank me, Peter,' I said. And went.

I had an appointment to keep, an appointment with my past. I left Peter keeping an appointment with his future. The man who'd arrived was one of the high-powered figures I'd seen around the Shirlands building, the woman a face I recognized from the business page of newspapers.

The waiter bowed as he held the door for me. He concealed his puzzlement beautifully. No, Peter's world was no longer my world at all.

Caledonian Road. Pentonville Prison. Sleet. That kind of afternoon.

They have a smell, prisons. A smell of despair and failure. The bunch of visitors going in had it too. My friend's husband had waved a wand and my permission to visit had arrived magically fast. I reported at the gate and then stood around, cold and wet and waiting. To cheer myself up I thought about the inmates who never ever had anything to do but kill time. One day at a time. For Dave Tanner five years of it, less remission.

He was a gaunt man, an old-looking Londoner although I estimated his true age to be around sixty. He'd been my father's contemporary which would have put him in that slot.

Tanner had nicotined teeth and fingers but the rest was pallor and grey hair. I strove to picture him robbing and assaulting but it defeated me. Caged, they were all pathetic.

He was intrigued by my inquiry but wary. Ray Donnelly's crack about my appearance made me wonder whether Tanner, if he had no young female visitors, mightn't scheme to drag out our talk over several visits. Convicted prisoners are allowed visits once a fortnight, for half an hour. If he prevaricated we could take months over it. He was answering slowly, it gave me time for wild fancies.

Reluctantly he spoke about my father. I prompted him with mention of Laughton who'd fallen to his death. Tanner, I'd heard, had also been angry about the dangers of the sites.

Hadn't he been a union man? Hard to accept now. That had been Tanner in a different incarnation.

He said: 'He was a man who wanted things done right, your dad. He never liked the corners cut and the dodgy methods. But they were the things that made the money. Dead men's lives didn't appear in the balance sheets. Yes, I remember Laughton. I wouldn't call him thick but he wasn't used to London. Didn't look out for himself, if you know what I mean.'

'I've heard that after he died my father planned to get something done.'

'Yes, but . . . Look, I don't know why you're getting into all this.'

'I told you, Dave. My gran's in hospital after a heart attack. She asks for Joe. She's afraid she'll die without seeing him again.'

There was a fine line of sweat on his top lip. He dabbed at it with the back of his hand. 'But, the thing is . . . I mean, what good does it do?'

'She hasn't much life left in her, and she's asked me to trace him.'

'It's a big old world. He could be anywhere.'

I laughed, echoing Bridie MacGuire. 'Or nowhere.'

His eyes became slits. 'What do you mean?'

'Oh I don't mean anything.' I sighed, drained by disappointments. Tanner was going to let me down as the other routes had. 'Yes I do, I mean I haven't found a soul who saw him after he left the corner pub. Well, I suppose even knowing he went into the pub is an advance on what I knew a week ago. Since I was four years old I've been taught that he walked out of the front door and was never seen again.'

Tanner nodded. 'Yeah, he called in for a drink. On his way to the site where Laughton bought it. Going to take a look around and then have it out next day with the foreman about the sloppy way things were run.'

I sensed a door opening on to the past, a door Tanner had preferred to keep locked. 'Did you go with him?'

'Me? No, I was at home. Union work, I used to do a bit of that. Uphill, it was. How do you unionize a trade that's full of Paddies, here one week and off to the Emerald Isle the next? What did they ever want with unions? Christ! *Me*, trying to change things by honest endeavour.' He shook his head in disbelief at the Tanner who used to be.

'Do you know whether he reached the site?' Maudie, the little mouse behind the bar in the pub that evening, had understood him to say he was going home first and out to the site later. He could have changed his mind.

Tanner hesitated long enough for his denial to be worthless.

I pushed him, not bearing to see the door slam shut. 'Please, if you don't know what happened at least tell me what you *think* did!'

Pushing had been the wrong method, he was evasive, grave. 'If Kitty Flynn's going to die, then she's going to die. Nothing that happened over twenty years ago is going to make a lot of difference.'

I swallowed and fought back my frustration. He didn't understand, but then why should he? It's facile to trust in a common human experience, apart from the very basics of life there isn't one. Dave Tanner's life and Gran's and mine were utterly different. How could I dare to blame him for not understanding how I was feeling?

'Just say it,' I pleaded.

He lit another cigarette, fragments of tobacco falling on to the table between us. Frugally he swept them into a minute heap, unwilling to lose them. He ran a tongue over cracked browned lips. Then: 'He went up to the palaces estate, those flats in Holloway. Laughton had been killed on Hampton. Well, Joe Flynn went up there to take a look. I reckon he saw enough because he told the security man he'd be back when the day shift began and he'd be speaking to the foreman.'

At last I was getting somewhere. Only the first step on a long, winding trail but at last I was taking that step.

Tanner said: 'He never saw the foreman. Before he left the

palaces he ran into Jock Currie. Jock was the law around there, not the foreman. A tough case, always was. Backhanders to get on the sites, anything like that was in Jock's line. A one-man bloody mafia, if you want to know.'

'Yes, I've heard of him.' A bad name from a bad period. The backnumbers of the newspaper had concealed him but he'd been a local legend.

Tanner sucked on the cigarette. He said: 'He's dead.'

'I know,' I replied. 'He died in Parkhurst serving fifteen years for . . .'

'No, Laura.'

And there was a pause on its way to infinity before his next whispered words. 'I don't mean Currie.'

'*Sweet Jesus!*'

The room was shaking. I was desperately cold, then burning. I had thoughts that never became words. And the words Tanner spoke to me were tangled, battered things that said nothing.

'Oh Jesus,' I gasped. 'My *father*.'

'Joe Flynn,' he said, with the pain of remembered horror.

I clutched for the proverbial straw. 'Is this real?' Was it guessing, not knowing?

'I'm not saying who was there and who wasn't,' he said quickly. And so I had my answer.

Tanner claimed he'd heard it secondhand, that he'd been told Joe Flynn had crossed Currie and been killed. Ginger MacGuire had had a role in it and within six months Ginger himself had died on his own unsafe scaffolding. Did I invent Tanner's vague hint that Ginger's death was in the nature of retribution?

Numb, I managed a hideous question: 'What happened to . . .'

'He's under Nonesuch House. It's what they did, isn't it, when they wanted to get shot of a body. Bury it under a building, everybody in the know's too scared to speak out and the body's never found. It's just like the man walked out of his house and disappeared.'

Breathing was difficult. *Of course* it was all dreadfully obvious, if you inhabited a world where you were prepared for that kind of disaster to befall people you knew. I wasn't. And Gran? She'd lived through those years in a way I hadn't. Plainly she hadn't been prepared for it either.

Oh, Gran. How was I going to tell her this?

Our half hour was up. Time for us to go, me out into the December bitterness to struggle with the unreality of what I'd learned. And Tanner back to his cell and the ersatz society of prison. He wished me a merry Christmas before he went.

A long way down Caledonian Road I realized I'd missed my turning. Taking the nearest street on my left I walked uphill. Wreaths were lashed to front doors. Christmas trees winked in windows. Children had sprayed imitation snow on panes to match the natural stuff outside. A snowman was lopsidedly creeping away in a front garden. There was even a real-live robin posing on a snow-capped gatepost. Why did nobody care that my father was dead?

I went into the gardens in Barnsbury Square. Snow lay unblemished on the lawns and bowed the camellias and lilacs. The roof of the gardener's hut and the dark earth were blindingly white. Everything in my world was violently reversed.

Standing beneath a stark tree, I shuffled my emotions, striving to get beyond shock but floundering from outrage to sorrow and always coming back to a stubborn refusal to accept. I'd never imagined him dead. And how could I, when he'd always been with me through the gift of St Lucy? I'd imagined him in a life far away – in Ireland or America, where the rumours had placed him – and I'd never found it in my heart to blame him for going there. A free spirit myself, I secretly admired a freer one. To deny his right to choose his own path, was to deny myself that right too.

The youngest, I'd been protected from the anguish of his

going, and mine was a family that absorbed its hurt. He was not cursed, he was simply absent. He wasn't there, therefore I'd invented him.

How genuine was it, that treasured memory of him squatting in front of me, hands outstretched as he fastened around my small child's non-existent neck the fine gold chain bearing the golden saint? How accurate, the recollected scratchiness of the bark as he stood me against a tree in the gardens and raised his camera?

A cat slunk from the gardener's hut and joined me under the tree, coiling its sleek tail around my legs and murmuring comfort. The tears were hot against my cheeks. I dried my eyes on gloved fingers and felt through pockets for a handkerchief.

The cat anticipated food, then, contemptuous of my failure, diverted its attention to a bush and posed there, sniffing Sylvia Plath's 'barbarous holly with its viridian scallops'. It was better than I was at the charade of not caring.

Tanner had opened one door to the past but he'd slammed the door to childhood.

'You've only got Dave Tanner's word for any of this and he's not the most reliable source,' I sniffled.

Suspicion set in. Suspicion that was born of hope. If Tanner's story was true, it put the responsibility for my father's murder on two dead men. Extraordinarily neat if the living were to avoid getting their come-uppance. No, I couldn't accept Tanner's version uncorroborated. What's more, I knew who I was going to confront.

There was a second gnawing doubt. How many people knew the truth and had let me grow up without it, turning aside my queries with lies and evasion? It had been left to Tanner, an outsider, to say what had to be said. My tribe had let me down. Me and Joe Flynn.

The cat dispensed with pride and strutted stiff-leggedly beside me as I crossed the garden and began my walk to Anna's house. This time I didn't fling my coat cosily by the Aga, I slumped over her table still wearing it, my hands folded around a glass of hot thick red wine as if it contained holy treasure, a truth. The treasure, the kitchen, the friendship were all smudged by my unshed tears.

Anna said: 'Oh, Laura.'

She said it like Mike Brenan had said it when I'd announced that Gran was dying and wanted my father at the deathbed. Pitying. I got furious with her.

I said: 'You think I'm a fool not to have thought of this, don't you? Stupid Laura Flynn who's supposed to be a detective and can't see the nose on her face.'

She was at her calmest. She welcomed my anger. 'No, I think it's too close for you to make your usual judgements. If he were anyone else's father you'd have said right off: well, twenty years is a long time, there's been no definite sighting of him, no word, could be he's dead.'

'And I'd have checked whether the death had been registered here or in Ireland or the States. And it wouldn't have been, would it? Murderers don't fill in forms reporting deaths. I'd have gone on believing he was around somewhere, happy. Anna, I've always believed in *happy*.'

The treasure blurred some more and I raised the glass for the first time and let the bitter dark wine and its infusion of herbs flow over my tongue.

Anna was saying: 'You're convinced that what Tanner says is true, but . . .'

I gulped another mouthful of wine. 'I'll seek corroboration, of course. But, yes, I'm convinced. So many snippets of information come clattering into place if Tanner's story is true. And I know he believes it to be true.'

She questioned whether it would have been possible to keep a man's death secret and I snapped: 'Secret from the police, yes. Secret from my family and their friends, yes. But an awful lot of other people would have known. And those responsible, they'd have been confident of the secret being contained. Think of it, Anna. A big immigrant community that sorted things out its own way and didn't go running to the police. Too many complicated allegiances and dependencies for tale-bearing. And don't forget this, most of them thought they'd be going home again with a pile of money, scattering and never meeting up again. They didn't know London was for ever.'

Why should she appreciate the depth of my hurt that the tribe had failed me? I'd never, as I'd gullibly believed, been comfortably protected by it, I'd been spurned. Not for faults of my own but because I was reaching for the handle on the cupboard where it kept its secrets.

No, she couldn't appreciate it, but I made her hear it anyway. We drank another glass each of the deep red wine and then I got up to go. The kitchen shimmered. No breakfast, no lunch except for a glass of Perrier in an expensive restaurant waiting for Peter, and now Anna's mulled wine.

I pulled myself together. She was saying I should stay on but I was suddenly desperate to be home. Alone. I'd used her as a listener and now I was going to cast her off, because my needs had changed. Anna, whom I chided for letting herself be used by the rest of her friends. Here I was, doing the same thing myself. I hadn't even asked her how the book was going.

She said, as she saw me off into the snow: 'Will you tell your grandmother what you've learned?'

I bit a lip. 'That's the worst of it. Once I've got more than Tanner's say-so, I'll have to. I can't feed her false hopes, I can't lie to a dying woman. It would be . . . like *them*.'

Anna threw her arms around me and held me a second before I stepped out into the white flurry that filled the streets.

Alone at the flat I made the telephone call I'd intended to make that morning if Ray Donnelly hadn't blundered in. I spoke to a supervisor at the cleaning agency, spun a story and received confirmation that Bridie MacGuire had been working at the gym the evening before I found my office entered and my Whisperer's lipsticked message.

Then I drank the coffee I'd begun to make before the call and, after a couple of cups, I forced myself to pick up the phone again. It wasn't that I felt like attending to any of this, merely that it was the only way I knew to stop my thoughts swirling as uncontrollably as the snow outside. I had a lifetime's memories to readjust, but not now. Not yet.

I dialled and waited. Ray Donnelly came on the line and I reported on my exchange with Peter at lunchtime. He was interested, pleased with what I'd come up with but that didn't stop him sniping at my methods.

'Remind me never to do a deal with you, Laura, if this is how you keep your side of a bargain.'

'Oh that's nothing,' I said airily. 'Peter and I have a history of lying to each other.'

'Is that so?'

I skipped away from the topic and retaliated. 'Mind you, you're not entirely reliable yourself, Detective Sergeant Donnelly. What about the mugger whose jaw turned out not to be broken after you'd used his delicate state to blackmail me into helping you look for Kate Mullery?'

'I can't hear a word you're saying, Laura.' He hung up, laughing.

I made a sandwich, showered, dressed in the fancy Kate Mullery dress and dried my hair carefully. The waves hung long and smooth down my back. Then I made up my face and I dithered over my two best pairs of ear-rings. I'd given up wanting to be alone. I was on my way to Polly's party.

Polly's party was near the Angel. A big house by the Grand Union Canal, it could have been the subject for Sickert's *Hanging Gardens of Islington*. She'd done very well for herself.

I hitched a lift from a friend whom I knew would be driving past my flat to get there. That way I arrived clean and neat.

In the car, in the dark, talking of one thing and another, I created a mask of carefree composure. The tribe had damaged me but I remained a member of it, I could be rejected but not removed from membership. Tonight I was going to take part in one of its dearest rituals, drinking and laughing and talking to excess. Wasn't it Wilde who described the Irish as the best talkers after the Greeks? Polly's parties were the best *craic* in town. Who, with an invitation, would care to stay away? Not me, not tonight, because I needed to look them in the eye, these open-hearted people with their black-hearted secrets.

'Laura! Darling!' Polly flung herself on me with an exuberant embrace. She'd taken to 'darling', along with Alaïa clothes and Emma Hope shoes, when she'd got rich. I don't know what the nuns who'd taught us at school would have made of her. But no matter, we all changed and an excess of Anglicized affection wasn't the worst one could do.

Wincing, she drew her cheek from mine. 'Everyone's so cold, it must be hell out there. Come and have a drink and get warm.'

She passed me on to a young man with a tray of wine glasses. My hand went for white fizz. All around me people were greeting each other excitedly, pushing across the room in answer to cries of welcome, casting around to catch the eye of new arrivals.

There was noise, warmth, closeness and above it all the sound of a *ceili* band with a Donegal fiddler, all aggressive rhythmic drive. I felt myself closing in. My face kept up the carefree composure but inside of me I was drawing away. Afraid to connect with the people there, simply afraid of them.

An arm slid around my waist. 'Laura, you're more beautiful than ever. Isn't that what all the fellas tell you, now?'

Automatically I smiled, joining in the banter. I'd known the man since I was tiny, he was being kind, it was only his way of rescuing me from the sidelines. He'd invariably been kind to me, but which side was he on? Was he one who knew about my father or one who didn't? A dozen faces concealed the same mystery.

Like a good guest I went through the motions of having a good time. I drank, too much, but so did everybody else. I was teased and did my share of teasing. I listened to gossip and I handed it out. Over and over I answered sympathetic inquiries about Gran, and I had no reason to suspect the sincerity of the questioners. Except that they mightn't always have been on the side of the Flynns.

And Polly herself? Where was she in all this? Her short blonde head bobbed, her huge ear-rings swung, as she mixed the people from her old life with the people in her new life. Lively, active, the centre of attention as she'd always been, even in a gymslip. Which side of the divide was Polly on? Connected to the Brenans on Mike's father's side, might she be linked vaguely with the MacGuires too?

I cut off these meandering thoughts. Too simplistic, I reminded myself. Not one tribe riven by one incident, albeit an incident central to the life of the Flynns. No, there were bits of numerous tribes edged together by history and the necessities of immigration.

A man beside me spoke. 'This is altogether too happy an evening for frowning, Laura.'

Mike Brenan.

Again.

I switched off the frown. Managed a smile. Pretended it didn't feel as though half the room were watching us and the other half were being nudged and about to.

I said: 'I thought you'd something else on tonight.'

'This sounded better.'

I was on guard. I thought: 'I'm going crazy, I'm actually wondering about Mike in the way I've been wondering about the rest of them. He can't have known anything. Can he?'

I dared myself to ask him and warned myself off. There were subtler ways of finding out if I genuinely thought it worth pursuing. I didn't have to turn the matter into a public spectacle, add to the sum of gossip.

'Convince me,' I said. 'What was the other thing?'

'A cruise on the river.'

'A bit touristy, isn't it?'

He was ironic. 'It's said to be rather thrilling, floating beneath a floodlit Tower of London at blackest night.'

'Yet you prefer Islington with the old crowd? We're touched, Mike. All of us.'

'Oh, it was only a business invitation,' he said. 'Shirlands are, as you might say, pushing the boat out to entertain people who do business with them.'

My spine registered the name. 'A pity you missed the boat, it could have been fun.'

'Ah but it doesn't start yet a while.' He read his watch. 'I might just go on to it.'

'I see.'

We looked at each other. I saw, I really did. I thought of Anna Lee's warning about letting Mike back into my life, and I thought about Shirlands's Christmas party and how much it would interest me to be there.

I said: 'I'd hate to offend Polly.'

'We both would.' He read his watch again. 'Half an hour?'

'Fine.'

We separated and he went to talk soccer to a man who claimed not to have missed an Arsenal home game in thirty years. I hooked up with a group of people who were wringing their hands over Kate Mullery. One of the men, older than me by far, was saying that he knew her parents quite well. He'd telephoned them after the news of her death.

He said: 'The pity of it is that she ever took up with that Digby man. The Mullerys couldn't talk her out of it, he'd persuaded her the thing to do was to come over to England and he'd the money to help her do it.'

A woman asked: 'Did they say what they thought about her getting engaged to this Digby?'

Other heads in the group nodded, adding their curiosity to hers. Another woman said: 'They can't have been happy about that, not at all.'

The man replied: 'They were puzzled right enough. Kate herself had never breathed a word of it to them and they reckoned they were close to the girl. As far as they knew he was a family friend helping her out financially. The idea of an engagement came as a shock, I can tell you.'

Then the young man with the wine swooped on us and the conversation broke into fragments as people held out glasses to be topped up and moved away in twos and threes as other friends caught their eyes.

I went upstairs, searching for an unoccupied bathroom. Polly's house boasts many bathrooms, or that's how it seems to the owner of a compact flat with but one. On the landing I met Mrs Brenan.

The grape silk had been replaced by a drift of plum-coloured chiffon. Why do I always describe her in terms of fruit? Bizarre, considering how unfavourably I view her. Anyway, there she was on the landing in front of me, pure elegance. The Mrs Brenan who beneath the trimmings was no more than Deirdre MacGuire.

I'd meant to confront her but not here and now. However, I plunged in and asked her whether she'd remembered any more. I did it clumsily, with a provocative remark tying her MacGuire second cousins to Joe Flynn's last moments.

Not only was I clumsy, but I must have been a mite fierce because she was backed up against a row of hunting prints and looking as uncertain of her future as the fox over her left shoulder. I heard myself saying: 'Not everyone's scared to remember. Why don't you admit you've been fobbing me off, you and the rest of the MacGuires? It's a MacGuire secret, isn't it? You've always known that much, at least.'

She was holding up her hands to ward me off. I took a couple of paces back. No need to get within scratching distance, I had her cornered. She was staying there until she'd provided me with explanations.

Her hand was clawing at the plum chiffon around her throat. 'Laura, please, you mustn't do this. All these accusations, these eternal questions of yours . . .'

'I've a right to know. *You* know, it's only fair I should.'

'I've told you . . .'

'. . . nothing! You've misled me. Gerry MacGuire's misled me. Bridie's threatened my life, echoing threats she heard long ago. Did you know that? Well, she has.' I parroted the death threats from my answering machine, the warning on my mirror. I said: 'But she said it to my face in the end. Mad as she is, she spoke the truth to me in the end.'

'Laura, move out of my way. I have nothing to tell you. You're obsessed with events that are long buried.'

I laughed in her face. 'Like Joe Flynn's body under Nonesuch House?'

And that's when the hand from her throat went to her mouth. I can't say she stared at me astonished that I knew the truth, because instead she turned her face from me. She doubled over and her body was wracked as the very chic Mrs Brenan was sick on Polly's carpet.

Almost sick. She retched, ineffectually, made it to the bathroom and she made it there with me on her tail. Never lose an advantage, never have a door shut in your face if you can help it. I waited while she heaved over the washbasin.

Her watery reddened frightened eyes gazed at me in the mirror. She mouthed 'Get out' but the words didn't come. She cupped her hand and sipped water, so confused she got the hot tap instead of the cold one. And all the while I was at her, taunting her that she was hiding the truth. The truth about murder.

Then she recovered herself, drying her face on the rich pile of Polly's blue towels. She cut me off furiously, falling back on her superior manner, the one I'd never permit to unnerve me again.

'These are wild and slanderous allegations,' she said. 'You've no proof to substantiate them and you never will. There's a roomful of people downstairs who could tell you your story is fantasy.'

I broke in, saying: 'It takes just one to tell the truth, and I've found that one.' No, I didn't reveal it was Dave Tanner in

Pentonville or that he'd attributed all calumny to two dead men. Let her worry longer.

She ignored what I'd claimed, saying the truth was that Joe Flynn had walked out on me and that every other man in my life had done the same thing.

The truth is unreasonably painful. I wanted to hit her.

A hand pushed open the door, a voice apologized and went away to find another bathroom. Mrs Brenan was haranguing me about my inability to leave well alone. I continued to want to hit her.

Instead, I forced myself to walk out, to leave her having the last word and as many more as she required. Thank God for the band jigging away below, drowning us out with their jollier kind of noise.

People were eating. I was in need of food but I felt sickened. Recklessly I took another drink, nonsense in my mind about needing it to steady me. The half hour evaporated. I floated casually towards the hall, one of Polly's helpers fetched me my coat. Too cold to wait outside, I dawdled in the hall.

Mike didn't come. I waited five minutes, then another five. And I conjured up a series of fanciful scenes to explain his delay, scenes that involved his mother relaying the row we'd had and forbidding Mike to see me again. Rubbish like that.

Well, there was a choice. I could hand my coat back and rejoin the party or I could leave. I left. I reached the pavement to see Mike's car pull away from the kerb a little way off. Why hadn't I done the intelligent thing and gone outside? I'd known his car must be there, and now he'd . . .

A taxi came down the street and I was in the road, arm outstretched. 'Westminster Pier,' I told the driver.

I sat in the back in absurdly high spirits. 'Cinderella *will* go to the ball.'

Westminster Pier was busy. The snow had stopped but the air was breathtakingly cold. I saw a boat, a squared-off white thing with open decks, a flat roof and glittering people on board. I paid off the taxi.

A man who'd plainly taken a degree in repelling boarders repelled me. No ticket, no admittance. My story about mislaying my partner didn't get me as far as the gang plank.

So where was Mike? Had he beaten the taxi to the finishing line, or had he changed his mind and gone home, or taken up with someone more promising, or was he still on his way? The last option seemed the likeliest as the cab had been quick.

I hung around, the cold crippling me through thin party shoes. Other cars came and other people boarded and there was no Mike. Another man took over duty on the gangway and I tried my luck again. The answer was still no, but he was more sympathetic. 'We're leaving in a minute,' he said, 'but you can catch up with us because we're calling to take on extra supplies at St Katherine's Dock.'

Resigned, I turned away. Once a bright smile and a pleasant approach would have got you in anywhere but everything's ruled by security now. Did I look like an assassin? Oh well, no doubt a taxi would come along and I'd get home in time for an early night. I was beginning to think more sensibly, the coldness was sobering.

But along with sobriety came frustration that my best chance of getting to Silver Hair and a few answers about Robin Digby and Kate Mullery was moving down river on the tide. When the taxi came I asked for St Katherine's Dock.

There was a rubber band in my coat pocket. I caught my hair back on the nape of my neck. I pulled my coat collar up, wrapped the coat around me and tied the belt. If no one saw my shoes I might get away with it.

At the dock I asked a couple of people before I lit on one who could tell me where a cruise boat might pick up supplies. I expected a building but found myself aboard a boat. A boat that wasn't going anywhere. A boat that was loaded with drink and crockery and food. Fine. Exactly what I wanted.

'I'm a waitress,' I said when a young black man asked. 'I've missed the *Myosotis* when she sailed from Westminster.'

He queried me without words. Then: 'Any boat that *sailed* I'd sure like to know about, sister.'

'OK, OK,' I said. 'I'm a landlubber, I confess. Now. When is she due here and please will you let me aboard when she comes?'

His eyes were sharp, nostrils smelling a rat. Maybe two.

I said: 'Please. I need the cash, I can't afford to miss this one.'

A slow smile spread across his face: 'Sure, sister, I understand.'

'Good,' I said faintly, smelling a rat or two myself. Anyway he let me on board, I mean further on board because I'd parted with terra firma some while before.

He followed me. 'You got a big job on tonight, sister. Big Brass. Know what I mean?' And I wished I could read his wink because written in it was a whole vocabulary I didn't speak.

There were two young women on the supplies boat, fussing over trays of food. Instinct made me suspicious of the man with the wink. I asked one of the women, they couldn't have been out of their teens: 'What happens when the *Myosotis* pulls in?'

One with wisps of blonde hair escaping from her cap said: 'Not a lot. She's asked for some glasses, that's all.' She watched my eyes go to the trays of canapés. She said: 'No, this lot's for the *Jemima*, she's due in afterwards. I'm going to shove this at them. They'll be half a mile down-river before they discover it's inedible.'

She laughed. Her companion with the hennaed hair laughed. I laughed.

I said: 'When the *Myosotis* comes, which of you goes on board?'

They both squinted at me. 'Why?' they said in unison.

I repeated the lie about being a waitress who'd missed the boat. I got the double squint again.

'Waitress,' said Blonde Wisps, very flat.

'My arse,' said Henna.

'Look,' I said, 'I have to be on that boat.'

More narrowing of the eyes. Blonde Wisps said: 'Well it

could be worked. I mean, don't think you've fooled us about the waitressing thing. We've seen a few waitresses in our time, eh, Maureen?'

'Certainly have,' said Maureen. 'And you know what, Doreen? This ain't one of 'em.'

I said: 'Please, I have to be on that boat.'

Maureen winked at Doreen and said: 'What's the usual rate for helping out a working girl?'

I already had my fingers around a twist of notes. 'It's this much,' I said. 'And it includes the cap and gown, OK?'

Four eyes blinked down at the ready money. Two voices breathed assent. Slowly Maureen undid her overall. Slower, Doreen took out the hairgrips that secured her cap to her head.

That's how I boarded the *Myosotis*, dressed as a skivvy and carrying a box of wine glasses. I was also, unobtrusively, I hoped, carrying my coat.

Maureen slid back a door beside her and the *Myosotis* was in position with a door to her lower deck open. The last I heard of my fellow conspirators was Maureen saying: 'I don't think I'd fancy it on a boat.'

And Doreen replying: 'It's not as if it's a boat with cabins.'

The *Myosotis* didn't linger, she gave me time to leap on board and, she surmised, leap back on the supplies boat. Instead I dumped the box of glasses and scuttled into the Ladies' washroom, where I shed the rubber band holding my hair, and ripped off the overall and cap which I rolled up and left on a shelf. I deposited my coat in the cloakroom and was ready to enter into the Christmas spirit.

It was a swell party. So many famous faces were there it was a gossip columnist's dream. There he was, Silver Hair, lording it. Not far from his elbow was Peter, smiling as I hadn't seen for a decade. And there was the woman who'd been lunching with Peter, and there was the man ditto.

Around them were a bevy of big business names and television faces, people who cared to be closest to the folks who were perceived to matter. Until this moment I hadn't thought of Peter as one of the folks who mattered. For heaven's sake, Peter was just Peter, the man I'd frolicked with and been disappointed with.

Hold on. How had this come about? He wasn't so very important he was only a . . .

Oh, I see.

So that's what he'd done. That's how he'd used the information I'd given him. He'd . . .

He saw me. I ducked behind a bunch of wine-swilling junior executives, but I didn't duck fast enough. Peter had seen me but he couldn't leave the people he was with, that would never have done. He signalled with a well-trained eyebrow and a minion moved in his stead.

'Excuse me, madam.'

I elected not to hear.

'Madam?'

I whispered from the corner of my mouth that if he wished to avoid a scene he'd better leave me alone. The man retreated confused by the nature of his instructions and the undeniable logic with which I prevented him carrying them out. Good, I like to see unthinking ciphers bested. Quite makes my day.

Unlike Polly's party there was no warmth in this one, merely the synthetic good humour you find where a crowd of people know that it's politic to give the impression of having a good time. The theatre and television folk were most practised at keeping the smiles in place, the captains of industry almost in the same league. Low down the scale one witnessed the occasional doubt that this was a sensible way to spend an evening, feeling disconnected from reality, conniving at a spurious affection for Shirlands in the hope of doing business with the company in future. Mike Brenan would have fallen into the last category.

I avoided Peter and I thought I'd shaken off his minion. I dived into conversation with an earnest young man who told me he was in plumbing equipment. He was plainly horribly impressed to be at a Shirlands party, and palpably not the sort of company I ought to be keeping. I wriggled away at the first gap in the throng and set my sights on Silver Hair himself. Time was hurrying by, there wasn't enough of it left for a softly softly approach. Besides, the Shirlands champagne was making me bold.

If Peter hadn't been doing his chivalrous best with a full-bosomed loose-necked woman I took to be Mrs Silver Hair, then I wouldn't have succeeded. The course of the next couple of hours would have been different. But Peter was doing his utmost and this allowed me to edge up to where Silver Hair was talking. I positioned myself so that when he moved in my direction, he virtually fell over me.

I can be very charming in accepting an apology. Luckily he was the kind of man who, on public occasions like that one at any rate, was elaborate in his apology. And what more natural than that I should fall in step beside him, making conversation all the way on to the aft deck?

Silver Hair? Yes, he has a proper name. According to the newspapers where I'd seen his photograph he was Reginald Monke. According to the colleagues and business friends around him that evening, and to the actors who were performing friendship, he was Reggie.

Reggie was handsome. It was no pain for me to cut myself off from the bathroom suppliers and the faces from the commercials and give him my attention. We stood on the deck, side by side, and pointed out the sights of London to each other. We got some of them quite wrong, as Londoners do, and we challenged each other mildly.

Behind us stood Reggie's wife, who claimed to know all the interesting buildings on both sides of the river and was, in my opinion, wrong about most of them. Peter did no challenging.

Six other people were on the aft deck too, but they were in a huddle at one side of the boat and talking together. I worried how long I could keep Reggie to myself and whether this was the nearest I'd get to privacy. A wine waiter joined us and the champagne was passed around again. The interruption threatened to dissolve the pattern we'd formed. I had to make a bid now if I was going to do it at all.

I'd spun a line about being an actress, because there were plenty of actresses there and I imagined a high actress count was popular at these events. I'm not *Mastermind* standard on the life of the actor, but I knew I wouldn't have to give much. All most people know is that many of them spend more time out of work than in it, and I expected to suffer nothing more severe than a tactful change of subject when I'd hinted at terminal unemployment. Reggie obliged.

How, though, to shift gear from resting actress with an interest in floodlit monuments, to nosy parker demanding information about Kate Mullery's death? In my hazy reasoning Robin Digby would squirm out of trouble unless Reggie confirmed his guilt. I still don't know a satisfactory way of achieving the change of subject. With champagne fizzing into my glass, I looked up at Reggie Monke and held his gaze, preventing him being distracted by the companions who had far better claim on his time as host than I did. 'Wasn't it awful,' I said, 'about that dress designer whose body was found in the river last week?'

And while he was saying gosh, yes, it was a dreadful thing, I tacked on the assertion that she'd been thrown into the water from the Shirlands site. We happened to be close to the area at the time.

Reggie looked from me to Peter, didn't catch his eye and tried one of the other men instead. He took a step away from me but I stopped him dead by saying in a low voice: 'She didn't drown, you know. She was murdered. And she was murdered because associates of your friend Robin Digby thought she was me.'

I heard the intake of breath. We stood side by side by the rail making believe we were admiring the view. The cold air cut my skin and the breeze whisked an icy spray across the deck.

He said: 'I don't understand what you're saying.' The affability was gone.

'You do. Robin Digby told you about the killing and you advised him to report Kate Mullery missing. Surely you haven't forgotten.'

'None of this is true.'

'Oh yes it is. You met him in St Albans one evening. At St Michael's Manor Hotel. You expected to talk about his efforts to get the Patels out of their factory and clear the way for Shirlands's access road to the riverside site. Instead he told you Kate had been killed.'

There was a long pause. I gave a sideways look. He had his eyes shut tight. He might have been praying he'd invented my words, that he'd open his eyes and find I had no more substance than the foam trailing the boat.

He opened them and I was still there. 'Who are you?'

'Laura Flynn. A detective hired by Kate Mullery to check out Bethesda before she did a deal with them. I wasn't quick enough. She did some checking herself. Just once. It killed her.'

He shuddered. Then: 'What do you want?'

'Only that you tell the police what you know about the matter.'

'Only that?' He was bemused. I think he'd expected something complicated or potentially expensive.

'Only that.' I waited and when he didn't reply I added: 'She was my client. All I can do for her now is ensure the truth comes out.'

'Robin Digby has been discussing all this with the police.'

'I know that. They also want him to tell them about the arson that destroyed the Patel's factory. Shirlands's name is already in the mire.'

Reggie Monke said: 'I know nothing about any of it.'

'A pity,' I said. 'I rather hoped you'd be prepared to remember and do your bit for law and order. Ah well.' I tilted my glass and drank off the rest of the champagne.

The group on the deck parted to let me through to the salon. The door was guarded by a man whose duty was to preserve the privacy of the favoured few. Peter came through the door behind me so fast the man had to skip out of the way.

'Laura!' Peter gave me his public smile and took my arm. I felt myself steered to one side, away from the stairs that I'd meant to take. He lowered his voice to a murmur. 'What the hell are you doing here? And what have you been saying to Reggie?'

'Actually I was invited to the party, Peter. And I was trying to persuade your Reggie to part with a little information. It's what we detectives do.'

He was exasperated. I was delighted. I said: 'I expect he's thinking it over.'

Peter's grip tightened on my upper arm. 'We did a deal, Laura. You were to keep away.'

I wrenched my arm free, made a show of rubbing it where it hurt. 'I was to be given answers first. I didn't get them. You did though, and you used them. What happened at your lunch today? A coup? A merger plan? Reggie's taking no chances with you, is he? Suddenly you're running with the top dogs because you've become dangerous to him.'

He put out his hand to me again but I moved and he dropped it uselessly. He cursed me. 'Do you have to be so sanctimonious? Kate's dead, but it was an accident. She wasn't even roughed up, she just died. And she's going to stay dead, Laura. Wrecking this company, or Reggie's career or mine, isn't going to alter that. Why don't you go home and forget about it?'

I wore the look of a woman being tempted. Then I said: 'The trouble is, Peter, my natural curiosity (for which your cousin Kate was prepared to pay handsomely) won't let me do that. It wants to know why you and your silver-haired MD aren't queuing up outside the police station to tell all you know and to limit the Shirlands involvement.'

The door from the aft deck opened and the group emerged, eager to be back inside in the heat. Peter switched on his smile and returned to them. I ran downstairs where it was more crowded and hotter still.

I hung around down there, falling into conversation with an assortment of people until I met a couple of Shirlands types who, well-primed with drink, found it perfectly reasonable to answer my inquiries about the current round of promotions that had boosted Peter into a higher echelon. They mentioned that he was very ambitious and they wouldn't be surprised if he didn't end up running the company. Once I would have treated that suggestion with disdain.

That's not a compliment to either Peter or to me. I'd lacked the imagination to picture him outside the context in which I'd know him, and he'd channelled all his energies into his work until there was nothing left over for his private life.

A young man with a winter tan attached himself to us, introducing himself as Tony. Apparently he was from one of Shirlands smaller offshoots, and, as my two informants didn't know him, the conversation about impending changes at the company foundered. We picked up another subject but nothing that interested me and when word went round that the Thames Barrier was coming into sight I found myself at a window with Tony while the other pair went outside.

Tony, I grasped, was more interested in me than in London's flood defences. So be it. He was good company and good-looking, and if there wasn't time for a full-scale shipboard romance then a gentle flirtation before we docked was all right by me. I quite fancied a lingering kiss as the *Myosotis* skimmed beneath Tower Bridge. But I intended to keep my eyes open. Floodlit, the bridge is a famously romantic sight and I wanted to enjoy the moment to the full.

Things didn't work out that way. It could have been tragic, it was thoroughly scary and, like much that's disastrous, it was shot through with farce.

Tony plucked a half-emptied bottle of champagne from a waiter and we went up on to a deck where we talked and drank and watched the dark tide surging. There were other couples out there, silent cuddling couples who took no more notice of us than we did of them. The *Myosotis* swung round. We watched the *Cutty Sark* then the Cascades flats slide by.

I was telling lies about being an actress. *Half* lies. That evening alone I'd played the roles of waitress and actress, I could convince myself my claim wasn't totally false. And Tony was telling lies too. I didn't know why I knew that, but I did. I thought he was probably another one in plumbing equipment, or worse.

While I was dismissing what he was saying about having his own computer company, and while I was calculating what the less impressive truth might be, I felt the warmth of his cold fingers in my colder hair and he was drawing me to him. I wanted to say: 'Hey, wait, I can't see Tower Bridge yet. We're only at Limehouse Reach.' Instead I relaxed into his kiss, savouring, forgetting about keeping my eyes open for Famous Sights.

The kiss was a memorable one, if only because it was the prelude to the scene that almost cost me my life. Behind me a door moved and I registered the last of the other couples leaving the deck. I opened an eye. Tony had one hand on the rail and the other tangled in my long hair and pressing me to him. He lifted the hand from the rail and his fingers caressed my cheek. Instantly I knew what was wrong with the computer story. People who give their lives to playing with keyboards and software have correspondingly soft hands. I congratulated myself that despite an evening of party going my instinct and my observation hadn't deserted me.

We were kissing again when the door creaked open. I sensed someone come close. I would have ignored it, but Tony broke off.

Peter said: 'Good. Make sure you keep her out of the way.' And he added, unpleasant as a stage villain: 'Any way you like.'

I jerked round, tearing my hair from Tony's hand. Peter exacerbated the situation by laughing at me. 'One good trick deserves another, Laura. I know how you came aboard and now I'm ensuring you don't cause any more harm. Tony will look after you. In fact I can see you rather enjoy being looked after by him.'

I revised all that nonsense about the soundness of my judgement. The alcohol and the motion of the boat combined to make me feel distinctly underpowered. I'd fallen into an especially humiliating trap and couldn't see how I'd have the strength to think my way out of it.

Haughty, I accused them both of despicable behaviour. Peter remarked that I could say what I liked as long as I stayed where I was until the *Myosotis* tied up at Westminster Pier. Tony was silent, except when he agreed to Peter's instructions.

Panicking, fantasizing, I wondered what Peter intended to do with me when the boat docked. Put me in a taxi, tell me not to be a naughty girl in future and send me home? Seemed unlikely.

What then? I asked him.

He wasn't saying.

Tony wasn't saying.

More panic, more fantasy. I looked about. Execution Dock crept away, the Prospect of Whitby. Pleasure boats scudded up and down unaware of the drama on the deck of the *Myosotis*.

'No, Laura,' Peter said. 'They wouldn't take any notice if you screamed your head off. They'd think you were another office girl drunk at a Christmas party.'

I gasped the icy air, wishing I'd drunk less and had a keener brain, wishing too he hadn't read my half-formed thoughts with such ease. Moving towards Peter I felt Tony's fingers lock into my hair again. I was being physically restrained, held prisoner.

Suddenly in my head I heard Gran's voice, chiding: 'Laura Flynn, how in the world do you get into such scrapes?'

Gran had liked Peter, in the beginning when we were hitting the high notes together. He'd indulged her fancy by letting her put a dash of whiskey in his tea. My judgement askew, I made an undignified appeal to what I remembered of his sympathy.

'Peter, I have to get to the hospital and see Gran. She's dying and I've something to tell her. I know what happened to my father, and I must pass it on before she – um – passes on.'

I'd won my audience. 'What happened, then?' he asked.

'His body's under Nonesuch House, on the palaces estate. He was killed because he was going to expose malpractices. The MacGuires were involved, other people too.'

Peter wasn't as impressed as he ought to have been. I caught my breath in a sob. 'For God's sake, Peter. How long have you known?'

'I'm not saying I've known. Where did you get it from?'

Denying him Dave Tanner's name, I exaggerated my inform-ant into the status of eyewitness. From Mrs Brenan's horror I'd deduced she believed the story too, but I didn't mention her to Peter.

And which side had Peter been on? Not on the Flynn's side, that much was plain.

'Laura, who have you told about this?'

'Nobody,' I said, editing out Anna Lee. 'That's why I must be at the hospital. Gran should be the first to hear.'

He snorted. 'If that's crucial, what a shame you gatecrashed this party instead of hot-footing it to her bedside.'

'You know why I came. I needed to . . .'

'Yes, yes, I know.' He cut me off, preventing Tony learning my reasons. Then: 'You'll never prove that story about your father.'

It was my turn to crow. 'As a matter of fact it'll be proved within months. Nonesuch is coming down.'

'Coming down?' His face hardened.

My councillor friend had told me, among other items of local news, when I'd called to beg a favour from her prison officer husband.

I said: 'It'll be reduced to rubble, then I'll have proof.'

Peter repeated his instructions to Tony to keep me there, and retreated through the door to the party. Being left alone in a clinch with Tony no longer appealed. I made a dive for the door, but he held a fistful of my hair and although I swung and kicked I couldn't break away. If he'd kept his distance and guarded the exit, then I mightn't have done what I did next. But he flung himself on me, pressing me against the rail while he grappled for a firm hold around my neck.

He was no fighter. He didn't know the moves I knew and given space I could have dealt with him. Space is what he didn't allow me. He crowded me, fumbling for the secure hold. Equally unscientific, I slid a hand around the neck of the champagne bottle and I brought it up hard and cracked his head.

He rolled against the door, barring the way. There were two other ways for me to leave the deck. One was into the water and the other was on to the roof. I made it to the roof.

Tony pursued, his shoes slipping. I'd kicked mine off for a surer grip. My plan, if I could glorify it with such a title, was to dash the length of the cabin roof and leap down on to the fore deck and seek safety in numbers. Tony's plan was to prevent that at all costs.

As the boat passed beneath Tower Bridge we were halfway along the roof, tussling like a couple of ill-matched wrestlers. Above us the dazzling triumph of the bridge, beneath us the midnight water.

I had another of those moments when a fictional parallel leapt up, reducing achievement or disaster to absurdity. The Reichenbach Falls, I thought. Holmes and Moriarty.

There was never a moment when Tony didn't have a grip on me. He was bigger and he was wilder. I'll claim that I was fitter, but I was also hampered by my floaty, flowery dress.

Tony helped me with that problem. He clawed a handful of the skirt, and I felt the fabric rip away. I heard no sound. The boat engine and the music and conviviality from below shut out everything else.

Freer, I landed a well-placed kick. He came full length at me, brought me down. We rolled across the roof. Stars. Bridge. Water. Stars. Bridge. Water.

Water.

I hung over the seething mass. It seemed a long, long way below and all too near.

Forcing breath into my lungs I heaved him off me and spun to one side. If I was in pain then the alcohol prevented me knowing it. If I was making a hash of a simple race the length of the cabin roof, then I was too occupied to be ashamed of it.

We fell again. I was on top of him. He began to slide. I shouted into his face: 'For Christ's sake, why are you doing this? You'll get us killed!'

I don't think he cared. 'Reggie wants you shut up,' he said through clenched teeth.

We'd come to rest near the edge. Panting, I managed: 'You're crazy!'

I was a fool to call him crazy. It got him on the raw. He swore and we began to slide again. He said: 'You shouldn't have come up here if you're choosy how you go down.'

And he swung his body so that all at once it was *my* head near the edge, *my* eyes looking to heaven for help. I didn't see any signs of help, only stars, a crescent moon and the skinny white trace of an airplane taking people home for Christmas.

Tony's hands were at my neck. On my throat. His weight was crushing me, his masculine strength counting for more than my hours of work at the gym. One of his hands discovered my chain.

He hesitated in the act of choking me, long enough to bury St Lucy in his palm, haul the chain up until my head was lifted by the pain of the fine gold strand savaging my flesh.

St Lucy, who'd always been my friend. St Lucy who'd been the link with my father. St Lucy who was supposed to find things and was helping my attacker find a novel way of throttling me.

I head-butted. I thrust an elbow into one tender spot and a

220

knee into another. And as the vice of his hands slackened slightly, I saw a figure on the cabin roof.

We were passing Traitors Gate.

Peter. He was a frantic blur, shouting although no sounds reached us. Not Sir Galahad this time. Peter, who'd never been any of the things I'd taken him for. I wasn't prepared to risk him again. As Tony's pressure on me eased fractionally, I hurled myself off the roof and down to the gleaming swell.

In my blackest moments I perceive my life to have been a dismal series of disappointments interspersed with the excitement of bad shocks. Hitting the Thames on a December night was the ultimate in bad shocks.

With first-hand experience to back me, I'll believe any of those outlandish claims that a person can't live in such water for 000000.23 seconds or whatever arbitrary figure you care to pick on.

I left behind a confusion of lights and noise and shadows and a bubbling wake, and I entered a dark silent world where I was conscious of nothing but weightlessness, the insistent pull of the current, and going down and down and then down some more. This shock was followed by the equal one of bursting back to the surface with my lungs screaming, and knowing I had to draw air into them however much it hurt because the only truth that mattered was that I was going straight back down again.

Down and down.

Up. I was trying a few uncoordinated strokes but it was time to go down again.

Down. Slowly.

Then fighting my way to the surface, limbs leaden, everything tearing.

I'd never known the river so wide, safety so distant. Too distant. The tide had carried me hurriedly away. The *Myosotis* was receding, unconcerned. I dog paddled. I'm a swimming-pool swimmer, maybe a Mediterranean beach swimmer. I don't swim in this muck, in this temperature. I dog paddled and looked around for the nearest bit of safety. The wake of a small fast boat hit me in the face and I ducked under again.

Very slowly I resurfaced and struggled to keep afloat. Through my stupor I became aware of a boat bearing down on me. I was too numb in mind and body to care that it was going to run me down.

Suddenly it was lurching above me. Then I was in the air, puzzlingly because I felt nothing but the sensation of being airborne.

Detective Sergeant Ray Donnelly was plucking me from the water.

I'd never expected to wake up in bed again next to Mike Brenan. That was another of those shocks I mentioned.

My expression conveyed as much because he moved back and I rapidly worked out that I was in my own bed and Mike was outside it, peering at me.

'Laura? Are you all right?'

Wonderful how people ask you that when you can't possibly be. I grimaced as I tried to speak and found my throat raw, a steam hammer at work inside my skull, and my lungs tender. 'Terrific,' I said.

He looked extremely happy about it. I was fairly happy myself, as I scrolled a memory bank composed of rooftop scuffles and midnight dips and a bevy of policemen arguing whether to take me to a hospital, while I was a sodden heap in the bottom of their launch. Ghastly coincidence, they were the crew who'd lifted Kate Mullery from the water. No, not coincidence at all. Bodies were their business, naturally they'd have detoured from their task in hand to hook up mine. Ghastlier yet, there was a shape in a body bag on the floor beside me. They'd done their night's work, I was a bonus.

Mike was speaking to me, I wasn't concentrating. He tried again. I said yes to the coffee and yes to the painkillers. He had them at the bedside with superhuman speed.

I began delicately. 'Mike, the room service is fantastic, but do you mind my asking what you're doing here?

He said I'd refused to be taken to hospital and I'd won the argument because he'd weighed in on my side with a promise to look after me if I insisted on going home.

'By rights you should have drowned,' he said, a shade smugly.

I palmed the painkillers and gobbled them before pointing out: 'I was too full of champagne bubbles for that.'

He spoiled my quip by saying: 'Yes, I told them you were drunk. Ray Donnelly believed me but the others had you down as a trauma case.'

'Thanks,' I muttered, striving for irony. 'I expect both diagnoses were correct.' My thinking was slow. 'Just a minute, were you in the boat as well as Ray?'

He had an involved explanation about meeting Donnelly who was looking for me. Together they guessed where I'd gone, were worried what might happen and hitched a lift with the river police, meaning to board the *Myosotis*. Anyhow, it was too complicated for me the state I was in the morning after. And so were Donnelly's reasons for letting me blunder ahead with my cock-eyed idea that only by confronting Silver Hair could I get the evidence the police would require to nail Robin Digby. Or something.

As Mike came to the end of his tale I grunted solemnly, making out that it was a professional matter and the logic certainly didn't defeat me as it defeated him.

He ended up with: 'You'll be pleased to hear that Digby has crumbled and admitted knowing about Kate Mullery's murder and that he's implicated Reginald Monke in the factory arson. Ray was going to tell you, if he'd caught up with you.'

'You mean I went through all that for nothing!'

The glittering amusement in his eyes proved it, although he tried extremely hard not to laugh and carried on as though I hadn't spoken: 'The pretty young man on the cabin roof has failed to convince the police that he wasn't trying to kill you –

how could he, when a boatful of them had a floodlit view of the scrap? And your friend Peter has persuaded everybody that he had no part in any of it, except to attempt to rescue you.'

'Huh!'

'Hmm, that's what I thought. Well, you know Peter, Laura. He'll do well out of this business, whatever happens to the rest. Heads will roll but Peter's won't be one of them. Talking of heads, how are the painkillers doing?'

'Brilliantly.' They weren't. He refilled the coffee-cup. I said: 'Talking of business, shouldn't you be at work?'

'Christmas Eve? No thanks.'

I shut my eyes in a spasm of guilt. Christmas Eve and I had presents to wrap and friends to see. And Gran to visit. Worst of all Gran.

Mike said: 'You've already had a Christmas present of sorts.'

'Meaning?'

'A man with crinkly black hair brought something for you. He said he'd tried your office and Debbie in the boutique sent him straight round here.'

'What is it?'

He said: 'It's in the kitchen.'

'Well, bring it in.' God, he could be irritating. Just like old times.

'I'll try, but . . .' He went out, leaving me mystified. I lay back and closed my eyes. Another week's sleep would be ideal, I'd settle for a couple of days. I'd politely get Mike and his helpfulness out of my life and I'd crawl beneath the duvet and . . .

And he was standing at the foot of the bed holding in his arms the biggest, ugliest cat I'd ever seen. Not a cat at all, a monster. Jaguar!

I shrieked and scrambled out of bed. 'That's Jaguar!'

The cat reacted by bucking, scratching. Mike scowled at me. 'Now can I put this thing back in its box?'

The thought of returning the cat to Mrs Lotti and her children for Christmas, filled me with purpose and energy. Tiredness fled, and I did my best to ignore the pain. I raced to the bathroom to shower and dress. I phoned the Turkish sweat-shop owner to thank him. I rang Chris Ionides who declared my car ready. I dashed around the flat organizing what was left of my day.

Mike sat watching, superfluous to my life. Well, he'd wanted it that way, I seemed to remember. He'd . . . But I couldn't enter into that, I had to sweep him out of the flat with all the charm at my disposal, and get on with the race against the clock.

He drove me to Chris's garage, remembering something else on the way. 'Ray Donnelly had a message for you about a cat too. He said you'd understand. It was – um – something like "Tell Laura that Digby shot the cat and made the funny phone calls to put pressure on her." '

'Oh, I see. Well, I had wondered but it seemed rather petty.'

'You told me your messages were from Bridie MacGuire.'

'They were. Ray meant Kate Mullery's messages. She had them too, there's a lot of it about.'

At the garage Mike transferred Jaguar's box to my car. Chris was in his happiest mood. He'd received Christmas cards from his remaining relatives in Cyprus, he'd got my car back on the road, and he was looking at the most extraordinary cat he'd ever seen. Jaguar was a marvel he'd talk about for a long time to come.

Chris appeared to pay scant attention to Mike, or to us saying our brief goodbye with an impulsive, swift kiss. When Mike had driven off, Chris asked me: 'This man has found the cat for you?'

'In a way.'

He teased me, laughing, saying the cat was a very special present. There were many questions in his face. I answered them. 'Just a piece of my past, Chris.'

'Ah, Laura.' He shrugged, exactly as he did whenever I walked in and said the car was bust.

Mrs Lotti's joy didn't fade like that. She squealed and

whooped and locked Jaguar to her bosom, and then she locked me to her bosom.

'Isa good Christmas present, eh, Laura? Is Jaguar come 'ome.' And without warning her apron was up at her eyes and she was dabbing up pools of overflowing joy. I left her like that, choosing to remember her that way.

Nonesuch was bleak as ever, but its aspect was relieved by two things: Mrs Lotti's ecstasy and my knowledge that the building was soon to fall. With it would go the mystery of Joe Flynn.

Did I feel anything special as I climbed up and down its forbidding concrete stairs, looked from its balconies across Pooter country, or plodded over the snow-streaked empty expanse where architects had dreamily imagined children would play? I didn't. Another day I might have, but this errand was too full of the happy ending to Jaguar's adventures.

Then I started up my car and pointed her nose up the hill towards the hospital. Gran next. The tough bit.

Rehearsing my words, I failed to improve on the stumbling first efforts. I was tempted to hope she was asleep, that I could put this off for another day.

The green lights in the Christmas trees near the ward had been mended. Gran was sitting up in bed, reading Father Mahon's hand. Out of their sight I heard her saying: 'Sure, Father, it's the same as I told you before. Would a hand go changing itself this way and that? Now listen well, or we'll be over the course again. Your Sun sign makes it stark plain that you're to look forward to an advance in your career.'

He gawped at his pudgy hand. 'Kitty, you know full well you said I was to expect wealth.'

'And don't they pay bishops more than they pay the poor parish priest?'

I stepped into the ward, teasing. 'It's all nonsense and the pair of you know it. How are you, Gran?'

I kissed her papery cheek. Father Mahon smiled his cherubic smile and touched my elbow. We all three spoke a minute or so and then he withdrew. I steeled myself to get on with it before I was sidetracked.

'Gran, there's something . . .'

She spoke simultaneously: 'Laura, if you don't mind my saying so, you're letting yourself go a wee bit. These late nights are giving you dark circles, my girl.'

'Gran, this is serious. It's about my father.'

'About Joe, is it?' She was smoothing the bedcover with her small age-mottled hand.

'Yes. You asked me to find him.'

'I was very sick, Laura. Imagining things and all that.'

'Look, Gran, I did try . . .'

'Delirious, I dare say. Do you know I was so far gone I imagined you and that Mike Brenan were here together. That gives you a measure of the wildness that was in my mind!' She shook with gentle laughter.

I thought I understood her, that she was dodging the subject. I'd failed and she was sparing me.

But I'd come this far and I was determined to get it over. 'Gran, it might happen again. You might be asking for him and it's only fair that you should know . . .'

She reached out and patted my hands. I hadn't realized that I was twisting them, the classic gesture of anguish.

'Hush, it's all right now,' she said. And she turned my right hand over.

I curled my fingers. 'No, Gran. I'm sorry, but you must let me say this.' I found it hard to get the next words out. Then: 'I believe he's dead.'

I wished I hadn't done it. She kept her hand on mine but it changed from a vital moving thing to an impassive weight that I longed to throw off. It was a while before either of us spoke.

Gran said: 'Laura, I'd one foot in the next world, you know. Father Mahon says that thing's common enough. He had a name for it, out-of-body experience. Well, if Kitty Flynn was out of her mind or out of her body I couldn't say, but I know that I talked with Joe. You have the truth of it, Laura. He is dead.'

Her cool acceptance made the truth undeniable. She'd succeeded in crossing the bounds of the five senses. This wasn't a game, showmanship, like her palm reading. We could both trust in this.

Gran was looking at me closely, frowning at the mysterious thing she was about to say but didn't fully understand. 'He said I was to tell you he's happy, Laura. Nothing else. Just that he's happy.'

The blue eyes closed but she didn't sleep. Her thumb stroked my hand, soothing away my hurt, regular as heartbeat.

The press pounced as I reached home. Photographers, reporters and two television crews. Christmas Eve, one of those quiet news days, and the police had tipped them off about the Mullery–Shirlands story and me. What they put out was wrong but flattering. They were eager for a heroine and, in defiance of the facts, claimed they'd found one.

My phone got busy. There were bread-and-butter jobs that couldn't save Flynn Detective Agency, but by the time the church bells rang in the New Year there was one that could. The client thought I was the ideal detective for the case. And so did I.